By the

fiction

MOM
Bangkok Knights
Yawn (A Thriller)
Bangkok Old Hand

non-fiction

Thailand's Coral Reefs
Diving Guide to Thailand
The Kingdom Beneath the Sea
Thailand's National Parks (with Mark Graham and Denis Gray)

Kicking Dogs

CreateSpace 2010. Previously published by Asia Books (Bangkok: 2000); bookSiam (Bangkok: 1995); Editions Duang Kamol (Bangkok 1991).

Cover illustration by Colin Cotterill (www.colincotterill.com).

Fiction

Printed in the United States of America.
Distributed in the United States of America through amazon.com and createspace.com.

For distribution/purchase in other countries please refer to www.collinpiprell.com.

collin piprell

kicking dogs

prologue

hard times

Selections from Arno Petty's Intelligencer and Weekly Gleaner

SOMETHING FOR EVERYONE. The Chao Phraya River, the heart of Bangkok, is enjoying something of a renaissance these days. Trendy hotels and restaurants are appearing all along its banks, while an ever-increasing number of luxury dinner cruises threaten riverine traffic jams in the evenings. Some of us, however, prefer a pre-boomtime ambience. Besides which, your average newspaper writer's income extends more to beer and a plate of *naem sod*, these delicacies being best served in a humble noodle shop perched out on a ramshackle wooden pier.

I DON'T GIVE A HOOT. I have been told for the thousandth time that my favorite beer snack of *naem sod*, fermented pork sausage, is a great way to get worms (trichinosis, to be more specific). Well, we've all got to go some way. If in my case it's with a beer and a plate of naem sod, then so be it.

THE NAME IS JACK SHACKAWAY, and I'm a kind of freelance journalist. You meet some interesting people when you're a hack writer living in Bangkok.

For example, the other day I was enjoying a few drinks with a pair of dubious characters name of Tommy Two-Toes and Wrong-Way Willie Wong. Actually, it was more than a few drinks, and these gentlemen were more than just dubious characters. They had robbed me, only a short time before joining me for these drinks I mention.

They were apologetic about this inconvenience they caused me, and more than somewhat embarrassed. Robbery, as they were careful to impress upon me, was not something they considered a class act, and they hoped I understood this was merely a temporary expedient. I could be sure they wouldn't be caught dead holding up

5

citizens for pitiful sums of money in the normal course of events. But times being what they were, you did what you had to do.

I first met these types when I was taking a stroll around a part of the city I had never seen before. I stopped on a little wooden landing down by the river, figuring I would have a smoke and watch the boats for awhile. Not more than three or four of these things had gone by, the landing gently bobbing in their wakes, before I became aware of two individuals who had appeared on the landing and who, it seemed, wished to talk to me. One of them was a big man for a Thai, heavy through the chest and sporting a busted-up kind of face. He was wearing a straw hat with a "Visit Thailand" hatband. His companion was shorter and skinny and he had a delicate gait, mincing and tottering along like he was walking on eggs. Eggs maybe full of dynamite.

The big one came over beside me and swung a rolled magazine up to one eye, sea-captain style, and started scouting the far side of the river. "You. Are you a tourist?" he asked me in tolerable English, never leaving off from his perusal of the other shore.

"No," I answered him.

"Me and my friend sometimes come down here to hunt for tourists," he continued. His friend tittered at that, and belched. I was thinking I could detect Mekhong whiskey fumes. I was also thinking that these characters were two touts with more than your average ration of brass.

"We are guides," said the big one. "Sometimes, we are guides. You want a guide?"

I told them I wasn't a tourist and thought about telling them to shove off. While I was looking for the precise words to communicate my feelings about touts in general and about these two specimens in particular, the big one ceased his reconnoitering of the Thonburi side with the rolled-up magazine and, I noticed, took to pointing a large pistol at my stomach. I had seen these pistols pic-

6

tured in the local newspapers, and, for lack of anything better to talk about, I said, "That is a homemade shotgun pistol, isn't it?"

"Twelve gauge," he replied, and he smiled. His partner was also smiling, and he was holding an open switch-blade pointed down beside his leg so I knew it was there but not so every Tom, Dick, and Harry would know it was there too.

Right away I leapt to a conclusion. "Would you fellows like some money?" I asked, smiling in a way designed to say that no matter what I thought of touts, I could see they were by no means touts and I was thoroughly delighted to meet two such resourceful gentlemen and could only wish them the best of everything and would do anything I could to help them out with their life-plans.

This attitude was not one I adopted on impulse. Not at all. I had been tutored in the etiquette of being robbed in Thailand by those who knew, and it should be common knowledge that the robbee — at least one who wants to remain in good health — is always very polite indeed to the robber. It is a good idea to smile a lot and speak in moderate tones. You should, if possible, look for positive things to talk about, and always, always be sure you have at least a modicum of loot to lay upon your new acquaintances. If they are professional enough to go through all the moves thought proper to their side of the transaction, and then find that they are wasting their time and now look like ninnies because you are broke flatter than a flounder, they will lose a substantial amount of face. Losing face is something your average Thai robber does not enjoy. Just to make himself feel better, while at the same time removing a witness to his embarrassment, he will probably shoot you. This is something your average robbee does not enjoy.

So, keeping all of this good advice in mind, I smiled and handed over the contents of my wallet to the little one with the funny walk, while the big one smiled at me and kept pointing his cannon at my midsection. I indicated that I was confused about what should be done with my wallet, now that it was empty. Did protocol suggest I hand that over as well, or should I perhaps keep it? With a flourish of his pistol, the big one told me I should keep it. The little one, meanwhile, gave the money to his partner and took to checking me out for my taste in chronometers. When he saw what I was wearing, he snorted in disgust and said to the other that their business was done and they should think about moving on.

They were backing away from me off the pier, and we were all smiling and nodding and I was saying "You have a nice day, now" when the wake from a passing boat hit the landing and the little one, who had been having trouble walking funny and walking backwards at the same time, lost his balance and fell against the big one, who also lost his balance and who furthermore fell into the river.

Though this was not the least funny thing I had seen in my life, I was reluctant to indulge myself in a hearty laugh. Last I noticed, for one thing, the 12-gauge pistol was still with the big guy when he went into the river.

There was a certain amount of confusion and thrashing about going on over by the water, and no else seemed to be doing any laughing, restrained or otherwise. I was getting the idea the big one couldn't swim, and the little one was for some reason disinclined to go into the water to help him, no matter his friend had all the money they had recently come into. Chances are he couldn't swim either, I was thinking, and this idea was reinforced by his mincing around excitedly telling me in Thai and in gesture that he would appreciate it if I helped his buddy out a bit.

If only I had remembered my lessons on the etiquette of being a robbee, I would have wished them both a good day and got myself out of there just as fast as I could go. It was not inconceivable that the big guy and the little guy too found this whole situation a considerable loss of face, especially since I was not entirely restraining my appreciation of the humorous side of proceedings. Not thinking about this problem, however, I lent a hand and in no time had our friend back on terra firma.

He was pretty wet and I was pretty wet, and even the little guy was pretty wet because he kept dancing around getting splashed on. I was happy to see that the big guy, notwithstanding everything, was expressing gratitude and that he had left his pistol in the river besides. I was thinking at the same time that it was maybe better if I had died of gunshot wounds rather than suffer the slower death of cholera compounded by typhoid and river blindness I was looking at now. I was not happy at having been for a swim in the Chao Phraya even if it was in such a good cause as to save the life of this robber.

The big guy, on the other hand, seemed in a pretty fair mood, despite the loss of both arsenal and some measure of dignity. He still had my money, at least, which he produced with an air of triumph and wrung out before waving it back and forth in the breeze to dry. His cigarettes were beyond repair, however, and this threatened to dampen his spirits, except that I had a dry pack of Krong Thep and I gave him one and the little guy took one too even though he didn't smoke and we all stood there, a bit chilly in the evening breeze, smoking and waiting to dry out. After a while, the big one spoke to the little one and then he turned to me and said, "You come and drink with us."

This was no doubt a better proposition than getting shot, but I felt I had to decline: "Well, I would like to, but, you see I have no money, and ... "

"*Mai pen rai*," he assured me. "Never mind." And the little one grinned, nodding his support. "Don't worry; we have money. Hey. We look after you."

So pretty soon we were sitting in a nice waterfront joint where you could watch the boats go by, and all the garbage and water

9

hyacinth as well. It was beautiful also to see the sun go down across the river.

"You like Singha beer?"

In truth, I didn't. I drank Kloster, but they were paying and I didn't want to appear finicky.

"You eat *naem sod?*"

Maybe you are familiar with this uncooked pork sausage, which is served with peppers and peanuts and onions and shredded green mango and which makes beer taste even better than it usually tastes. Everybody also tells you that eating naem sod, besides all its other advantages, is an excellent way to get parasites, if you want parasites, which I didn't; but after my dip in the Chao Phraya one or two more varieties of parasite was not likely to make much difference to my general well-being, so I said, "Yes, I like naem sod. By all means let us have some of this stuff."

For a while, then, we drank beer and ate naem sod, as well as *yam woon sen, yam pla duk foo,* and some other kinds of food that went very well indeed with beer, only you never seemed to have enough of either beer or food if you took these things together. While we were trying to have enough of everything, we got acquainted. The big one let it be known he had picked up his English mostly in Vietnam, along with some other useful skills he acquired from the US armed forces while learning to be all that he could be. He had also benefited from some time spent in Singapore, where he had been a guest of the government and where he had lived in a small cell with a fellow soldier of fortune, a guy from Brooklyn who was a specialist in international movements of gold.

So the big one did most of the talking, since the little one didn't speak English and he didn't understand my Thai. We talked of this and that, and what a crime the taxes on beer were, and pretty soon we had spent all their loot, and the big one said he was still thirsty and so did the little one. And so was I, come to that, so I took off

10

my belt and showed my new friends the 500 baht I had zipped up in a secret compartment, and their spirits brightened no end. In fact, in no time all of us were feeling hardly any pain, and the others decided they could take me further into their confidence. The big one turned out to have the name "Willie Wong." Actually, he told me, he started life in Hong Kong, where he was known as Wong Wei, but somewhere along the line he came to be called Wrong-Way Willie Wong; and I could call him Willie if I wanted to.

Willie also told me he and the little one had been partners for some time already, though robbery was not their first choice of pursuits, and his partner's name was Tommy Two-Toes. As near as I could make out, given Wrong-Way Willie's special brand of Brooklynese and my own approaching state of total leglessness, the following was Tommy Two-Toes' story.

Some thirty-five years before, Tommy had been born in a town in the south of Thailand, down near the Malaysian border, and he was named "Thongbai," which was a fine and traditional Thai name. He was orphaned at an early age by hard liquor and high emotion, not his own, and he was forced by circumstances to leave the state school system not too long after that. The remainder of his education was a liberal one, the institutions of learning he attended having been organized along informal lines, and classes having been held in the streets. Growing up and entering into various loose associations with a motley society of Thais, Malays, and Chinese, most of them with educational backgrounds similar to his own, young Thongbai acquired a fairly cosmopolitan outlook on life. At the same time, it came to be generally agreed that "Tommy" had a more up-to-date feel to it as a handle than did Thongbai.

As time went by, Tommy made his way up in the world and he got hitched to a lady named Toy, proceeding to learn whatever could be learned from this latest lesson in life, which was popularly known as marriage. Then, in the course of still some more time,

Tommy decided this thing called marriage deserved further investigation and he married yet another lady, this one also named Toy. Toy Number Two, however, lived in another town where Tommy had certain business interests and which was conveniently located at some distance from Tommy's first domicile. For a year or so, both Toy One and Toy Two remained comfortably ignorant of the other's existence, and Tommy was thinking life on the whole was more than just okay.

It was during this time that Tommy came to be referred to as "Tommy Two-Toys" by his business associates, English *noms de guerre*, as I say, being thought to have a more-than-somewhat sophisticated cachet in these circles. In no time at all, "Tommy Two-Toys" had caught on at most levels of the community, the name having a nice ring to it. Before long that was what everybody called him. And the first Mrs Two-Toys, for one, couldn't help wondering why.

Finally, of course, she found out. To say she was not pleased went some way towards describing her reaction to the news, and she saw she was in danger of losing a considerable amount of face unless she took immediate steps. Going through Tommy Two-Toys' office one day, while Tommy was away on business, Mrs Two-Toys found a couple of sticks of dynamite in a filing cabinet, and she got a good idea. She had saved some money from the household accounts, and now she contacted a person who made a living compensating for losses of face and so forth, and in the course of time this public servant arranged to put the dynamite up under the bed of the second Mrs Two-Toys, together with a pressure fuse. He did not do this, of course, until one night he happened to know Tommy and his second wife were out at a party and would be getting back late and tired and no doubt in a hurry to hit the sack.

Unfortunately, from her point of view, the first Mrs Two-Toys could not afford the best technical help, and things did not go exactly as planned. The second Mrs Two-Toys was still in the toilet when Tommy threw himself down on the bed and was surprised to find himself tossed right back into the air by a loud explosion that also blew most of the toes off his feet. In fact, the medics managed to save two toes and they told him he was lucky at that. Tommy never for a minute suspected that his condition was the work of a business rival, since he knew that this class of technician would not leave him two toes or much of anything else either. Besides, Mrs Two-Toys Number One never even came to bring him flowers in the hospital.

Once out of the hospital, Tommy saw he had to take stock of his life. Deciding he had learned already all there was profitably to learn from marriage to two Toys, and reasoning that business was not so good anyway, what with two very sore feet and quite a lot of grinning and joking behind his back on the part of his brothers-in-business and the community at large, Tommy Two-Toys, who was now more commonly known as Tommy Two-Toes, headed on up North to see how the land lay in those parts.

Tommy could see right off that patrons failed to abound in the northern provinces, and opportunities to ply his various trades were not much in evidence. Times were so hard he actually found himself performing manual labor just make ends meet. It was not for this he had spent all those years getting a liberal education, and he was not in good spirits for a young man in the prime of his life if only you overlooked the condition of his feet. Around this time Tommy's luck changed. The old-boy network came through, more or less, in the person of one Wrong-Way Willie Wong, a friend of a friend of an old associate from down South, and Willie had a proposition for Tommy.

As it happened, they fared very well as partners for a time, doing one kind of job and another, though mostly one kind of job.

Log rustling in the northern forests was a pretty good racket, though they did not themselves actually rustle the logs. They provided more of a service for log rustlers, what you could call public relations. Mostly what they did for their clients was they talked to members of the public who were not happy with the clients for one reason and another, and Willie and Tommy changed the attitudes of these citizens, or at least they fixed it so they didn't bother the clients with their unhappiness any more. Together they did very well, because Willie had this useful physical presence and a facility with all manner of firearms, while Tommy was a master of the Look.

"Show him the Look," Willie told his friend, and Tommy showed me the Look.

Even though I was long since dry all over and more than a little fortified with strong beer, I could feel small furry things creeping up my spine. I nodded in admiration, and I said that Tommy did indeed know how to give a person the Look. The last time I had just that feeling was only a short time before, when it was Willie's 12-gauge pistol that was giving my midsection the Look, and Tommy's Look was neck and neck for first place, or maybe even a nose out in front. Tommy was clearly pleased at his success and he gave the Look to an innocent bystander at another table, who paid his tab and left in a hurry, and Willie had to tell Tommy to ease off.

"But it gets pretty bad up North, now," Willie continued. "You find soldiers and policemen and I don't know what up there who won't let you do your job and who don't take money and who you can't scare. It's a real crime. So we come down here to Bangkok. There has to be work in the city for men like us. You get all these people, *na?* There must be all manner of unhappiness and misunderstandings of one kind and another that need to be fixed. But it's hard to get your start. It takes money to make money. Money and contacts. "Robbery, now, that's a loser's game. I mean, what did

Tommy and I get out of this day's work? I mean, after all."

I said I was sorry and Willie said it wasn't my fault. Anyway now they were thinking of being gunmen, though it didn't help that they had lost their only gun in the river. It wasn't much of a gun anyhow, come to that, said Willie. Nowadays you needed at least an 11mm automatic, though an M-16 or a grenade launcher carried even more punch in terms of both image and impact. Of course it was not easy to conceal a grenade launcher on your person while riding around Bangkok on a motorcycle. But an 11mm pistol cost 12,000 baht and even a used M-16 would run you 4,500 baht. Willie asked me did I know how much just the ammo for an 11mm pistol cost? I didn't know, and it turned out Willie couldn't remember so he asked Tommy who told him five baht a round, black market prices, of course.

"Do you hear that?" said Willie. "Pow, pow, pow. Hey. Before you know it there's a whole night on the town blown away."

He told me that was why you needed such a heavy caliber weapon: nobody in the business could afford target practice, so you had to get up close to your man with something that looked impressive and made a loud noise so even if you missed you scared him to death.

What they required, then, was something to start — only enough to get their basic equipment together.

I told them if I had anybody I wanted blown away they would be the first to know but, unfortunately, I didn't want anybody dead right at that moment.

It was not necessary to want somebody dead, Willie was quick to assure me. Hey. Maybe I just needed to throw a scare into someone. Maybe my landlord, for example? Or some business associate?

Willie got Tommy to give me the Look again, except he had to slap him around a bit so he would open his eyes first and give me

15

any kind of look at all. What I finally saw didn't look much like the Look, even though I had to admit his eyes were open, and this time I didn't feel the furry things up and down my spine.

I wasn't feeling much of anything, by then. Willie himself, he said, was remaining upright in his chair only due to a discipline he had learned in some secret martial arts practice. Furthermore, as he pointed out, Tommy had left off giving the Look and was asleep face down in what was left of the woon sen. On top of that, the proprietor wanted to close up and go home, and we had spent all the money anyway.

It would be better, said he, if we got together again upon another occasion and continued our interesting discussions then. Maybe he would tell me how he first came to be called Wrong-Way and we could talk about me buying some shares in their new enterprise. Kind of like a "quiet partner."

This proposition got me to thinking, and I came to see it was time for these two gentlemen and myself to seek our separate destinies where we might. So I said to Willie that he had related an interesting history and I was pleased to meet a man of such accomplishments as Tommy Two-Toes, not to mention Willie's own good self, but I regretted to say I was leaving the country in one week never to return.

Willie was sorry to hear this, he said, and then maybe we could go to my joint right away and discuss a small business loan since he knew I was a good sort and my terms wouldn't be too hard, even though these were hard times we were living in.

I said we would do this thing as soon as I came back from the toilet, only I never came back from the toilet. I got in a taxi and I got out of that part of town, maybe forever.

part one

a bad time to quit smoking

Selections from Arno Petty's Intelligencer and Weekly Gleaner

HIRE A SPECIALIST. The Land of Smiles has one of the highest murder rates in the world. Most of these killings are crimes of passion involving friends and family. A lot of them, though, are the result of 'business disputes,' where for a fee persistently annoying individuals may be removed by gunmen who specialize in such matters. The going rate for a newspaper columnist (a foreign one) is about 15,000 baht, or 10,000 baht for a Thai. Reporters can be done for less. Yo, Izzy Scoop: are you out there and listening?

HAVE THEY GOT A UNION? In the run-up to the general election, the police department has said it plans to keep tabs on the 1,000 gunmen it has on its books in the Central Region alone. Why, if these people are gunmen, are they only on the police records and not in jail? Is it just for taxation purposes that these records are kept, or what?

OVER THE NEXT FEW MONTHS, I got to tell the story of Tommy Two-Toes and his partner Wrong-Way Willie any number of times, and I got to enjoy more than a few complimentary beers while doing so, which went some way towards helping me recoup my losses of that day. Eventually, o f course, other characters and other stories pushed Tommy and Willie out of the limelight. Next thing I knew, I even forgot I never wanted to go into that part of town again.

I had other things on my mind. Like eating and paying the rent, for example.

Propriapist Publications (New York) still hadn't mailed me my check for *A Dick for Dorothy*. How was it they could tell me Arno Petty's pornographic A-Z series of novels was fast becoming a cult phenomenon back Stateside, hurry up and send the next one, but they wouldn't even up the ante? All they would say was they might make it an extra grand a book, after we got past "F." After *Flora's Fauna*, God help me.

Meanwhile my friend Hippolyte Lafleur — sometimes known as Izzy Scoop, although that's a secret — put a word in for me down at the Bangkok Examiner, and I got what you could almost call a serious assignment, even though the money they talked about giving me was not what anybody would call serious money.

And so that was how one day I wound up in a snooker room down by the waterfront at Klong Toey, this snooker room being what you might call a colorful place. I was thinking it was too bad I didn't have a camera with me, and then again I was also thinking it was not too bad. The joint was harboring a number of your classic shady characters, and it was a safe bet these low-lifes were no assembly of male models, unless, that is, you were thinking of modeling brass knuckles.

Chances were pretty good, in fact, these boys were not in the mood to have their picture taken by me or by anybody else either. And it was not as though I could sneak a quick shot or two on the sly — I was the one Westerner in the place and this fact was not going entirely unnoticed. The only way I would stick out more like a sore thumb, I thought, was if I had my nose painted for example bright blue or else I waved a camera around.

I was there because I wanted to talk to some gunmen. It was not that I sought their professional services. Not at all. I was a peace-loving citizen, and there was nobody I wanted dead at the moment except for maybe one newspaper editor, now that I thought about it. Maybe a couple more editors, too; why not? But no, I was merely writing a story about gunmen. Only I knew very little about gunmen other than that bumping people was a real growth industry in some parts of Thailand, with assassins getting thick as flies, and with not enough police they had to watch the even-numbered gunmen on some days and the odd-numbered ones on other days. And no matter how much these boys looked after business, there always seemed to be more business conflicts and suchlike that needed resolving, and more people who would pay good money to establish their own peace of mind.

So I had to get some background, and I had an appointment to see a couple of individuals I was told were adept at ridding the scene of bothersome folk. For a suitable fee, they did this, and sometimes only for practice. I was supposed to show up alone and sit with a Singha beer and a *Bangkok Examiner* and wait till somebody came to tell me what was what. And that was what I was doing.

This snooker parlor was the place to talk to gunmen if you wanted to talk to gunmen, or so I had heard, and looking around me I had to think I was not being misled. Just about anybody I saw could have been a gunman. But I told myself to relax. These were merely a few citizens having a quiet game of snooker. That's right. The real desperadoes were the guys I had arranged to meet and whom even then I sat waiting for. This thought made me drink my glass of beer down and pour another one.

I don't really care for Singha beer, to tell the truth, but you didn't get Kloster in this class of establishment. Even if they did have it nobody would drink it, drinking Kloster beer being considered effete and foolhardy besides, since anybody who could pay extra just to be seen sitting around drinking a premium beer with a fancy foreign name deserved to have what was left of his money appropriated by people who specialized in appropriating other people's money and then redistributed to the truly needy, let us say, for example, the salt of the earth who by preference drank Singha beer.

No, these boys drank Singha, and I was drinking Singha. I could also smell Mekhong whiskey, which was likewise de rigueur in

21

these circles, and cheaper than beer besides. Three tables down from where I sat there were a pair of bullyboys and they were putting back the Mekhong sodas and shooting fast, hard snooker like they knew what they were doing. Both were stripped to the waist, and they were covered with blue tattoos — lizards and dragons on their arms and magical Khmer script all over their backs. It was not only on aesthetic grounds they were thus decorated, by no means: these tattoos were meant to ward off everything from bad luck and bullets to the common cold. These two specimens were also wearing a couple of chunky amulets on chains around their necks. Looking at all this, you had to get the idea their world was a dangerous place and, seeing the various scars that also decorated their persons, you might have thought they could use one or two more amulets and maybe a Khmer postscript just there on the lower back where there was room if you wrote small.

Half the guys weren't wearing shirts, and the other half had their T-shirts rolled up to let the sweat evaporate off their bellies. You could believe you were looking at boxers, dockworkers, lads who could tote hundred-kilo sacks of rice up those ramps in the godowns along the river ten hours a day with half an hour for lunch and no double time on Sundays.

I was sorry I had quit smoking, because it's almost impossible to hang around a snooker room successfully without a cigarette. I was concentrating on being invisible, though of course not so invisible my contact might miss me. Despite this, I was the object of any number of looks from the denizens of this joint, not to mention some comments in Thai that I did not quite get. One word was coming up more than once, however, and that word was *farang*. Farang means "Westerner," which is not the worst thing you can call a person, though there are different ways of saying this word. Some ways seem to mean "Westerner-who-is-a-welcome-guest-in-this-place-which-is-our-turf," while other ways have the flavor of

"Westerner-who-bears-much-resemblance-to-a-dog-turd." Even if I allowed for some paranoia on my part, I had to think the farangs I was hearing smacked more than somewhat of the latter model.

With hard men in Thailand, it is not generally recommended you look them in the eye too long unless, of course, you wish to communicate the idea you are made of sterner stuff than they are. And unless you have some experience in fighting with fists, knees and feet, not to mention all manner of objects both blunt and sharp, it is unwise to communicate this idea. So as to avoid sending this message, then, I was not looking at anybody's eyes. I was looking instead at a big painting that was hanging in the shadows, gracing the otherwise bare wooden planks of the wall opposite. An oil painting on black velvet of a bare-busted blonde lady, it was hanging fairly radically askew, and I was wondering why they hung the picture in this way. It could be they thought it added to the homey ambience, along with the crusty spittoons and the smell of stale piss and beer and sweat. While I was so musing, a dark spot on the wall above the painting suddenly moved. It twitched and crawled along the top of the picture-frame, and the picture tilted some more. It was a fact, I told myself not for the first time — Singha beer had mind-bending qualities beyond those attributable only to alcohol, and I would never drink it again unless, of course, there was no Kloster beer at hand. Then I saw that the dark spot above the picture was no dark spot at all. It was instead a large rat with glittering eyes, a large black rat that abruptly dropped to the floor, leaving the lady with the big bust rocking in her frame.

I felt a chill, no matter this was Bangkok and as usual hotter than the hubs of hell, the lazy big ceiling fans doing little to alleviate the situation.

Then I felt another chill, and this one made the first chill seem balmy by comparison. There was a guy looking at me, and there was no looking away from those eyes. What I was getting was the

Look, and it was none other than Tommy Two-Toes himself who was giving it to me. There he stood, tottering away on his bad feet. Then he moved closer, and he lurched along like he was on strings, his puppeteer no doubt keeping him just off the ground so Tommy's feet didn't hurt too bad and he wouldn't get pissed off and give him the Look.

You ask if I am the type who has chills at the drop of a hat. I assure you that I am not. A slight frisson at the drop of a rat, perhaps, as I have already admitted, but other than that I am normally as cool as a cucumber, or possibly cooler. What I was getting in the way of the Look from Tommy, however, would have made a mountain gorilla blanch and leave the room. If you could have harnessed the Look, it would have been just the thing for riot control.

I was trying to find a smile, and I started to say "Hi, Tommy" when there was a sudden diversion. The two tattooed types with the Mekhong sodas had agreed to disagree about something. One of them slammed his cue down hard on the table, and they stared each other right in the eyes which, as I have already said, is inappropriate behavior for anybody trying to win friends and influence people in these circles. I couldn't understand exactly what they were saying, but one guy was obviously suggesting something along the lines of "Egad, sir. You displease me more than somewhat!" and the other gentleman probably answered him with "I give not a fig for your displeasure, my good man; and I give even less for the services of your sister who, as it is commonly known, cheats at cards and smells of fish besides." Or words to that effect. Before you knew it, of course, they had called each other *hia*, giant lizards, and there was no turning back.

They immediately moved on to various tests of each other's magical defense system, and set about trying to add to each other's collection of scars. The ritual proceeded with the kicking off of the flip-flops, and then with spirited attempts to kick each other's heads off as well. The rest of the assembly backed off to a prudent distance, and I saw some of them were busy making bets on the outcome of the contest.

Just as they started to wave snooker cues around as well, and it looked as though some damage might finally get done after all, Tommy stepped in. He flung a brass cuspidor gonging up hard against the wall, and everybody froze. They looked at the splash of mess on the wall and at the cuspidor, which had come to rest on the floor between the men. Then the fighters looked at Tommy, and there was black death in their eyes.

Tommy tottered on his mutilated feet, bracing himself against a table, and then he unleashed the Look. Death going eyeball-to-eyeball with the Look was no contest. The two rowdies started blinking nervously and backed away, all animosity forgotten. They put the cues down carefully on a table and they gave everybody sickly grins before they left.

I was also making my way along the wall towards the door, thinking I had had enough local color for one day and possibly I liked travel writing better anyway, when Tommy refocused on me and said, "*Sawasdi, farang.*" Howdy, farang was no doubt better than many things he could have said to me, and this version of farang seemed to be mainly a warm and welcoming one.

He came over and said like this in Thai: "*Where have you been all this time, long time no see. Hey! Are you the farang writer who wants to talk to somebody upstairs? Imagine that. Isn't it a small world?*"

I think that was what he said, anyway; I found it hard to understand his Thai. In any case, it seemed we were old buddies, and why didn't we shoot some snooker while we waited to see our man; it wasn't time yet.

Tommy couldn't stand on tiptoe to rack the balls, not having enough toes to stand tiptoe on, so he had to lie flat on the edge of the table, legs straight out behind. While he was racking up the balls I asked him, "Where's Willie?"

This got me a funny look, and he said, kind of quiet like, "*Willie who?*"

"You know — your old partner, Wrong-Way Willie Wong." I spelled it out for him.

Tommy ran the rack back and forth on the table making some noise with the balls, and he said, "*Never heard of him.*" Then, in a quiet voice he added "*Kowchai* (you know what I mean)*?*" He got down off the table and gave me a look that wasn't the Look, but which was nevertheless a warning the Look would not be far behind if I didn't get smart and forget about anybody named Willie real quick. Which I did, but I couldn't help but wonder why I had to do this thing. Maybe Tommy and Willie had had some sort of falling out.

The other boys in this snooker parlor warmed right up to me, once it was clear I had business there and somebody knew me and all. You didn't get that many foreigners down in this part of town, I guessed, and I was something of a celebrity. Already I was getting called Steve Davis. After all, Steve Davis was a foreigner and I was a foreigner, and this was a snooker room and Steve Davis was the world-champion snooker player; therefore I was Steve Davis. This much seemed reasonable enough. The local lads had great respect and admiration for this noted practitioner of the snooker's art; possibly Sylvester Stallone and Jackie Chan enjoyed better press as foreigners in Thailand, but that was about it. Actually, I was thinking it was too bad I did not resemble Steve Davis a bit more, as this would probably have increased the value of my stock around the place no end. Unfortunately, I was at least twice as robust and only one-fiftieth as knowledgeable about which end of the snooker cue was which, and not even his most distant cousin could have really mistaken me for Steve Davis.

Anyway, everybody crowded around and wanted to know how

long I was going to be in Thailand and how come I could speak Thai? It did no good to tell them I spoke Thai just as well as I played snooker because, after all, I was Steve Davis. They also wanted to know if I could eat hot food, and did I like Thai girls? I know they asked these questions to show they liked me; it didn't matter that every Thai I ever met asked me the same things. So for a change I told them yes, I ate Thai food and I liked hot girls. This joke, I had to think, did not translate into Thai because nobody laughed. But maybe they didn't understand my Thai in the first place.

Tommy made a few shots, and then I scratched, jumping the cue-ball right off the table. The guy who retrieved it for me congratulated me on a very amusing shot and smiled to let me know he knew I was only hustling. Tommy made a few more shots and I scratched again. Tommy pretty soon got pissed off. It was hard to make a shot even if you did know how to shoot, what with all these fans hanging around, and he told me it was time to go upstairs. My groupies gave me a rousing send-off, telling me I was always welcome, let us have a friendly game next time. They were glad I liked Thai girls. When I looked at their faces, I could see they thought that was where I was going now, to meet some nice Thai girl. It was that kind of place, I guessed.

There was a door in the back of the room, in behind the beer counter, and we walked through a shed into the open air, where we went along a wooden boardwalk across some wet ground into the next building. A nervous individual with one clouded eye and an enormous goiter popped up as we came in, but he relaxed as soon as he saw Tommy. They exchanged a few words I didn't catch, and Tommy and I continued along to a dimly-lit staircase. On the second landing, sitting on a chair outside a door, there was a big, handy-looking dude dressed in a sarong. The door was clearly built to resist shock and it had a sliding peep-hole.

The guy got up and banged three times on the door. Somebody appeared at the peephole, and then I heard a drop-bar being lifted and the door opened. Tommy went in first and I followed. We found ourselves in a plain room — unpainted wooden walls, a few mismatched chairs and a card table, and a dirty mattress on the floor with a TV and video machine at one end. There was another door opposite, but it was closed. A Mekhong girlie calendar hung on one wall; the calendar was for July two years earlier. Probably because the girl that month was such a knockout.

There were two men in the room. A scrawny lad of twenty years or so, with blue-tattooed arms sticking out of a tank-top that read ZOOM, BANG, BANANAS was perched on a chair up against the wall under Miss July, a wooden match between his teeth and a pair of shades hiding his eyes. A long-barreled pump-action shotgun stood against the wall beside him, and a bandoleer of 12-gauge shells was slung diagonally across his chest. His chest was only eight or nine shells wide. I thought maybe he was doing his Rambo imitation, though he needed a good fifty pounds of meat on him if he really wanted to look like Sylvester Stallone. Was this one of my gunman? I asked myself. I hoped not. But he moved that matchstick back and forth between his teeth like a real pro. And his eyes might have been deadly, behind those shades, who could tell?

Tommy ignored him. He talked to the other guy, a pasty-faced party with wall-eyes and a slavish manner. He looked something like an Asian Jean-Paul Sartre as a young man. But Tommy called him Somsak. He told him to go downstairs and get a *ben* of Mekhong whiskey, a half-bottle, and bring some soda and ice. Also he wanted some food — he said bring us *yam tua thot*, some deep-fried peanuts with chopped fresh chilies and spring onions, and *moo yahng*, that nice barbecued pork with hot sauce.

"*You like Mekhong?*" Tommy asked me, even though Jean-Paul Somsak had gone already and it was too late to order anything else.

28

So I said sure, what the hell.

I sat down and put my pocket tape-recorder on the table.

"*What's that?*" said Tommy, and Rambo pushed his chair away from the wall and came down with a bang to sit forward, motionless, eyes intent on my little Hitachi.

"It's my tape-recorder."

"*No.*"

"No tape-recorder?"

"*No.*"

This was going to make life unnecessarily difficult. It was going to be hard to use my notebook while I ate and drank and tried to make sure nobody shot me all at the same time.

I shrugged and started to put it away, but Rambo indicated he wanted to see the machine.

So there we sat. Tommy was silent; he just looked at me. His face was alert, but he didn't appear to expect anything — he was merely sitting and looking. I wondered what I was supposed to do. Rambo was playing with my recorder, back on his chair against the wall, busily chewing his matchstick. Who was it I was supposed to interview, then? Maybe it was Tommy. But how was I going to interview him in Thai? Here in Thailand I sometimes got sent to the toilet when I was only trying to order pork sausage.

Rambo was singing Carabao's nice song "Welcome to Thailand" between his teeth into the mike — in the process, I guessed, erasing the interview with the high-ranking police officer I had managed to get only after long negotiation. Then there were three bangs on the door, and Somsak arrived with the drinks. I decided a little Mekhong was a good thing after all.

And just at that moment the other door opened.

it's a small world

Selections from Arno Petty's Intelligencer and Weekly Gleaner

HIGH TIMES. The US embassy advises American nationals that if they discover their children are doing heroin, then the only real hope of saving them is to get them out of the country, and the sooner the better. Heroin is so readily available and so cheap, at least for the middle class, that the prospects of your kid giving it up are minimal. Or so goes the received wisdom.

RECYCLING THE WEALTH. In your explorations of Bangkok, you sometimes come across men and women wading waist-deep in the city's canals, straining the black mud with woven baskets. They are panning for amulets, coins, bits of things that people have thrown in over the years as gifts to the spirits. Later, you will find these small-business people with their treasures spread out on the sidewalks for sale to passers-by. Others, a more exclusive guild, paddle their sampans along the river and use long-handled baskets to scoop out everything from plastic bags to soft-drink cans, later selling them back to street vendors or else to scrap dealers. Whole communities of slum dwellers, meanwhile, eke out a bare subsistence by scavenging on municipal garbage dumps.

EVERYBODY SAYS THIS IS A SMALL WORLD, and that is so. Standing there in the doorframe four-square and wound up tight, a spring-loaded cement truck on a hair-trigger, who did I see but Wrong-Way Willie Wong, a.k.a. Wong Wei, man about Bangkok, originally from Hong Kong.

In Thailand you get your *nak laeng*, your toughs who make their way in life ignoring all the rules that normally keep polite Thai society smiling. This is their power. It's a kind of terrorism: the pre-

30

dictability of conventional social discourse no longer holds. In Thailand everything is smiles and *wai*-ing — bringing your hands together in greeting up against the forehead as in prayer; it's all excuse me and no, please, you are first. *Jai yen yen* — keep a cool heart, maintain your cool; showing your emotions, losing your temper is a sign of weakness. Self-containment, calm and control is strength and it is the Buddhist way. That's right. Right up to the moment somebody cracks. Then you find no nicely graduated escalation of the situation, where all parties to the piss-off can see where things are going and take steps to defuse it before irreparable damage is done. No, here in Thailand everything is smiles one second and blind mayhem the next. That's why the country has just about the highest murder rate in the world. There's a high value placed on control, but there aren't enough safety valves to take the pressure off. When a citizen blows, he blows right up.

And *nak laeng* capitalize on this. They ignore the polite conventions; they don't play by the rules. They're already outside the game, out there in that nasty, unpredictable jungle where anything goes. The conventional controls are already off, and the tough uses this perception to control the situation — you don't step aside, and you're dead. You return the stare one second too long, and you're dead. Some nak laeng is drunk and he thinks you're laughing at him, and you're dead. This prospect disconcerts your average square. He's got everything to lose, but this guy who wants to relieve him of only part of that — whether it's his money or his self-respect — behaves like he's got nothing to lose. So most people try to fix things in a way that makes any nak laeng in the vicinity happy. And this is how these types make their living.

But a man like Willie was in another class altogether. You only had to look at him to see this. He radiated authority. Tommy had it too; I saw that in action downstairs when he sent two nak laeng outside, and all it took was the Look. Guys like these were coming

31

from somewhere that terrorized your Joe Naklaeng, never mind Charlie Citizen.

And here was the Willie whose name I couldn't mention downstairs.

"Willie!" I said.

"You!" he answered me.

Having expressed our mutual surprise, Willie and I stood there for a minute fresh out of topics for conversation.

"You are the writer?" Willie asked me in tones of disbelief.

"You are the specialist I've come to talk to?" I asked in similar tones.

Tommy looked pleased, just as though he had engineered the whole thing himself. Rambo played back his rendition of "Welcome to Thailand," and he looked pleased. In fact by now everyone was looking pleased, except for Somsak, who was merely looking eager to please. Tommy told him to get some drinks on the table, what was he standing around gaping for? I think that was what Tommy said; anyway Somsak poured the drinks.

Willie, it turned out, was indeed the notorious gunman who had agreed to tell all to the press, only the newspaper was to keep his name out of it, right?

He remembered our previous encounter well, and he wondered how I had managed to get lost that night, after we had had such a good time together, getting along so well we had even talked of forming a partnership. But truth to tell, we all wound up so plastered he wasn't sure it was me who got lost or them. Anyway, he was glad I did not leave the country and it was good we could do business together again. I should have a drink, he said, and ask him anything I wanted to know. One thing he had these days, he told me, was lots of time on his hands.

Willie looked at the half-bottle of Mekhong Tommy had ordered. "Tommy, Tommy, Tommy," he said. "This is our old friend

32

the *farang* who is now a newspaper writer and who drinks and eats with us like we are brothers, and you order one *ben* of whiskey for what?"

Willie looked over at Somsak and Somsak jumped up with an anxious expression sliding around his face.

"You. You go down and get another bottle of Mekhong. A big one. And also bring some naem sod. That's right. Our farang friend can eat Thai food."

This time, to tell the truth, I would have liked to say no to the *naem sod*, but my instincts told me etiquette forbade. Besides, what were a few parasites to stand between old friends reunited at some providential whim?

Somsak was fixing drinks. I got a glass of Mekhong soda that was mostly Mekhong, I judged by the color. And I saw no reason to change my mind when I tasted it. I told my friends I was working, this time, and I didn't want to drink too much. Especially since I had to take notes; I couldn't use my recorder.

"Drink up, *farang*," said Willie. "We are old friends, and I know you can drink, drink all night, no problem. Only maybe you disappear, sometimes."

Somsak served drinks all around; and even Rambo took the matchstick out so he could get at the whiskey. Somsak poured himself a shot as well, I noticed; but Willie said something to him, and Somsak went over to dump it into Tommy's glass. Tommy was half finished the first drink already.

I was wondering why Somsak didn't get a drink, but what I asked was this: "What's with all the locked doors, and why can't I say 'Willie' to Tommy downstairs without getting the Look?"

Willie rolled his shirt up over his belly and got himself comfortably arranged on his chair, taking a good two-handed grip on his drink.

"It's a long story, *na?*" said Willie. "Last time we see you we are not in real good shape, our only hardware on the bottom of the river and not enough money to buy beer at breakfast next day; the hangover is enough to kill us. Never mind our quiet partner and main hope for the future disappears into the night. We don't even get a 'See you later.'"

Willie looked at me accusingly.

Tommy wasn't listening; he couldn't follow the English. He was playing with a switchblade knife, dropping it again and again between his knees, trying to stick it into the floor. Somsak was over on the mattress watching a Chinese kung fu movie on the video. Rambo was still up against the wall, Mekhong soda in hand, matchstick in place, but you couldn't tell if he was watching the video or what he was doing, with those shades on. I knew he wasn't asleep, because the matchstick kept traveling back and forth, from side to side between his teeth, except when he took it out to make way for the Mekhong.

"I don't know what happened," I told Willie. "One minute I had to find a toilet, and the next minute I was across town somewhere and you and Tommy were nowhere to be found. Maybe I drank too much. Or could be I was tired from all the day's excitement. You know how it is."

Willie said he knew. He could see I was a straight shooter, basically, only I lost track of myself from time to time, and he could understand that, after all.

"But now, I hear, the newspaper wants to find out about gunmen," Willie said. "So, no problem. Hey. Ask away."

Willie wanted to let me know we should get this interview on the road. He wasn't sure how long he could hang around, in fact. These days he liked to keep moving. So I got right down to business, and in no time I was learning all manner of interesting things.

I learned, for example, that big 11mm automatic pistols such as the one Tommy had on the table in front of him tended to be favored, hereabouts, because they had a nice punch — they often finished off your assignment even when you missed the vital organs. One other advantage, of course, was that gazing into that big, black muzzle tended to keep the mark kind of spellbound. This gave you a chance to make peace with his spirit before you pulled the trigger — from what Willie told me, I got the idea it didn't do to have disgruntled spirits roaming around constantly annoying you, if you were a professional hitman.

I asked about the fee schedule gunmen such as themselves applied when negotiating a contract.

"You mean, how much to bump a man?"

"Yeah."

"That can be anywhere from 10,000 baht, these days, all the way up to about 200,000. Where you get somebody with lots of protection, plenty of influence — that's where it costs you. Actually, you can get as much as a half million, but that's generally for some square, somebody polite, *na*?

"Tommy and me, of course, we mostly take on the fatcats, you know what I mean?" Willie was waxing expansive. "The *seua nawn kin*. Driving their Benzes, jiving their minor wives …"

"I see." Here was an angle for my story. "It's like you resent these bigshots with the money and the power, right? Strike a blow for the little man, social justice and all that, eh?"

Willie looked at me pityingly and asked me what I was talking about. He turned to Tommy, and he told Tommy I was calling them a couple of Commies or something. "Hey. Those bigshots are smart," Willie said to me. "They got it made, and they got nothing but my respect. You don't think I take these Benzes and these sweet *mia noi* with their fine clothes and soft voices? You crazy? No, you have to respect these guys.

"But the thing is, that's where the money is, bumping fatcats. What's somebody gonna pay me for bumping, say, a reporter?"

35

Just about nothing, I hastened to agree.

"Ten thousand baht. Tops," he told me.

I was worth five hundred bucks US. Less than that. So why were my life insurance premiums so high? Not that I paid any.

I passed my glass over for a refill, forgetting for a minute I wanted to stay sober.

"Yeah, we bump enough of these fatcats, only we can hang onto the money for a change, and you find us behind the wheels of those fancy big cars, eating in those fancy big restaurants ..."

He repeated all of this in Thai for Tommy, and I saw Rambo was listening in with no little interest, as well.

"How else are guys like us gonna make it? *Na?* I'm gonna work on the docks, I'm gonna get rich? And Tommy, here, with his bum feet he can't work on the docks, he's gonna sell meatballs on the street? Sure, and die poor and die young. You can have it. Hey. No, you gotta take your chance where you find it. It's just business. After all."

Willie got a real serious look on his face every time he said the word "business." Tommy also looked pretty solemn, and he said *"Chai, chai. Yes, yes. Bisnet."*

"But, like I say, that's the kind of money it takes to bump somebody. Just to shake him ... that depends.

"The way it usually goes, Tommy and I get our man alone some place, and I show him some hardware while Tommy shows him the Look. Chances are that's all it takes. But some jobs are different, *na?* Like not too long ago, a client wants us to throw a little scare into one of his business competitors. Loosen the guy up a bit, you know? Get him to listen to reason and everything.

"This guy, his name is Fast Vanich. He's not a man you can get alone some place for a talk, and you don't get close enough to show him the Look or any hardware either. Unless this hardware is somewhat bigger than an automatic pistol, let us say for example

36

something about the size of a battle tank. One problem is, he has a small army of bodyguards.

"Tommy and I get to thinking, seeing we can't discuss things directly with him, maybe it's better we kick the dog instead. This approach has more class anyway, when we think about it. You know what I mean?"

In Thai society, my girlfriend Mu had already told me, more than once, it is not polite to express your annoyance directly. It is better you smile at the object of your annoyance, while at the same time you put the boots to or otherwise batter some other item in the vicinity, such as a passing dog. If you do this right, the real object of your displeasure can have the fact of this displeasure brought home to him quite forcefully, and meanwhile he cannot fault your sense of propriety.

But Willie wanted me to know that he was speaking only figuratively, when he spoke of kicking the dog. They had by no means been about to kick Fast Vanich's dogs, which were several in number and bad-tempered Dobermans besides, the type who do not take kindly to getting booted. Not to mention they would have had to climb over a three-meter wall topped with broken glass and electrified barbed wire even to get close enough to these mutts to kick them in the first place.

Tommy thought they could throw poisoned meatballs over the wall, this being in his opinion a sounder procedure than trying to kick a bunch of Dobermans. "But I like dogs, generally speaking," said Willie, "and it is not a dog's fault if it's born a Doberman and not real friendly, and I just as soon not have all these dead dogs on my mind."

But then Willie and Tommy got a good idea. Fast Vanich had this godown along beside the river, and they checked it out and found it was full to busting with all kinds of fine stuff. It seemed Fast Vanich was into import-export. He had everything from color

TVs to antique plastic dancing elephants on hand, and rumors had it that once in a while some of these *objets* contained certain substances that could realize a very high profit margin, as long as the authorities didn't get wind of this information first. So Willie and Tommy figured it this way — they only had to remind Fast Vanich of the impermanence of all worldly things, and maybe a small explosion in this warehouse was just what it would take to do this. A few 24-inch Sonys up in smoke, and Fast Vanich would figure it was time to cut his losses and talk turkey. So they did this at night, when nobody would get hurt, only a night watchman or two; and it was nice and polite — not too direct or anything, I had to understand. Fast Vanich would see he could talk to their client and nobody had to lose too much face or anything. What were a few television sets to a bigshot like him? After all.

As an example of kicking the dog, Willie told me, this godown caper had the dog kicked all the way into next week. "You have to think Tommy is probably out of touch when it comes to demolition jobs, and we overdo the explosives a bit. And besides this the piles the joint is built on are most likely rotten. What with one thing and another, anyway, the whole warehouse goes into the river. It's what you call overkill."

This miscalculation was good news for many of the small businessmen downriver from the job, mind you. Willie told me the favorite collector's item had been the plastic dancing elephant, which often turned out to be stuffed with bags of No.4 heroin. The cushions with the Temple of Dawn embroidered on them had also been popular, since many of these objets were filled with an unusual grade of ganja, sweet maryjane, and the cushion covers made good gifts.

"Overall, it is good promotion for our services," Willie said, "since people in general are quite impressed with the spirit they hear we bring to our work."

And my friends did play hardball, I could see that. They were also drinking enough to make them impressive individuals even if they didn't make a habit of blowing things up when they weren't blowing people away. I was getting the idea they were keeping up with me, the bottomless farang. You couldn't let some pissant foreign pencil-pusher drink you under the table.

My next question was interrupted by a sudden "*Whish, whish, whish, thud. Whish, whish, thud; thud, whish.*" I had heard these sounds earlier, on the kung fu video, except this time it wasn't the video, it was Somsak who was shooting boots and fists in Rambo's general direction. Somsak was making whishing noises and pounding his chest to simulate the sound of blows.

While everybody was watching this performance, I whipped my Mekhong into the ice-bucket again.

But Tommy was annoyed with Somsak's antics, it seemed, because next thing he decided to level his pistol at Somsak's head. I was thinking this couldn't be happening. He wasn't going to shoot old Somsak in the head, was he? Then I saw if there was anything worse than getting the Look, it was getting the Look over the gunsights of an 11mm automatic pistol. But Somsak didn't notice. What he did notice was that Rambo had left off being unconcerned by all this whishing about. In fact Rambo put down his glass, stood up, and kicked Somsak in the stomach. Somsak's eyes bugged out and he staggered back to fold up on the mattress, wheezing and gasping and looking surprised.

Rambo sat down again to watch the video or whatever it was he did behind those glasses. But first he turned those Blues Brothers shades on me and stared till I had to think something was up. What the hell was this? I asked myself. Then I asked Willie: "What the hell is this?"

"Never mind the boy. He doesn't like *farang.*"

"*Farang!*" said Rambo, the first thing I had ever heard him speak, and he used the "Westerner-who-bears-much-resemblance-to-a-dog-turd" version of farang.

"His father was an American GI," Willie told me, "on a little R&R from Vietnam, *na?* And he finds this nice girl on New Pet-chburi Road. He bangs her up and goes away and the boy never gets to see his own poppa. It pisses him off, he says."

"Okay, I guess," I said. "But why did he kick Somsak in the stomach? Somsak is no farang, even if he does look something like Jean-Paul Sartre."

"He kicks Somsak, but he means you."

"Oh."

I was still surprised Somsak let everybody treat him like a dog this way. He was bigger than Rambo, for one thing, and he looked stronger. "Doesn't Somsak have a gun?" I asked Willie.

"Nobody in their right mind lets that guy have a gun. Hey. He's a good boy, but he is watching the video and doesn't notice when they hand out the brains in this life. He's not all there in the head, *na?* Especially when he's drinking. We don't let him drink."

Right at this moment there was a knock at the door. *Wham, wham.* Not wham, wham, wham, like when Tommy and I arrived, but just wham, wham. Not much of a difference, I was thinking, but it was truly remarkable the reaction it got from my compa-nions.

Rambo was suddenly crouched down in the corner with the shotgun pointed along the wall towards the door. Tommy was on the other side of the door with his pistol held high. Willie, in the meantime, was making his way on tip-toe out through the other door, the way he had come in earlier. Then I saw what Somsak was good for. Tommy waggled his gun at him and he was the one who got to answer the door, which he proceeded to do quite cheerfully; you could see he liked to help. Willie was right; the boy was no Einstein.

Willie was waving at me frantically, so I got up and followed him through the door. I was quite pleased to get invited out of the room just then. I wasn't sure exactly what was what, but it was clear something was up, and that something was no surprise party for somebody's favorite cousin.

I was standing in what I thought was a closet, only Willie reached up and pulled something, and the back wall swung away to reveal a flight of steps. I kept waiting for all hell to break loose, but there was merely the sound of muffled voices and then some muffled thuds. Willie was also puzzled, and he fiddled nervously with the M-16 assault rifle he had found somewhere since we came in here.

After a minute we heard a tap-tap-tap on the door, and Willie hugged up against the wall beside the door and tapped back with the barrel of the M-16, three times. Then we heard tap-tap-tap-tap-tap, and Willie said it was okay; it was Tommy. Open the door. I was no Somsak: I opened the door, but with no enthusiasm whatever.

It was Tommy, however, and he reported there was no problem. It was only a boy from downstairs with the food, and he didn't know the code knock.

What about the guard on the landing? Willie wanted to know. He looked not very happy.

He had been asleep when the boy came up, Tommy said. The boy was afraid to wake him because this dude was a hard man and generally bad-tempered, as well.

I could see Willie was not very happy, indeed. He said, "Where is this guard, I want to talk to him." He said this in a way that made you glad you were not the guard in question.

According to Tommy, however, the hard man was indisposed right then; he was downstairs getting his face taped up. I saw Tommy was back to wiping and polishing his pistol; the paper he was using had red stains on it. Maybe blood, I guessed.

"I swear," said Willie. "The kind of people you have to work with. *Na?* It isn't easy to get good help, not these days. I am glad when this all blows over, and things get back to normal. Eh, Tommy?"

Tommy looked noncommittal. He stripped his automatic down and started to clean it part by part.

not standard

Selections from Arno Petty's Intelligencer and Weekly Gleaner

HEAVEN ON EARTH. One senior official has suggested that the government should designate certain areas as 'Paradise Zones.' Within the limits of a Paradise Zone, not only would prostitution be legal, it would be regulated by the Interior Ministry. What a great idea. At the same time they could declare them AIDS-Free Zones, and then just sit back to watch the revenues roll in.

'LANDMARK DECISION.' Some years ago, five girls were found chained to a wall in the back room of a brothel on Phuket, this brothel having just burned down. The proprietor of this establishment was actually sent to jail for three years and, as though that weren't enough, a court has this week decided that he should pay the mother of one of these girls 95,000 baht in compensation. The girl had been the chief source of income for her family, after all.

THE GREENING OF THAILAND. Golf is the current passion of the affluent. Membership exchanges advertise in the papers; and memberships are traded like pork bellies. Only pork doesn't tend to run between 400,000 and 1.5 million baht per belly.

SOMETIMES Tommy and Willie shot people and sometimes they didn't. Sometimes they only reasoned with them, maybe blowing up their warehouses and suchlike.

"But we are also in the protection business," Willie told me. "Kind of a security service, you could say. Take this time not too long ago, when we are up in the boonies, up North in a joint called Happyland. Hey, Tommy? That was some job, *na?*"

Their job was to assist a guy name of Paiboon. Paiboon was the man who ran Happyland for their client, and the problem was this: there was a gunman of some reputation named Dit who was telling their client's man Paiboon that he should give over a large sum of money or else see both himself and his business meet untimely ends. Already two female employees had disappeared and three more had been knocked up, though nobody believed this was Dit's doing, no matter what he said.

"But Paiboon starts to get nervous and unhappy, and he asks our client to send some help. That's us."

I asked Willie how about the police?

"Cops? This guy Dit *is* the cops."

I expressed surprise at this, but Willie told me it was no big deal. Your average gunman in these parts was a cop. "I mean, you just about gotta do something extra; no cop can feed a family on what they get paid. It's a crime, what you get paid for an honest day's work in this country."

I was writing all this down, wondering would my editor print it. Generally it wasn't a good idea to say such negative things about the police.

Tommy had his gun put back together again, and he cocked it, running the slide with a nice clean snick. When Willie filled Tommy in on which caper we were talking about, Tommy suddenly sat up straight and got interested. "*Mangda!*" Tommy spat this word, and he had a look on his face you could see why people hired him as a consultant when they had business problems.

Willie told me Tommy had no use for mangda, though I already had this idea anyway. But I was confused. Mangda? I asked him. The only mangda I had ever heard of was a big beetle they sometimes mashed up and added to *nam phrik gapi* — that sauce they made for raw vegetables — and the only reason I knew this word was that I wanted to ask every waiter who ever served me nam

44

phrik gapi, was there any mangda in this stuff? It was not that I was squeamish; I was not. But I could never get used to the idea of eating bugs, except maybe for fried grasshoppers. As long as the oil was fresh.

Beetles were okay with Tommy, according to Willie, but it wasn't beetles we were talking about — it was pimps he didn't like, and pimps were also called mangda.

When I asked him why, this could give me some color for my story, he said the male mangda climbed up on the female and rode around on it. Just like a pimp.

This was interesting, I told Willie. I had never known pimps upcountry rode around on ladies, before. But he didn't laugh.

"*Dhamma*," Willie pronounced in grave tones, "the teaching of the Buddha tells us that 'right work' — a good job — is one part of the Eightfold Path."

I had never seen Willie look self-righteous before, and I made a sound something like a giggle, though I coughed and pretended it was some whiskey going down the wrong way. Tommy was giving his imitation of a choirboy, as well; no doubt it was this talk of dhamma that was doing it. Willie went on to tell me that Tommy in fact used to live in a temple, when he was a boy; that was where orphans went, and he knew all about such matters.

I said okay, but what about shooting people — the Buddha was not down on this activity?

"It's not the same." Probably tired of self-righteousness, Willie tried indignation for a change. "Your average pimp kills the girls while they are still alive. *Na?* He is a bloodsucker. He feeds off human life. He takes, takes, takes; he never gives back."

I was thinking there was also something one-sided about killing a person, and I couldn't help but ask Willie what he thought of this. Was he sure there was nothing wrong with shooting people?

"Listen," he answered me. "It's only karma."

45

"Karma? You are not trying to tell me they merely bring it on themselves, are you?" I laughed at this humorous idea. But Willie wasn't laughing.

"You could say that. Yeah, that's right," he told me, though I could see even he had to think that proposition over some more.

"The thing is, to do this job right, you got to be a professional. Isn't that right?" He turned to Tommy and told him the same thing in Thai. Tommy nodded seriously and rammed the magazine on his pistol home before sighting it in on Somsak's face. Somsak smiled and blinked. You could see he hoped Tommy was just kidding some more.

"You're a professional," Willie said, "you can't go around playing God. Hey. You don't know if somebody really should be dead or not. After all. You can't know about his karma, his past lives and like that. Maybe he asks for it. But, for sure, if it happens, then you know he asks for it somewhere along the line, because that's karma. You follow?"

"I see what you mean," I lied. I noticed Tommy had put his gun away, and I guessed Somsak's karma was okay for the time being.

"So you got a job to do, you do it. You don't ask questions. You don't think 'Hey, this is not a bad guy, I don't mind playing snooker with him; I better call this contract off.' No, you don't know if his karma says he lives or he dies, so you take the contract and do the best job you can and you don't worry if it's right or if he's a good guy or not."

I was nodding and smiling and trying to let Willie know it was okay with me if he went around shooting people, but we should get on with our interview. He didn't believe I was convinced.

"Everything that happens in this life, good and bad, happens because sometime in the past, or sometime in some life you lived before, you do something that asks for it. Na? You make lots of merit — you do lots of right things — you look after your momma

46

and poppa real well, you do your time in the temple, you be true to the people around you, and one day you get born all over again and next thing you know you can't do anything wrong. Everything is roses no matter what happens. Even if people are taking out contracts on your life and so on.

"But you do a lot of wrong things now, and in your next life it's like trying to row a boat in mud, everything you do."

Willie stopped talking. He and Tommy seemed dispirited, all of a sudden.

"More whiskey!" said Willie, and Somsak jumped up.

I had Willie's observations regarding this life and past ones noted down; but I was thinking it was time I got some more hard material for my editor, or he was going to send me back to interview a couple more gunmen. I couldn't believe I ever did anything so bad my karma had this on the agenda.

What exactly was it they had to do; what kind of business did this Paiboon run? And why did Tommy say *"Mangda!"* in exactly that way? I meant with a look on his face like the first time I had a big mouthful of *nam phrik gapi mangda* and somebody told me what a *mangda* was.

Willie informed me their client's man Paiboon was a pimp — a rich pimp, mind you, since he ran this very large brothel, but a pimp nevertheless. And Tommy hated pimps.

"Still, Tommy's just the man for the job. He knows what's what in the brothel business."

I was surprised to hear this, given what Willie had already told me about Tommy and pimps.

"Tommy lives in a brothel when he is a boy."

"I thought you told me he lived in a temple."

"That's right, he does," said Willie. "But he also lives in a brothel."

It seemed that after Tommy had done a year or two as a temple

47

boy with the monks, he got tired of the spiritual pace of life, seeing he was getting on towards the age of ten, and he started to think it was time to get out into the world and make his mark. So he came up with a job running errands in a brothel, where he got room and board and more tips than he had ever dreamed of. Plus he got to enjoy all the fringe benefits any boy just coming of age liked to enjoy while living in a joint jam-packed with young ladies with soft spots for little men who were orphans and who were at that age where there was only one thing on their minds, except for Tommy, who thought about making it big as a man to be reckoned with outside the whorehouse as well.

"It all gives Tommy a taste for variety he never loses.

"But the thing is, this brothel burns down one night, and everybody gets out except for three ladies they find the next day chained up in a back room, turned to carbon. One of these ladies is Tommy's best friend, who the boss already tells Tommy has to go over to her hometown to see her mother who is sick." Tommy was just a young boy, Willie went on, but he got this good idea. He found some electric blasting caps somewhere, and he wired them up to the ignition switch one day when he was supposed to be cleaning the boss' car, a really good job, inside and out. The caps were in a five-gallon can of gasoline, which was in the trunk. It probably shouldn't have worked, but it did. And it gave the boss, his driver, and some other dude a quick preview of what it was like where they were headed next. Word soon got around what a good job Tommy had done, never mind he was only a kid, and before you knew it he was apprenticed to some guys who specialized in blowing things up, where these things annoyed people with money plus little patience with annoying things.

"So it's where Tommy gets his start in life, only he never loses his feeling about pimps."

The more I learned about these men, the more impressed I was.

There was a refreshing directness about them. Thais are generally more circumspect. I didn't know I was getting the sort of material I needed for a story, however. Even though I was just about sober, I couldn't seem to keep track of where things were going. In fact, nobody knew where they was going, was my guess. Everybody had taken to staring off into the middle distance, maybe trying to get the Big Picture.

At that moment a big tough old cockroach started to lumber across the floor, probably thinking all the time it was scuttling. You could see life was like rowing a boat in mud, and possibly it had been a mangda in its last life. Rambo came off his chair and put his foot down on the creature, rubbing it out slowly and with relish. The cracking of carapace and rupture of innards made me hope this poor bug had made lots of merit in this life and would come back with better prospects next time.

As a matter of fact, I was surprised Rambo was this direct with it, when he could have kicked Somsak in the crotch instead. Just so the cockroach would know what was what, I mean. Rambo sat down again, matchstick in place, and he leaned back up against the wall. And he stared right at me, though the opaque windows of his glasses gave me no clue what was going on behind them.

Then we all looked at the remains of the bug for a while, and we thought about this and that. I mostly thought about how I hated cockroaches as much as I hated mangdas, and about how mashed cockroaches, on the whole, were worse than live ones.

Willie belched and said to Somsak, get some more food. And more ice. Then he took up the story again, telling me how him and Tommy, they settled in up North in Happyland and stayed for a while.

No matter how Tommy felt about pimps, their job was to stick like glue to this mangda Tommy couldn't stand being around. Not only did they have to stick close as flies to shit, they were supposed to see to it this villain Dit never got to do him any damage. Even though for two baht Tommy would have severely damaged Paiboon himself; in fact you could have kept your two baht.

Tommy didn't like Paiboon. On the other hand, he made quite a few friends among the resident employees of the establishment. So did Willie, come to that. To tell the truth, if it hadn't been for all the friendly ladies and the free account at the bar, Tommy and Willie could have gotten quite bored. Before long, though, they started to feel like nothing more than baby-sitters; and where was this guy Dit? They began to think he was only a rumor. There was nary a sign of him. Even though two more employees turned out to be pregnant, and Paiboon's second cousin who lived in Korat had a motorcycle accident, Dit did not come forward to take credit. It made Paiboon uneasy; things were too quiet. At the same time, Willie and Tommy were themselves getting restless, their talents being wasted this way.

"It gets so bad Tommy is thinking of getting married," Willie told me, "just for something to do. One handy party from Ubon reminds him of his first wife, Toy Number One, the lady who blows him up back down South."

One afternoon, then, just for something else to do, Tommy went around checking out Happyland for its safety features, and he decided right away the joint was a death trap. He told Paiboon he needed fire escapes and fire extinguishers all around the place.

"Paiboon says like this, he says, 'You think I'm made of money? I've got money to burn, I already pay a small fortune to keep you two bums around here drinking my best booze and, no doubt, giving half my staff the clap besides?' So Tommy gets drinking, one afternoon, and he goes around looking for a back room full of girls chained up, or something. Paiboon's men try to stop him, but Tommy has got the Look and his 11mm pistol, and they don't try too hard." Willie started to laugh and he said something to Tommy. Then they were both laughing, and I asked them what was up.

"Tommy finds this one big heavy locked door, way down in back, and he wants it open, but nobody will open it. So then he gets the idea this is where you find the girls in chains. He yells stand away from the door and he shoots the lock, never thinking it may be hard to stand out of the line of fire if you are chained to the wall. Luckily, there are no girls chained to the wall, with or without bullet-holes in them. What they find is Paiboon and his driver, and they are embarrassed about something. Could be it's because the driver's pants are on backwards. Then Paiboon gets mad and fires all his men because they can't stop one skinny gunman from interrupting him in the middle of an important business meeting.

"He tells us he calls our client and he has us fired too; what do we think the score is? We are supposed to be here to take care of Dit, but maybe it's better he hires Dit to take care of us instead; and whose side are we on anyway?

And this is the way it went, Willie told me, the kind of stuff that was going on, and Paiboon was about as happy with them as they were with him.

Things went from bad to worse, in fact. Happyland was short-handed, what with all the men Paiboon had fired, and now this low-life wanted Tommy and Willie to double as minders; he seemed to think their job was also to keep the girls in line, and not let them go AWOL and suchlike.

Normally, Tommy and Willie would not argue if you told them they should stay up close to a bunch of nice women and keep an eye on them. That was pretty much all they had done since they took this contract, anyway. But when Paiboon told them they had to make sure these ladies stayed in line, and didn't go off on their own or break any house rules, they told him right back this was no part of their job. Their job was to bump Dit, if this guy Dit was really real and if he ever got around to showing his face in the neighborhood. They weren't any prison guards, and nobody should ask them to put the muscle on these honest working girls, many of whom were already pals. What did he think they were, anyway? Mangdas? Paiboon finally had to hire back the men he had gotten rid of before. He saw he was losing some amount of face, and who was responsible? These prima donna hired guns who were costing him money and all they were doing was enjoy this paid vacation. So he beat up a girl named Bon, who was one of Willie's favorites, only to let Willie know he was not happy.

He kicked the dog? I asked, and Willie said that's right; I was learning all about Thailand.

Now, Willie was a man of some delicacy, and he did not shoot Paiboon. He wanted Paiboon to know he was also unhappy, so he merely started an argument with Paiboon's good friend the driver. This argument Willie resolved by throwing the driver out of a third-floor window, and Paiboon turned out to be short one driver and one friend for awhile.

Paiboon didn't talk to Willie for some time after that. Meanwhile, Tommy got to drive Paiboon's Benz for a couple of days while Paiboon looked for a new driver. Tommy liked driving the car but, of course, with his feet in the shape they were in, he really needed feather-touch power brakes, and he drove the Benz right into the back of a ten-wheel truck. Tommy said thank my ancestors I had the seat-belt on, though Paiboon could see no grounds for gratitude in this.

"That's some car, eh, Tommy?" Willie said. "One day soon our luck changes, *na?* We drive our own big black Benz with smoked glass all around and about ten big spotlights on the front. Back seat full of *mia noi*, minor wives."

But to return to his story, Willie told me things did not improve between them and Paiboon.

And Paiboon finally went too far. "Right in front of everybody, he calls me a Chinaman," said Willie.

I said I thought he said he was from Hong Kong.

"Nobody calls me a Chinaman. So I call him *nah phooying*, 'face-of-a-woman,' and *katoey*, 'ladyboy.' Which is only the truth, after all. But this gets him real mad, and he calls me a *hia*, so I shoot him in the face."

Well, sure; of course you couldn't have people going around calling you a big lizard. Not in front of everybody that way. You just about had to shoot them in the face. After all. But Willie did it right, he wanted me to know — he got right in there close enough to ask Paiboon's pardon before he pulled the trigger. He used Tommy's pistol. Tommy, meanwhile, was keeping a few of Paiboon's flunkies in line with the M-16.

"Asking Paiboon's pardon?" I said. "But you already told me he annoyed you more than somewhat."

"That's right; he does. You should know, however, it is the custom among pros like us to ask the target's pardon before we bump him. It is polite, *na*? It shows you are doing this thing with a *jai yen yen*. With a cool heart. Anybody can kill a man when he is hot."

Needless to say, in any case, their client back in Bangkok — Mr Bamrung — was not overjoyed at the way things had worked out.

"Mr Bamrung?" I asked. "You're not talking about 'Bam-Bam' Bamrung, by any chance?"

"That's the man." Willie tried on a modest expression.

I was impressed. I was more than impressed. Bam-Bam Bamrung Klangsongboon had been very big stuff, indeed — a bigshot among bigshots, never mind his name sounded like somebody just fell out of a window into an alley full of trash-cans. His sudden passing had been headline news.

So it was easy to believe that it had been death for Willie and Tommy on the streets, and that for a while they had had to go under deep cover. finally, though, they saw things couldn't continue

53

the way they were. So they took out a contract on Bam-Bam. This was not just because he was making it more than somewhat hot for them on the street, right then, but also because Willie had picked up a bullet-wound or two during the last caper — merely flesh wounds, but he was still not feeling up to par.

"Or else, of course, we look after business ourselves." Willie pulled the collar of his T-shirt away to show me a big puckered red scar.

It was inappropriate that they should hire inferior talent to deal with such a prominent man of affairs. But, now that Paiboon had passed away, Dit the invisible gunman suddenly materialized, so they hired Dit to do the job. When Tommy and Willie explained they wanted him to take care of their client Mr Bamrung, who was Paiboon's boss, Dit could see this was a suitable way to bring matters to an honorable close.

And Dit did a good job for them. It was maybe his training as a policeman, who knows? As a matter of fact, he was disguised as a cop when he pulled the hit — sure, he was a cop; but he disguised himself as a Bangkok cop. A smooth job.

A masterpiece, according to Willie. And although it cost them everything they could borrow and steal, as well as their whole stake, many of their personal problems had been ironed out, and it looked as though it was time to get back to the business of living. The way things had turned out, the only people who wished Tommy and Willie ill were people who were not about to translate such ill-will into action. Not with two desperadoes such as they now enjoyed the reputation of being. A lot of people didn't even want to get close to them. Word had it they were just a bit unpredictable, and not a little direct when they decided to act.

It did not escape me either that there were better people than this to hang around if you wanted to stay bored, and maybe get to grow old and have many grandchildren.

"Nobody likes a man who's a pimp and a woman-beater," Willie was saying. "Not too many people, probably not even his own mother, are sorry to see Paiboon go. And there are a lot of folks who sleep better with Mr Bamrung passed away, as well."

Still, as Tommy kept reminding him, business was business, and when a gunman took a contract he was expected to honor the terms of that contract, those terms rarely including the extermination of the contractor or contractors themselves.

"We get a reputation for not being standard," Willie told me.

wrong way

Selections from Arno Petty's Intelligencer and Weekly Gleaner

BARING ARMS. Maybe you were wondering what those signs in Thai on the doors of the bars on Suttisarn Road and similar venues are all about. These areas have been declared Weapons-Free Zones, you will doubtlessly be relieved to know. So check your Uzis at the door, okay?

GOOD NEWS? The city is declaring key areas of Bangkok Traffic Violation Free Zones. From now on, drivers on these designated roadways will cease and desist from driving in ways detrimental to the public welfare. So it has been decreed, and what a relief. Of course up till now the entire city, if not the country as a whole, has been a Free Zone for traffic violators ... Just a minute — this proposed scheme *is* something new, isn't it?

I COULDN'T SAY I WAS SURPRISED. That Tommy and Willie had come up with this reputation for being not standard, I mean. But I was glad to hear everything had gotten straightened out in the end; it sounded as though they were smelling of roses, all in all. So I was wondering why Willie was still keeping himself scarce, I couldn't even say "Willie" in the snooker room downstairs.

Willie wasn't one hundred percent comfortable with this question. He held his glass out to Somsak and waited till it was full of whiskey. After he had taken a long pull at it, he belched delicately and he ate a stuffed chicken wing, a specialty of the kitchen next door. "Try one," he said. "They're good."

He was right; they were. They were stuffed with shrimp and pork, and they came with a nice hot-sweet sauce, full of honey and chili peppers.

"We have another little problem, still," said Willie finally, and he repeated this in Thai for Tommy, while he chuckled ruefully.

Tommy did not chuckle, ruefully or otherwise. He said like this, he said *"Ting-tong,"* which was Chinese slang for "crazy." Then he said something about *tamruat*, which were policemen. As I got the story, then, it seemed they managed to find some work here and there, and before long things were looking up again. Willie even traded his M-16, which was really only useful upcountry, and started packing an Uzi machine pistol, which was just what the doctor ordered for city jobs, where it was generally better to keep things out of sight till you needed them. Willie was going on about the rate of fire an Uzi gave you, and talking about its dependability, when he suddenly got this dejected look about him: "But I have to sell it to meet expenses. This past month is not an easy time."

"Tell the farang the story," Tommy suggested.

In a nutshell, then, what I heard was this.

Willie was having dinner at a fancy restaurant on the river with a young lady of no mean charms. He was feeling very pleased with life; he had this foxy lady and his Uzi and money for food and drink. The sun was going down and the river was beautiful in the sunset. The beer was cold. There was a cool breeze, and the lady had her hand on his knee. This was it, he was thinking — now everything was coming together, and this was what his life had been leading up to. This was his reward for always doing his best even when the times were hard.

"Then the waiters push a couple of tables together and a gang of uniformed policemen sits down." Willie looked deep into his empty glass and said all this talking left him thirsty. He sent Somsak downstairs for more whiskey and soda. And ice. He said here, take the ice bucket.

It was hot in there, and I wished I had another drink of water. I happened to look over at Somsak, who had stopped at the door. I guess he was thirsty, too; I noticed he was drinking from the bucket. He took it away from his mouth for a minute and looked surprised. Then he laughed and tilted that bucket back like it was a shot glass and he was Wild Bill Hickok come to town after a long drive. Then he went out.

I still wondered why they didn't let Somsak drink, but I thought I should find out pretty soon, because by now he had sucked back just about all the Mekhong originally meant for me.

Rambo followed Somsak out, saying he needed the toilet.

With some more prodding from Tommy, then, Willie went on with the story.

He said we all knew what a threat to a man's peace of mind your average cop was, not to mention one's life and limb, and suddenly here we had a whole tableful of these big lizards right next to him. Naturally, Willie started getting edgy right away, and he wished there was no bunch of policemen sitting there. They were probably already drunk, but they quickly proceeded to get drunker still. From Willie's point of view at that time, parked there with one foot in Heaven, it was hard to imagine some more annoying fly in the ointment. If there was anything worse than a number of loud drunks, it was a number of loud drunken cops. Especially cops with big pistols strapped to their hips and walkie-talkies they were waving around like official scepters or something. They probably thought it made them special in some way; they could talk to each other over a distance without yelling. But they were yelling anyway.

"*These are merely a few boys having a drink,*" said Tommy in Thai, and I was surprised to hear Tommy taking the side of a policeman. "*It's like you never make a noise when you drink? Ting-tong!*"

"*You are not there when it happens, na?*" answered Willie, "*So you don't know how it is that night.*"

Willie was a man of the world, after all, and he could have probably handled it, ordinarily. If only it hadn't been for this one especially loud and unappealing individual who kept flourishing his walkie-talkie with arrogant abandon and who kept eyeballing Willie's lady friend, who was by no means flattered at this attention, just frightened. Willie wasn't sure what to do, he said, though his instinct told him it was time to leave; his lady decided she wasn't hungry anyway. He gave the cop a look or two, but it didn't do any good. If only Tommy had been there with The Look. Then the pig stood up, all flushed with drink and self-importance. He had the walkie-talkie raised high in one hand while he shifted the gun lower on his hip with the other, this hip being cocked at an angle designed to piss Willie off even without the gun and the walkie-talkie and everything.

"*Now I see it, then; of course, everything is okay now — the guy is standing wrong. That's how it all happens. Of course.*" Tommy didn't really look relieved or anything, however.

Just then, Willie continued, he caught the law officer's eye, and it was plain the young cop figured it was incumbent upon Willie to look away first. Willie was not accustomed to looking away first, though he could see it might be a good idea this time if he did, and then maybe leave quietly with his lady while the leaving was good.

"*I was gonna leave then,*" he told Tommy.

But he didn't leave. Exactly at that moment the cop fumbled his walkie-talkie in mid-flourish. In fact, he dropped it right into the big steaming dish of *tom yam kung*, which is a tasty hot and sour shrimp soup. This got everyone's attention right off. Most of the other patrons of the restaurant looked away again immediately, though, their expressions showing nothing. You could see this was a big loss of face for the cop and to all his buddies as well. It was not a good idea to drop your walkie-talkie into the soup in public. It did not help that Willie could not restrain a hearty laugh at the proceedings. As soon as he didn't restrain this laugh, of course, he figured it was a mistake. But what could you do? After all.

Now the cop was reaching for his pistol, and Willie saw he had decided the best way to save face and to forestall further laughter was to shoot Willie. Of course Willie was not the type who took kindly to getting shot, and rather than see this thing happen he brought out his Uzi, which he hadn't had a chance to field test yet. The gun worked fine. It caught the kid and held him dancing in a stream of bullets for a second before Willie turned his attention to the other police officers present. They might have been drunk, but they weren't slow, because most of them were already diving off the restaurant into the river. Two went for their guns instead, but the Uzi chopped them down before you could say cheese it.

Willie got his spare clip into the machine pistol, and he said to his date they might as well leave; it was good she was not hungry. She was happy to leave, it turned out; but she would just as soon not leave with Willie or ever see him again either. This hurt Willie not a little, he told me, but there was no time to talk it over and he got out of there without further ado.

"All that happens only a month ago, and the police are still annoyed, from what we hear. So I figure on lying low for a while."

I was more than somewhat impressed by this account. I was so impressed I started to think about lying low myself, merely because I was in their general vicinity. I could believe the police were annoyed. To tell the truth, I started to get nervous I was even in the same part of town; it would not be healthy when the shooting began, the local police not being notoriously accurate and furthermore being often short-sighted and unable to distinguish a law-abiding citizen like myself from a bona fide bumper-off of cops by the job lot such as my associate had turned out to be.

"Well." I smiled broadly. "I guess that's all I need. It should make a good story. Thank you. See you around, now. Look after yourselves."

As I got up to leave, there was a triple knock at the door and

Willie said get that, would you?

It was Somsak, and there was clearly something wrong with him. His eyes were glazed over more than usual, and he was walking funny. At first I thought he was imitating Tommy's walk, and I thought what a dangerous thing to do. Then I saw it was only Somsak trying to walk a straight line.

"*Somsak!*" Willie said. "*You are drunk? What is this?*"

The bottle Somsak set down was not full, the way you might have expected a new bottle of Mekhong to be.

Somsak belched loudly, and you could see Willie, for one, was offended.

"*Cops.*" Somsak let go another resounding burp. "*The cops are downstairs.*"

This had an electrifying effect on the room. Tommy was suddenly mincing along towards the closet at a rate of knots, moving much like Howdy Doody on hot coals. He had his pistol in one hand and the Mekhong in the other, probably for balance.

Willie never lost control. He told me to stay where I was; I would be all right. But maybe I had better pay for the interview now. Quickly, he wanted to say. This was the first I had ever heard of payment, but you didn't argue with a man of Willie's caliber, not when he was holding an M-16 and he was in a hurry. I gave him 1,000 baht. Anything to get him out of the room. He looked hurt, so I forked over another 1,000 baht and I said, "Good luck; you better go."

Somebody was hammering on the door and yelling; it sounded like Rambo. But that couldn't have been right, because next thing old Jean-Paul Somsak let fly at the door with a blast from the shotgun. This operation left Somsak sitting stupefied on his ass. It also stopped the knocking.

Then there was another loud bang. Somsak was still holding Rambo's shotgun, and now he was staring up at a hole in the ceiling. From upstairs you could make out the sound of a woman screaming and there was the sound of hurried footsteps leaving the room.

Which led everyone present to believe this might be a good policy generally, and we all ran into the closet. Except for Somsak, who was taking time out from shooting up the joint to vomit.

Now we could hear heavy footsteps on the stairway outside.

While these unidentified types you had to suspect were policemen thundered up one staircase, we were moving down another just as quietly as possible. It was getting dark, but I could make out Willie and Tommy ahead of me as they hot-footed it outside and along a planked walkway. It occurred to me, don't think it didn't, that there were better places to be under the circumstances. Running along this boardwalk in Klong Toey with these two gentlemen, so armed and so sought after by the local gendarmerie, was not my first choice of venues. But the alternative was to be in the room upstairs with the smell of cordite in the air, not to mention puke, waiting for a gang of annoyed and no doubt heavily armed policemen to bust in, chances are shooting first and asking questions later, by which time it probably wouldn't matter my Thai wasn't so good and I couldn't answer very intelligibly.

So there I was. And in a minute we were on a ramshackle wooden pier in the twilight, where we found two longtail boat taxis tied up. The drivers didn't seem surprised to see three men, two of them carrying firearms, running towards them. Only when we get up close did one of them show any excitement: "Steve Davis!" he cried.

Needless to say, Steve Davis was not there, and I was pretty sure he wasn't even in Thailand. No, it was me he was talking to, and he was one of the snooker room lads I had met earlier.

Tommy and Willie jumped into the other guy's boat and told me to get in quick. I said to them like this, I said I wished them well, but I had an appointment up the river the other way; perhaps we could get together again at some future date.

Although this was something I devoutly hoped would never come to pass, as I stood there by the river waiting for the sound of gunfire behind me. But Willie said, "Yeah, we'll be in touch; tell it like it is," and Tommy said, "*Sawasdi, farang. So long.*"

I jumped in my boat and waited till Tommy and Willie had headed off one way, out towards the port, the big motor screaming, and then I told my driver to go the other way, and hurry.

"Steve Davis!" he yelled at me as we made our departure. "Do you like Thai girls?"

I was still listening for gunfire, however, so I didn't answer him. And for a second I thought I did hear shots, but it was off in the distance, in the direction Tommy and Willie had made their getaway.

If I lived to get home and get to my typewriter, I figured, I might have enough material for a story on gunmen. I hoped so. I didn't want to do any more of these interviews. They made me tired.

Rambo had never given me back my recorder, I suddenly realized, and I wondered how the editor would go for 2,000 baht and a new recorder on expenses. And Mu, my girlfriend, was going to have a few words to say about these matters. At least I didn't have to pay for the food and drinks this time. Come to that, I guessed nobody did, unless they were screwing it out of Somsak.

I still hadn't found out how Wrong-Way Willie Wong got his name. But I could live with it now if I never knew.

part two

traffic is just murderous these days

Selections from Arno Petty's Intelligencer and Weekly Gleaner

HAPPY DAYS. Soon everybody in the country will have a couple of Benzes, not to mention pots full of chickens. Dearie me, yes; the race to NIC-hood (Newly Industrialized Country status, for those of you from outer space) is bringing on a New Day for us all. Now if only we Bangkokwallahs also had somewhere to drive our Benzes, and some air to breathe, especially when we can't be sitting in some fine car with the air-conditioner going flat out.

ANOTHER TYPICAL WEEK. Five Aussies found dead of drug overdoses in guesthouse rooms. Two Germans in the same shape in Pattaya. One Swede dead of alcohol poisoning. Twelve Nigerians busted for possession of heroin at Don Muang Airport. Various 'dark influences' removed 30,000 acres of pesky forest and paved over thirty miles of sandy tropical beach. Another 2% of the country was covered in golf courses. Seven powerful businessmen, victims of 'business conflicts,' were found dead of lead poisoning behind the wheels of their Benzes, except one of them who was driving a Volvo. Millions of children in Bangkok, meanwhile, continued to flirt with lead poisoning just by breathing the rich city air.

IN BANGKOK laborers made ninety baht a day, if they were lucky. A freelance writer was even luckier than that, sometimes.

Just think—90 baht a day, and a Big Mac cost 50 baht. A bottle of beer in a five-star hotel could go for 110 baht. And a little tiny Camembert cheese was almost 100 baht; these laborers had be grateful they didn't like cheese, though many freelance writers had no such grounds for gratitude. My girlfriend Mu looked at me like I was crazy if I bought one Camembert every three months.

Bus fares were going up again, I heard, and I guess I could handle that. Though many could not. The people who wanted to build the Skytrain said they would have to charge twenty baht basic. Sure, and you were making 90 baht a day or maybe less, and you could spend 40 baht a day just getting to and from work. No problem.

Meanwhile you got all these Mercedes-Benzes and BMWs stacked up at the traffic lights; it was almost an embarrassment to be seen in a Toyota Crown or a Volvo. And you could buy a Benz for a few million baht, since there was only 600 percent duty on one of these nice pieces of engineering. Of course if you were rich you didn't have to pay this duty; there were ways around it, and some of these ways came up across the Malaysian border. And a few of the Benzes, I saw, now had gold hood ornaments; I guess since there were so many Benzes around these days it was no special distinction to be seen in one unless it was 24-carat. At 90 baht a day you worked for some time to save up for such a car, even if you cut corners on your food expenses and such-like. Even if you made more than 90 baht a day, as I did sometimes.

These were some of the thoughts that were occupying me, this hot day in July. I had spent all the money from the gunman stories, not to mention the piece I did on that deputy minister Wrong-Way Willie put me onto, the one who had interests in whorehouses all over the south. That one had created a little stir. I was surprised the paper used it. Anyhow, the money from that was long since gone. Though now I had had a new score to tide things over.

And what the hell, I was thinking. Bangkok was home. Even when a guy was broke half the time and had no Benz, not even a Toyota. Even with a hangover. Even though I was trying to kick tobacco again and wasn't finding any part of existence entirely comfortable. Even though my woman, Mu, was not altogether happy with me right at the moment. Even though there were men with guns somewhere out there and they were looking for me. Of course I didn't know about that part of it at the time.

This day I was riding along in a taxi with my old Royal typewriter on my lap; I was going to sell it to a shop down in Chinatown. I didn't like to part with this classic machine, but just recently I had gone hi-tech. I had bought a nice Taiwanese IBM computer clone and a pirate word-processing program that turned me into a writing factory compared to what I had been able to do with the antique Royal, and which besides gave me lots more time for drinking beer and suchlike. So I was thinking life could have been worse.

Only a couple of weeks before that, I had got back from a trip to Burma, where I had to see about getting another visa so I could live in Thailand some more, and Burma did me a favor by having something like a revolution right in the middle of my vacation-cum-visa run. Now your average person is often not happy to find revolutions in countries he visits. And I understand this attitude. But your average person is not a freelance journalist with a chronic shortage of good things to write about. Which is something I am. And right then Burma stories were selling like hotcakes, even my stories.

So things were more than just okay, and I was smoking a big cheroot with the window open because my driver was not so keen on big cigars. What my driver was keen on was "rive shows," and he thought I should be keen on them too, never mind I kept telling him to for Christ's sake shut up and drive, I was an Old Hand and I didn't let taxi drivers take me to see live shows.

"Good. Is good. Lookee, lookee only. Man-woman show. Fucking."

But that was Bangkok these days. Everybody out to make a buck, it was boom times, NIC-hood in the air. Thailand was going to be a Newly Industrialized Country. One of the five Tigers of Asia. The whole country was one big feeding frenzy, with condos being built on top of condos; the skyline was a tangle of building

67

cranes, and people were slapping up hotels or else department stores anywhere other people had forgotten to put condos. You added the banks and the tour agencies, and you got the whole show paved over with glitz. Tourists carried in money by the plane-load, with 6 million of these public benefactors expected that year. And Thailand had stopped lobbing artillery shells across the border at Laos, and had taken to bombing them with baht instead, it being more cost effective to use money I guess, though I have never understood economics. Turn the Southeast Asian battlefield into a marketplace; this was the new plan. They had sold the Thai forests already, so now we had Burma to supply teak for the nice houses for the nice Thai people who were running this market that was no longer a battlefield, except maybe for some little problems, like where for example the Burmese were wiping out the Kareni. Hey, it wasn't just because they were a bunch of dirty separatists; no, they were also messing with the traffic in logs across the border, and anybody could tell you that you didn't want to screw around with Commerce. And you didn't hear much from the communist insurgents in the south anymore; it was hard to sell communism when there was the scent of money to be had in the air and, who knows, a car in every garage besides and a couple hundred more air-conditioned shopping malls to amble around in. What did your average Marx or Lenin know about any of that? I ask you.

The TV and newspapers were full of taskforces and master plans, not to mention working groups and crackdowns. Everybody was having a hell of a time, and it was projects here and projects there, and my goodness, wasn't it a shame the way the shit settled all over your Benz in this city? It was this pollution; somebody should do something, maybe set up a taskforce. It wasn't just the government and big business, either; school boards and who knows probably even noodle vendors had to have their master plans and taskforces these days, or they weren't up to date, which was one measure of anything's value these days, whether it was up to date or not. These were exciting times. Everyone wanted a piece of the action, including my driver this day I was telling you about.

"You want lady?" he asked me.

"Shut up and drive."

"You want rubies? Sapphires?"

"Just drive."

"Snake farm?"

I was thinking I should get out and walk; it was as fast anyhow, given the traffic. Even the motorcycles had a hard time going any-where; half a dozen of them were swarming around my taxi right then, waiting for an opening. Some of them carried two passengers, some of them with girlfriends modestly riding side-saddle so I couldn't look up their skirts. It was better, you had to think, they ran the considerable risk of falling off the bike and creaming them-selves than some stranger got to look up their skirts. There was one with a whole family of four on it — momma and poppa and two toddlers sandwiched in between.

I could hear the sound of voices through the window: "You! You!" This was what Thais of a certain class did when they noticed a foreigner such as myself and they had some time to kill. I ignored them, but they went on in a similar vein. "You! You!" they said. I guessed they didn't mean any harm, though it smacked more than somewhat of baiting the farang.

Just for something to do, I timed the light, and I saw we had been sitting there already for ten minutes. I held the computerized traffic lights, those early signs of NIC-hood, responsible for this inconvenience. It was all only show, anyhow, like a lot of other things I saw around me. In fact, they had traffic policemen every-where you looked, supplementing the hi-tech light system probably according to some master plan. Like there wasn't enough noise in this city as it was, Bangkok police kept the traffic moving by blowing whistles at it and waving furiously. When they wanted a lane to come to a halt, they stopped blowing and turned their backs on it, which took some courage, I had to admit. It was like pulling off a veronica with around fifty giant bulls bearing down on you all at the same time. Personally, I would award any one of these officers a couple of ears and a tail.

This morning the radio news was purring along with the government line, so happy with its statistics. The only news on Thai radio was business news and the only business news was good news, said the government. In the middle of this the announcer informed us this year there were thirty percent more "units" of automobile sold than last year, and wasn't that something? We were all getting rich. Never mind it looked as though the whole city was going to seize up tight. There were too many cars already, and one morning soon we would get up and think about going to work, and everybody would suddenly notice we couldn't go forward and we couldn't go backward either, so we would get out of our cars and walk; and where was the NIC-hood when nothing in the place moved unless it walked? But it is hard to ask questions like these during a feeding frenzy because everybody is generally quite busy, and they don't listen.

"Jesus Christ!" I hollered, meaning to signal some alarm to the driver.

He had found an opening in the traffic and we were out on the expressway, gamboling along like a colt let out to pasture in the spring. The thing was, at the same time he took this opportunity to cut loose, my driver saw a temple, and I had to think this temple meant something special to him, because he took his hands off the wheel and brought them together up to his forehead in what the locals call a *wai*, he wanted to show his respect, and we veered off across four lanes of traffic, which inspired much spirited honking of horns all around and lots of stylish swerving of vehicles to make

70

way. By comparison, revolutions in Burma left me feeling quite relaxed.

I forgot to mention that my driver was no ordinary driver, and the taxi was no ordinary taxi. In this age of approaching NIC-hood not to mention gridlock, Bangkok cabbies were getting nervier and nervier about asking an arm and a leg to venture into traffic at all, and it seemed the process of getting a fair price was starting to take a disproportionate amount of my time. So this day I had turned away from four or five cabs in disgust, and almost thought about getting on a bus, never mind the heat and the fact there was no place to sit on the buses anymore; they started their routes with all the seats already occupied, I don't know how they did it. I was looking around for one of these public services when I heard a car-horn croak at me and then a person also croaked "You! You!" and I looked and it was a Mercedes-Benz, about 1957 vintage, body-work done with a ballpeen hammer, bottle-green paint slapped on by hand. The driver was older than the car, probably ninety-five or so, and it looked like somebody had also worked him over with a ballpeen hammer some time in the past, though he wasn't painted green.

"Where you go?" this individual asked me. "I have car." He climbed out of the Benz, maybe checking to see if he could still stand up on his own, and he wanted to know which hotel I was staying in. The condition I was in, I wished he wouldn't mess with my head this way; I got the crazy idea the whole planet was on tilt. This geezer grinned at me and listed to one side. He toppled over a bit, took a crabwise hop or two to catch up with himself, and then stepped back to his original position. He went through the whole routine once more, and then he asked me again, "Where you go?"

I told him where, and right away I said, "fifty baht, okay?"

"Okay," he answered me, just like that, and I couldn't believe that was all there was to it.

And I was right. He got in the front again and slammed his door. I jumped in the back and my door also shut after I slammed it two or three times. You could say car and driver were about equally clapped out. Where you got the taxi lurching, the old man would go into a spasm: one shoulder would convulse and his head would twist around till he was looking into the back seat. Where the car shuddered, the driver trembled as though he had the DTs, and he made funny wittering noises. first I thought it was the valves.

But now we were out on the highway, out of the worst of the traffic. It took some time to get the car up to thirty-five miles per hour, this machine being no dragster. But I was grateful we were moving at all, because the air-conditioner was busted and now there was a breeze through the crack in the window. I closed my eyes and thought nice thoughts about the Burma articles and about money, and I was almost drifting off to sleep when I heard what sounded like a death rattle from the front seat and my eyes popped open. We were doing about forty miles per hour now, thanks to a gentle downgrade we had come upon, and we were weaving from lane to lane in a way that made me think Bangkok buses weren't such a bad thing after all. Probably the driver was trying to guess which side the much faster traffic from behind was going to pass on.

There was another death rattle. The driver had one of his convulsions and he twisted around to look into the back seat. "You want crocodile farm?"

"Keep your eyes on the road, okay?" I suggested. Actually, I kind of screamed it. "You crazy bastard!" I added.

The blare of horns prevented the crazy bastard from hearing this, however. He swerved into the next lane just as a gaily decorated ten-wheeler truck came up on us and shot by at somewhere around the speed of sound. Then he whipped the car back into the lane we had left before, causing a Toyota Crown to go into a squealing four-wheel drift. Trembling and twitching, grinning and drooling, the driver continued his exploration of all the four lanes while I thought about this and that, mostly about how I didn't really want to go where I was trying to go anyway; and why hadn't I stayed at home? This was a good day to stay at home. Or maybe to go wait for happy hour at Shaky Jake's. The Benz was doing all of forty-five miles per hour by this time, and there was an alarming chatter coming from somewhere up under the hood.

"You want rive show?"

"I don't want anything! Don't you understand? Nothing! I want *nothing*. Just drive." I slid down on my seat, out of sight of the road and the traffic, telling myself not to get so excited. But it was only that I didn't want to die right then, not with money in my pocket and my hangover almost cleared up. You know how it is.

There was silence from the front seat. Then, in surprised and respectful tones, he said, "You want Buddha?"

I got out the pipe I had brought along for emergencies. I stuffed it full of nice dark tobacco and lit up, puffing hard to get it going well, laying down a cloud of smoke that sent the driver into spasms. I had the idea he was trying to say something to me, but he couldn't stop gasping and wheezing long enough to get it out. I puffed some more, but he had managed to get his window wide open, which mostly cleared the front seat of smoke. Possibly he still had smoke in his eyes, however, because he suddenly cut off a Volvo tour bus coming up from behind like the Cannonball Express, and I couldn't believe he meant to do that. Those tour buses don't ever lose at chicken. It's a point of honor with them.

I fingered the amulet that hung on a silver chain around my neck. My girlfriend Mu had given me the thing as protection against injury. A doodad from some temple upcountry. Big magic. GIs on R&R from Vietnam liked to pick these things up in the old days, I hear, and some of those boys, anyway, got back Stateside in one piece. Who knows? Maybe it was because of amulets. This one was a tiny silver Buddha-like figure with its hands over its eyes. What it wouldn't look at couldn't hurt it. That's what I would tell Mu, anyway — just like the Thai public, who were getting railroaded by business interests into selling off their forests and their beaches and their children, and not saying a thing about it. Mu didn't laugh. You had to take your magic charm seriously, if you wanted it to work for you. Mine had four extra hands, actually, the deluxe model, and they covered four other openings I guessed your miscellaneous slings and arrows of outrageous fortune might look for.

Mu's world was full of spirits and magic. She didn't like it when I razzed her about this, either. And I couldn't say anything negative about Thailand. Anything Thai was okay, as she explained to me again and again, because it is the Thai Way. And I knew dick about the Thai Way, was the unspoken corollary to this proposition, so what could I say?

This woman Mu was not a standard model of Thai woman, in some ways, though in other ways she was, through and through; and she was as a consequence twice as hard to fathom as your average Western woman, who was in my experience already pretty hard to make out.

We came off the expressway, and we were almost there. Now I would be able to flog my Royal and then try to hit happy hour at Shaky Jake's. Only we were in heavy traffic again. The air was not moving and the heat was making me sweat into my shorts and my hangover was coming back. It was so bad I couldn't even smoke my pipe. We were stopped at a light, and the exhaust fumes were settling on my spirits like a pall. This was giving me a headache, as the motorcycles percolated through the boiling traffic to condense up front, up by the light. Some of the drivers were honking horns

74

probably for practice, since nothing was going anywhere, except for the steady trickle of motorcycles. I was thinking for the hundredth time I should get a motorcycle, it was the only way to get around in Bangkok these days, except I knew I would kill myself the first time I forgot I had had a few beers and tried popping wheelies on Sukhumvit Road. I was also thinking about Mu, and I wondered whether I should bring her some fruit, after I got away from Jake's, maybe a great big durian.

Then I heard "You! You!" from just outside the window again, the traditional baiting of the foreigner. Some jerks on a bike. I tried to ignore them, practicing my *jai yen yen* for Mu, learning the Thai Way, maintaining my cool like I was a frigging saint or somebody, when there was a sharp rap on the glass beside my head.

"What the ...?" I turned my head to give them this short lesson in colloquial English I had in mind, only I found my glare being returned by the muzzle of an automatic pistol, enormous through the glass at a range of eighteen inches.

I heard "You" again, repeated more softly this time and furthermore punctuated by the bark of a gun. My head snapped back as soon as the shooting started, and I twisted around to hit the seat, sliding down onto the floor with the typewriter on top of me. The pistol barked twice more.

The cabbie first screamed like a woman. Then he started making funny noises; you would have probably thought somebody was tickling a sick goat in the front seat, if you didn't know different. I could have wished he would clam up, though, there being enough turmoil as it was. I was wedged down on the floor of the back seat, my eyes still shut tight against the blast and the glass and the prospect of about one second's life left for the living, which was less than I had planned on up to this time. My ribs hurt like a son of a bitch, though, which was reassuring, since it seemed to argue that I was not dead after all. What it was, the corner of the typewriter was digging into my chest trying to pass itself off as a bullet wound.

Suddenly I noticed I wanted to do some screaming myself. But all I did was holler "My eyes! My eyes!" Why I did this thing, there was this searing pain in my eyes, and a sick feeling in my guts as I reached up to check for blood, for bits of sharp glass imbedded in flesh. All I could find, however, was some liquid that was only tears and this gritty substance, which I rubbed at cautiously. One eye cleared enough to see, and I put my fingers to my nose and sniffed. Pipe ashes, cold ones at that. Stung like a bastard, you got pipe dottle in your eyes. Lots better than glass, mind you. Or bullets. My pipe, though, was no more. I guess the first bullet caught it as I threw myself back, smashing the bowl, exploding dottle and bits of briar all over the inside of the car. The second or third shot ricocheted off the underside of my typewriter. There was this *bedwaanggg*, just like in the old Wyatt Earp TV shows. It didn't look like a mortal wound, though. Those old Royals were built to last.

I started to laugh, now. This laugh was too high-pitched to qualify as a chuckle, and it sounded weird even to me, as though I were listening to somebody else, and this person maybe wasn't as entirely happy as he would have you believe. By the time I pushed the typewriter up onto the seat and wriggled out of the back seat and got out on the pavement, though, I realized that I was okay, just about as good as new and possibly better, since I could detect no trace of the hangover at all. It could be adrenaline is a cure for hangovers. There was already a crowd of people having a good gawk at this crazy farang laughing away at a taxi full of bullet-holes.

It was like a miracle or something, I was thinking, as I fingered my amulet some more. I also thought about that article I sold after Mu gave me this thing — the one where I talked about the history of these items. "Many Thais actually believe these charms protect them from bullets and knives," I had written. "I don't think I care to test that claim." This was still true; I didn't care to test it.

76

Traffic was now moving, to the extent Bangkok traffic ever moved, and behind the cab there was the blare of horns. We were getting cars, tuk-tuks, motorcycles, and buses turning and making their way around, accelerating past with angry looks at me — who was this klutz standing in the road with a shot-up taxi? They couldn't glare at the driver; he was still out of sight in the front seat praying to various agencies, most likely, and imitating a sick goat.

contributions to the tea and biscuit fund

Selections from Arno Petty's Intelligencer and Weekly Gleaner

ENOUGH FOR TEA. The new chief of police in the City of Angles (or is that 'Angels'?) is talking about giving Bangkok's finest a pay raise. Would that this be true. Law enforcement officers can't possibly subsist on current salaries (which are often less than the legal minimum wage), so it should not be surprising if unofficial income supplements are de rigueur hereabouts.

SURVIVAL THAI LESSON. *Yord nam-man* translates as 'oil for the machine.' Locally, the English euphemism tends to be 'tea money,' and this refers to the little gratuities that enable public officials to buy tea when they are thirsty, thereby favorably predisposing them towards reasonable claims upon their official time.

THE POLICE WERE ANNOYED at this non-standard hold-up in traffic. Down at the station house, when we finally got there, they seemed mostly interested in why I had so many visas to come to Thailand, and what was my job? And didn't I know there was a revolution on in Burma, and did I use drugs? Or, maybe, smuggle them? So this was the way things went. I was a sitting duck in this shooting gallery Bangkok had become, at least from my point of view, and I had to admire the way these law officers managed to hide their concern for me. They were real professionals, I told myself.

After a while I saw it was a good idea to make a contribution to the Precinct Tea and Biscuit Fund. I asked if 300 baht would fill the cookie jar or not, and they indicated not — 2,000 baht got you the imported ones with the cream filling. So I said 500 baht, I was short of the needful, what with all this traveling to revolutions and everything. They had to know how it was. In the end they seemed very pleased with 1,000 baht. They wished me a good day, and said they would look into this shooting of my typewriter at an early date. But I shouldn't leave town just at the moment, or change addresses without notifying them. My driver, they informed me, figured I owed him for all the bullet-holes in his hack. Then one nice policeman told me confidentially that the driver's car was a wreck even with no bullet-holes, and it should never have been allowed on the road in the first place. Much less to be used as a taxi for which the geezer had no license. He told me this and he told me that, and before long I was getting the idea a couple of hundred more baht for doughnuts or something would fix it so maybe the old man's car was not an issue any more. It was only an act of God, after all, this mysterious hail of bullets.

I could see the old man over in another corner; chances were he was discussing taxi licenses and other arcana of this modern world, and no doubt he wanted to make a donation to the Policeman's Benevolent Fund if possible. This idea was reinforced when he came over and asked if he could borrow 500 baht for just such a purpose; he was sure I didn't mind, since I practically owed him a new Mercedes-Benz anyway. In fact I did want to help, even though it was awkward for me, since I had told the police I was fresh out of funds already. It was too hard to convey these difficulties to the geezer in an undertone, so I laughed loudly and slapped him on the shoulder, which sent him into his topple-over-hop-to-catch-up-step-back-into-place maneuver, and then I shook his hand, leaving behind a crumpled-up purple banknote. This behavior puzzled him, I am sure, but he got to spring his car, and he offered to take me wherever I was going for free; he would even throw in a trip to the crocodile farm. Frankly, though, I had had enough excitement for one day, and I went out on the street to find a real cabbie and hoped that this one wouldn't want to take all the loot I had remaining, which was nothing like the fortune in easy money I had begun the day with. But such is life. And I was still alive, which I had to admit was something.

I decided to forget about Shaky Jake's, it being late and there being not enough money to buy all the beer I thought I needed. I wanted to talk to Mu anyway, so I went straight home.

the key to mu's libido

Selections from Arno Petty's Intelligencer and Weekly Gleaner

TAKE IT EASY. When in Rome, do as the Romans do. When in Bangkok, do pretty much whatever you want; but remember that certain institutions—notably the Royal Family, the Buddhist *sangha*, and the military—are above criticism. Remember also to respect the strictures concerning pointing feet, touching others on the head, etc. Any good guidebook will give you the essentials. Otherwise, relax. *Tham sabai*. Thais are some of the most tolerant and fun-loving people in the world.

DON'T LOOK. More than one male visitor to the city has remarked on the essential modesty of Thai ladies. Even those ladies who make a profession of being such. This may come as a surprise to those who witness some of the upstairs shows on Patpong Road, especially admirers who then go home with a performer and often find it difficult to convince the artiste to remove her towel after the shower.

ANOTHER LOURDES? The authorities have it that the bars of Patpong Road are still AIDS free, despite the fact that some brothels upcountry have already tested as high as 80% HIV-positive. This miracle is no doubt due to some divine decree that nothing should ever be permitted to interfere with Commerce and the inflow of foreign currency.

I GOT STUCK with the handle Jack Shackaway. If you think that's something, then get this: my girlfriend's name was Mu. That means "Pig," in Thai. But don't get the wrong idea — this lady in no way resembled a pig. She was probably fat when she was a baby, so they

81

hung this moniker on her; and, unlike the baby fat, the name stuck.

I was happy this lady was not too fat, this day I got back from the shooting. Mu was sitting on the edge of the bed in a towel, fresh from her shower, luscious. She was frowning. I had known this lady pretty well for a whole month before she let me see her without any clothes on. She would come to bed in a towel, and wanted the light off when we made love. In the night she would say do that some more, it's nice, as I ran my hands ever so lightly all over her body looking for Caesarean scars and suchlike. So I was relieved finally when she loosened up one evening, and I got to see there was nothing wrong. Nothing at all, in fact; quite the contrary, you might have said, and I could have wished she wasn't so modest still. Sightings of her unclad body were rationed out like some precious non-renewable resource. It could be I'd never get jaded this way; I tried to look on the bright side.

At this particular time I had Mu's panties pulled down over my head, and I was peering at her out of a leg-hole. To tell the truth, that was all I was wearing just then, except for a conservative pair of powder blue Y-fronts Mu had bought me the week before. I was Cyclops rampant, you could have said, although I didn't want to explain this idea to Mu; it would take too long and furthermore probably spoil the mood I was trying to create.

"Hey, you!" I grunted at her. "*You*."

"Disgusting!" she told me. Even when I zoomed in on her and ogled like crazy through my frilly porthole on the world, she was still offended. She wrapped the towel around her more tightly, and set her pretty little frown a bit deeper. She edged away from me on the bed, and I was hurt.

Thai women are as a rule modest. Too modest, is how I would put it. For a gang of ladies who have some of the finest chassis this side of your favorite adolescent dream — not to mention their warm and generous personalities — they are most unkindly reluc-

82

tant to let the rest of mankind view this commodity. Part of the problem is their religion tells them that the lower parts of the body are base in nature, and should be kept out of the public eye. The head, on the other hand, is the highest and, therefore, the noblest part of the person. So for me to have Mu's undergarments on my head was disrespectful.

"This is my head," I told her. "It's okay if I'm disrespectful to my own head. I know I'm only fooling around." This sounded reasonable to me, but Mu was a Thai, and she was giving me the idea this was not the Thai Way, whether it was my head or not.

"This is not funny." That was her opinion. In fact, she had been telling me all about my general ignorance of all things Thai, and about how this was going to get me killed, sure, because even if nobody else did this thing then she was going to, one of these days.

Mu was too serious sometimes, especially when it came to sex. She was the first to admit this. It had something to do with her childhood, no doubt, though we couldn't figure out what, exactly. She was never forced to study geometry while being sexually abused, or anything of that nature. Or so she said. But it was nevertheless the fact that as soon as sex appeared on the agenda, she was likely to get more and more subdued until you could have described her as totally morose and not have been wrong.

This was at first very frustrating, as you can imagine, seeing as how the lady was built along lines designed to turn young men's fancies to thoughts of unrestrained love-making. Even men who were not so young, such as myself, but who only acted like they were.

"How old are you?" she asked me. "Sometimes I think you are just a little boy. And you are supposed to be a big 'freelance journalist.' How can a little boy be anything?"

By accident, one day, I learned that there was a way to brighten Mu's outlook on the business of having a good time in the sack. I discovered this by rolling off with a big sigh of satisfaction and then falling down between the two beds. It could have happened to anybody. I thought I was on a double bed as usual, but we were in a Pattaya Beach hotel with twin beds; why I hadn't pushed them together in the first place I don't know.

As soon as I disappeared down between the beds yelling "Holy shit!" and furthermore landing with my butt in the ashtray, I took to hollering even ruder things, and Mu got the idea this was something funny, so she took to laughing fairly immoderately from my point of view at the time.

Still, it was worth it to find this key to Mu's libido. Because even though just before my abrupt disappearance from view I had given what I liked to think was my all, Mu turned into a glutton as soon as she stopped laughing, and she was set to go once more or maybe even twice; could be she was hoping to see me fall out of bed again, this was such an entertaining sight. She was so enthusiastic it rubbed off, and I surprised myself, if not her. For all I knew she thought it was normal.

I would have fallen out of bed any number of times for the good times we had that day. And now I knew that foreplay with Mu meant getting her laughing. Once that was out of the way, the main problem was keeping up. So this day I got back from having my typewriter shot, I was engaged in foreplay. "I take your panties off my head, you take my shorts off." I inched closer on the bed to make this job easier for her. Mu and I were best friends and lovers too, despite what I told you already about her frowning and all, and she set about doing what I suggested, even though her gloom didn't lift noticeably. An innocent bystander at first might have thought she was a morgue attendant about to unwrap a cadaver.

Then I was unwrapped, and she was speechless for a minute. For here was Cyclops rampant all over again, a one-eyed happy-face painted in three bright colors, and it was nodding and leering

84

at Mu in what I thought was a very fetching manner.

She gasped a couple of times, though not necessarily with admiration, because then she said, "You must show more respect." She looked stern as she brushed her hair back from her face and took a closer look at this outrage she had found in my shorts. Then she started to laugh. Only a little, at first, like a starter motor on a cold morning; but it picked up, and finally the whole thing was a great success, because she laughed and rolled around till tears came. She grabbed the one-eyed trouser snake in a fist and shook it back and forth, telling it how naughty it was.

"Is it poison?" she asked me. "The paint, I mean."

"No," I told her. "It's only vegetable dye."

Mu was by no means the same shy maiden I first took up with.

And I guessed I was forgiven, for the time being, for not knowing the first thing about getting along in Thai society; and I snuggled down with Mu, thinking I would get a nap and wake up later feeling even better.

Then there was a crash from outside the bedroom, and Mu said, "I wish Bia would be more careful."

I could hear Granny yelling "What? *Arai na?*" over and over, and this was followed by a general hubbub of voices, most likely all of them telling Granny nobody said anything. There was another crash, and I could hear Cousin Sombat hollering for a little peace and quiet, he had to get his rest.

home sweet home

Selections from Arno Petty's Intelligencer and Weekly Gleaner

ALL FOR ONE, AND ONE FOR ALL. Western men have been known to misconstrue what is happening when they marry a Thai lady. Suddenly, as often as not, they discover that there are two cousins from upcountry who need a place to stay while in the city, two sisters and a nephew who have educational requirements entailing money, not to mention one uncle and a great-aunt who are both sick and who need expensive operations before next week. A typical reaction is to decide you are being victimized. Not so. Not usually, anyway. In fact, in this society when you marry you take responsibility for the whole extended family, which with some of these families is a very extensive crowd of people indeed. But it works both ways. When you're in need the help is there, no questions asked.

BOOMING BUSINESS. Pirate music tapes are big business, hereabouts. All those vendors blasting us with their samples up and down the streets are franchised by 'influential people,' not to say 'dark forces.' And it's funny: when public officials occasionally get it into their heads that maybe this country should start honoring the international conventions on intellectual property and copyright in this regard, some of those same officials start to experience very bad runs of luck, coming up with broken limbs or sometimes even hand-grenades on the back porch.

IT SEEMED STRANGE; everything was normal when I got to my little street only a short time before you found me in bed with Mu's panties on my head. The truth was, I was just as happy to be alive as not, and maybe more so. I appreciated the songs of the birds and the shouts of the children playing in the road. The late sun slanting through the fronds of the coconut palms on the other side of the temple wall, furthermore, cheered me no end. I could even just about ignore the construction cranes looming everywhere high on the horizon and the thumping of the bass from the tape vendor down the lane.

Everything was more vivid than usual, a shade more real around the edges. I was thinking that if I could talk to Mu, maybe go to bed with her and lie around for a while, then I would feel better still. Because to tell the truth I was feeling somewhat edgy no matter how much the sun was slanting and how many happy children were playing.

The tiny, twisting alley that led to my apartment might have let two thin people pass. The boardwalk was only three planks wide. At the mouth of this alley there was a vendor with a cart, a two-wheeled wooden cart with a glassed-in box full of vegetables and stuff. This was Big Lek the *somtam* lady, who made green papaya salad with poo, little fermented black crabs, or even without these critters if you weren't in the mood for gastroenteritis. Mu always said the *somtam poo* was good for her figure.

Big Lek liked to speak Thai to me, since I was probably the only *farang* she had ever met who spoke any Thai at all. Only she seemed to reckon if I spoke some I had to speak the whole shtick, philosophical excurses and all, at least judging by the complexity of the raps she laid upon me at times. While she was talking, she would slice and shred papaya and tomato and lime, and she would pound chilies and garlic and so forth in a stone mortar, her forearms big and swollen like a construction worker's. She gabbled away like a 45-rpm somtam lady stuck on 78, and I never got more than ten percent of it even on a good day.

Right at that moment what I mainly understood was that Mu was home already, my beautiful girlfriend, *suay jangleuy*. The somtam lady had seen her go down the alley an hour before; when were we going to get married?

I couldn't shake this feeling of weirdness — here I was with a gut-shot typewriter, it was lucky it was not me instead, and this lady was rabbiting on just like nothing was amiss, giving me the idea furthermore it was still possible to marry Mu if I wasn't careful. I showed the lady where the 11mm slug had ricocheted off my typewriter, and I tried to tell her, "*Khon mai dee*, bad men, *song khon*, two of them on a motorcycle, *kheun motosai*, and bang bang, you know? *Chai na krap?* They try to blow my jesus head off. *Taay laeow.*"

"*Chai, chai*," she told me. "Yes. *Motosai mai dee.* Too much noise. Motorcycle no good. *Chai.*" And she grinned at me fondly; it was so nice to have this tame farang to talk Thai to.

You have a day like that — getting yourself shot at, getting to chat to a gang of policemen, getting driven around town by an ancient kamikaze pilot who not only takes ten years off your life but also shakes you down for an extra 500 baht so even if he can't plug the bullet-holes in his cab he can get his license back. You do all that and you never even get around to flogging your typewriter, which is actually all you had in mind in the first place, except for hitting happy hour at Shaky Jake's, which you never get to do either; and you think it's nice to get home and relax — to drop this typewriter some place, your arms feel like they're going to fall off if you have to carry the machine another step.

Two grinning urchins were sitting in a pile of pink and purple orchids on the landing outside the door to my apartment. They were responsible for the manufacture of these modern improvements on nature, deftly twisting and turning bits of crepe paper into flowers that never wilted, only gathered dust and hung around forever depressing people. I didn't recognize these two craftsmen, and I guessed they didn't know who I was either, even though I was the master of the house, because they said "*Farang! Farang!*" with some excitement and tried to sell me paper orchids. "You!

88

You!" They told me. "Ten baht!" I had to step over them to get at the door.

The door was bolted, as usual; and as usual when I hammered on the door I heard sudden silence followed by mysterious scurryings and rustlings from inside. The flower children on the landing hollered "*Farang, farang!*" some more, and then the door opened a crack to reveal a girl who brushed her hair away from her eyes so she could see me, and I recognized Mu's sister Bia, who also recognized me, which was nice, and she let me in.

In Thai *bia* means "beer," and Mu's sister was named Bia because Mu's papa generally drank whiskey except for one night — chances are the same night Bia was conceived — when for a change he was drinking beer. I noticed she was wearing one of my shirts again, three times too big for her and the shirttails hanging out. I wished she wouldn't wear my shirts all the time.

The door didn't open wide, even after it was unbolted and the chains dropped, so I had to sidle in. There were large bundles of sugar cane stacked up against the wall, which explained why the door didn't open all the way. Sugar cane. I didn't even ask. Bia told me Mu was having a shower. Then she stood there looking at me. At least I figured she was looking at me. Bia grew her bangs down so you couldn't see her eyes. And no matter what she said, she couldn't see a thing with her hair that way, with the consequence she was always tripping over things or falling down the stairs. She thought she had little eyes, which as any Thai lady will tell you aren't *suay*, they aren't beautiful, so she grew her hair down over them and saved her money for an operation. I told Mu her sister would never live to get round eyes, the way she was going, and there was nothing wrong with her eyes anyway, except they were covered with hair. If she had any money she should get an operation on her brain, which might in fact be defective. But Mu told me I didn't understand Thai girls. Which was not news to me.

89

Bia asked me would I like some tea; I said I would like a beer. She turned to go in the general direction of the kitchen and she fell over a stack of wicker baskets. As I helped her up, I noticed bruises on her otherwise lovely legs. Big fresh black and blue splotches overlapping the yellow and blue ones left over from earlier encounters with her environment. I asked her what happened, and she told me she fell down the stairs; it was Mu's fault. Mu had even got people working out on the stairs now. It was getting so you couldn't turn around without falling over something, Bia told me. And then she fell over a big box of crepe paper on her way to the kitchen.

There was certainly no shortage of things to fall over in this joint. You looked around, you could find evidence of untold numbers of business enterprises in various stages of realization ranging from "let's try this sometime" to "that's the last time we're ever going to deal in used electric hairdryers."

These were Mu's "bisnets." She had short-term, medium-term, and long-term enterprises of all kinds. Or she used to have, anyway. Her main long-termer had been the box of fish. "What the hell is this?" I had asked, when first I encountered it. "This is a box of fish," she told me, though it was really a five-foot aquarium tank that held two golden arowanas that she had paid 8,000 baht apiece for. That's 16,000 baht, and these specimens were each about the size of a good baitfish. This was only 160 Camembert cheeses, as I pointed out to her; 320 large bottles of Kloster beer, and she had spent this sum on two fish? Yes, she told me, plus 1,500 baht for the tank and another 1,000 baht for various pieces of furniture to make the fish happy, since these were not your run-of-the-mill fish, and they should of course have the best facilities we could provide. The idea was that after some time, like about seventy-five years, these prize fish would be worth a total of 200,000 baht. And who knows, maybe Mu was right, except that Mu's cousin Sombat fed them Mekhong whiskey one night, only trying to be friendly, and they starting floating belly up till finally Mu had to admit they were dead. Sombat to this day is probably the least favorite cousin of them all. Those fish never got big enough to qualify as lunch, much less as a retirement plan.

The fish box was now a showcase for stacks of Dayglo bathing suits, which turned out to have a high turnover in the short term, and which furthermore didn't go around floating belly-up when you poured whiskey on them, something Sombat was not likely to do in any case, having learned his lesson once.

I have already talked about the sugar cane and wicker baskets, not to mention the paper-flower factory out on the landing. Then you also had the coils of rope that Cousin Rhot braided and knotted up into horses, tigers, deer, people — you name it. He wasn't around right then, but over by the coils of rope I saw an almost completed dragon three feet long, incredibly detailed, life-like, even though it was only knotted out of plain hemp rope.

There was quite a bit of rope around, but that was nothing compared to the clothes. There were clothes in boxes, clothes on racks, and clothes draped on the sofa. There were clothes everywhere you looked. These clothes came in a variety of electric colors and designs that kind of shrieked at you, if you stumbled across them on a bad morning. There were dresses and shirts, trousers and shorts, even a collection of neckties, over on the bookcase, which would have made excellent gifts for everybody you ever hated.

There was also food. I walked into the next room and found tubs full of vegetables, bags and boards full of meat, bunches of aromatic herbs hanging about, fruit in baskets. Some of this was simply on hand to feed the hordes of relatives, neighbors, waifs, and other assorted hangers-on that Mu liked to keep about the place. And me, of course. The rest of this stuff went towards a va-

91

riety of bisnet ventures, such as the *satay* wagon Cousin Lek trundled around the neighborhood every evening, selling tasty sticks of grilled pork with peanut sauce. That was Little Lek, I'm talking about. Big Lek, on the other hand, you have already met. She was the somtam lady out on our lane; for all I know she was also a cousin. (*Lek* means "little" in Thai, and Big Lek was probably little some time in the past, back when she got her name.) And there was more, only I could never keep it straight, who was doing what, or even who was who and what was what.

I guessed that was why my brand-new computer was already pressed into service keeping account of Mu's many business interests. My computer. Nobody seemed to realize this was my bread and butter; this was how I made my living. I had only just moved the machine in and already, if Mu wasn't doing her accounts on it, then Bia was in the bedroom practicing her touch-typing or having Cousin Maem teach her about spreadsheets. Mu said it was no problem; when I wanted to write, I could write. "Bisnet was bisnet," in the meantime, and why couldn't she use the computer when I wasn't there? She was right — there was no reason, none I could think of that held water.

Though I did suspect Bia was spending too much time in our bedroom, and she wouldn't leave off wearing my shirts. But this I didn't mention to Mu because I was not sure myself what it signified.

Anyway, when you got tired of stumbling over business enterprises, there were lots of people to fall over instead. These diverse and interesting folk kept things from getting boring, it is true, though I came to feel I wouldn't mind a little boredom now and then. But as Mu said, all this was the Thai Way, and she was probably right, since she was the expert on the Thai Way in this house.

*

When Mu came out of the shower, she was wearing a loose

shift tied up behind her neck, the bright cotton clinging appetizingly to her body, her hair glistening wet and smelling of herbs. She was the reason I put up with the rest of it, the stuff that went on around here.

"Jack," she said, she didn't even tell me howdy. "What is this typewriter doing here? I thought you were going to sell it." So the first thing she noticed was another marketable commodity sitting on the floor beside the sugar cane. Most people wouldn't have noticed the Brooklyn Bridge if you parked it in the middle of this chaos.

"Mu," I said, figuring it was best to get straight to the bad news, and not beat around the bush. "Listen. Somebody is trying to kill me. And they ruined my best pipe, the Italian one with the big bowl. They shot the goddamned thing."

"Your pipe? You're smoking again? You tell me tobacco is too expensive, you're never going to smoke again."

"Mu, they were shooting at me. Trying to kill me. They blasted my typewriter, for Christ's sake. They filled the taxi full of holes as well. And they got my pipe. The Italian one."

"What? Your typewriter? They shot your typewriter? Is it okay?" She took to rubbing at the smears of lead on the undercarriage, where I showed her. "It still works okay; you can still get a good price for it?" Mu may have been a hard-headed businesswoman, everybody said she was, but I never doubted her basic concern for me, which was why I was still with her, never mind we were going to wind up married if I wasn't careful.

"Mu, it's me they were trying to shoot." I could hear impatience in my voice, which told me I was under some strain.

"You? Somebody try to kill you? Oh, my darling! Who?" Now she was running her hands over me, searching everywhere probably for more smears of lead.

This was a good question. The only person I could think of off-

93

hand who might have wanted me dead was Mu, if only she ever found out where I was that night I told her I was doing some research for a story on Celadon ceramics. Even though I never saw sweet little Ann again, and I had sworn to myself not to screw around any more; I was living with a fine woman and I owed her something even if we never did get married. "Mu, I don't know who wants me dead. Maybe it was a mistake; they probably took me for some other guy."

Mu got thoughtful and right away after that she looked more than a bit anxious. "The police!" she said. "What about the police; are they coming here?"

I guess she was worried that they might want a piece of the action when they saw all the business interests she had going in the joint. But I told her to relax. The cops were finished with me for the time being, and probably for ever, if I read correctly their interest in murdered farangs with too many visa runs in their passports.

"Tell me again," she said. "These two men, they shot at you? With bullets?"

What kind of shooting was it with no bullets? I wanted to ask. But then Mu sometimes had trouble with English, and God knows my Thai was no great shakes. Mu was no doubt distraught, besides, and not entirely sure of what she was saying. Nevertheless, she was reacting in a strange way, I thought. She seemed more angry than worried. You got the feeling if Mu had these inconsiderate types at hand, she would have given them a piece of her mind.

"It was only one man who shot at me," I told Mu. "The other one was driving the motorcycle."

"Did they say anything?" Mu was finally getting around to looking worried, I was pleased to see.

"Sure. They said 'You! You!'"

"Jack. Serious. Did they say anything?"

"No."

In fact I was thinking this was funny — whoever paid these jokers to take a shot at me was not getting his money's worth; I didn't even know why I was getting shot or who was concerned enough to arrange this little matter. Personally, if I wanted somebody dead badly enough to set it up, I would want the guy to know what was what.

"Maybe it was only my typewriter they were after."

"Oh, Jack; please listen to me. I tell you and I tell you again: you have to be careful. You are too *jai rawn*, too hot tempered. You can't do what you do in Thailand; this is not America. You don't understand. You will get into big trouble one day, if you are not careful."

This was not big trouble I was in already?

But sometimes Mu seemed to think I went around deliberately trying to get us all in hot water, what with writing about subjects I had no knowledge of and furthermore never listening to her advice. "I told you, you have to be careful who you write about in your newspapers. This is Thailand. You can't just say anything you like. You have to think about people's face."

And the week before Mu got so angry with me, she threatened to leave. This was only because I had a slight altercation with the bozo who set up to sell music tapes in the lane outside our building. It was the usual thing — a big wooden table and a tape-deck with two fifty-megaton speakers so the vendor could play samples from daybreak till after sundown. Usually he played a variety of rock'n'roll, both Thai and Western, but this one week he was blown away by Milli Vanilli, and he played Milli Vanilli over and over and over till everybody for 500 yards around could appreciate the finer points of these artistes and all the stray dogs had long since left for some place they could have a quiet nap of a hot summer's afternoon.

Don't think I was not impressed with this public servant's re-

95

solve to provide the neighborhood with nice music all day, and for free; but sometimes I had problems concentrating as it was, working at home and with deadlines to meet. So maybe I could be excused if only once I went down to complain, to explain to this goof I was tired of Milli Vanilli, and I was tired of him and tape vendors in general; it was probably best he move his operations to some other venue while he was still intact enough he could move; and so on. I was as persuasive as could be, and smiled a lot, and finally even helped him start to move his stock off the table. Being in a hurry, I just kind of turned the table over, seeing as how we were having trouble communicating; he couldn't seem to get it through his head that this was now a Tape-vendor-free Zone. There were some hot words, finally, and a gang of interested citizens gathered to attend the debate, which I finally won, since the vendor and some buddy with a pick-up truck eventually moved everything away.

When Mu heard about this discussion I had, she was so upset I wound up giving her a lecture on how to stay cool. "*Jai yen yen.* Cool, cool," I reminded her, which got her even more steamed up. Anyway, she couldn't understand why I didn't want to have to listen to somebody else's music all day long every day. If you could believe her, she had never noticed the tape vendor till I started this hassle.

Another thing I freely admit I don't understand about the Thai Way, is the way everybody thrives on deafening levels of noise, the louder the better, preferably coming from as many different sources as possible. In the restaurants and nightclubs, on the streets, at temple fairs — wherever you go it's the same thing. Your average visitor to Bangkok asks you how people can stand the constant noise of the traffic, the screaming tuk-tuks, the motorcycles with their mufflers off, the tape-vendors every fifty yards along every street. What they don't understand is that this is just the background — if a Thai is really enjoying life, they'll see to it there's lots more noise than that.

Then there was the noise in my apartment, where I wrote my stories and had trouble even with no noise trying to communicate with Mu and Co. A real estate agent might have called this the "ambient noise," only a real-estate agent would never have mentioned this ambience unless he absolutely had to.

While Mu was trying to get to the bottom of this latest tomfoolery of mine — this going around getting shot at — Thai pop music was coming from a bedroom; I didn't know who was in there. Some Western rock group was meanwhile screaming at each other on little Jit's tapedeck. Jit — I didn't know for sure how he fit into the scheme of things, probably he was another cousin — was asleep on the floor beside the tapedeck. Cousin Noi was pounding spices in a big stone mortar and singing a broken-hearted Thai love song that had nothing to do with the radio song, the rock piece, or the music leaking into the joint from the new tape vendor out in the lane, the one who set up shop just two days after the last one had left. This music-lover had no Milli Vanilli, and so far I was maintaining the old *jai yen*, a "cool heart" to make Mu proud, even if I knew some day soon I would kill the son of a bitch.

Noi was going pok-pok-pok with her big mortar and pestle, jamming away with Cousin Daeng, who was going chop-chop-chop with a cleaver, cutting up some meat on a board in the kitchen. Keeow, a roly-poly thing with dimples — I wasn't sure if she was a cousin or not — made up the rest of the rhythm section, pumping the treadle on her ancient sewing machine as she took up the hems of three gross of sundresses Mu acquired had two seasons before, and which, she had decided, would now sell better if they were four inches shorter.

As if all this wasn't interesting enough already, you had Bia falling down at more or less regular intervals, and Granny, who was deaf as a post, hollering "*Arai na?* What? *Arai na?*" trying to clarify what everybody was saying to her, even when most of the time nobody was saying anything at all to her. Granny was stabbing skewers through pieces of pork for Little Lek and glaring at everybody, especially me, whom she wouldn't understand even if she could hear anything. And, finally, there was Cousin Dok, who was a *katoey*, a transvestite. He was practicing being a girl, as usual, by shrieking away in a falsetto and flapping about batting his eyelids till you might have thought he was having an epileptic fit. He was also saving up for an operation, he said, though his was going to cost a lot more than Bia's. They could have both gone to the same brain surgeon, for my money, and got a two-for-one special.

Dok was shrieking and simpering at Mu's cousin Meow the Hairdresser, who was laughing and shrieking right back. This was what Thai girls call having a good chat. Meow yelled something at Bia, who then fell over Cousin Sombat, who woke up and yelled at her for her thoughtlessness; he had to get his rest, since soon he would be going to work in Saudi Arabia which, as anybody would have told you, was enough to make you tired. Sombat had already been going to go to Saudi Arabia for two months, at that point. Ever since I fronted the 1,300 dollars he needed to pay his job sponsor. Once in a while I asked why he didn't go to Saudi Arabia, now I had come up with this money, at no small inconvenience to myself, I might have added, but nobody really explained it.

"Wait," they told me. "We must wait."

So if you're starting to get the idea I lived in Bedlam, you're just about right. Only it was worse than that. It was enough to make you tired even if you weren't almost shot to death, and more than somewhat worried on that account. All I wanted to do was talk to Mu and get her to give me a massage and tell me everything was going to be okay. And so on. But it wasn't always easy to get a little privacy. It was enough to make you edgy.

And all Mu could tell me was this was the Thai Way, and I had to "adjust myself." It was because I was not adjusting myself successfully, I had to understand, that people were shooting at me, and things would only get worse if I didn't wise up.

On top of that, I couldn't even smoke in my own apartment. Granny had problems with asthma, though how her lungs differentiated between normal Bangkok air and tobacco smoke I didn't know.

That night, after I gave Mu the surprise in my shorts, I tried to take the edge off things some more by having a few drinks with Cousin Sombat and Cousin Dok. The ladies, even Mu, kept a steady stream of tasty snacks coming from the kitchen, lots of crunchy-hot-salty-sour stuff that kept you wanting more cold drink no matter how much cold drink you had already, while Bia, sweet thing, kept our glasses full no matter how often she walked into things and fell down till the floor was awash in Mekhong soda. She fell against me at least twice, I had to notice.

Dok worked at his fluttering and shrieking but seemed to get more masculine the drunker he got, while Sombat talked about the things he was going to do with all the money from Saudi Arabia, only he still couldn't tell me when he was going to go away and get this money. Then everybody sang songs in Thai, except for me, who just made noises in rough approximation to these popular tunes.

Mu finally threw us out, and half a dozen of us went to the club down the road. There we drank some more and I smoked even though I'd quit; and we got to listen to an endless series of Thai ladies climb on stage in party dresses and try to make louder noises than the electric organ and drum machine. Eventually they took off all their clothes and walked around kissing members of the audience instead, which was aesthetically more pleasing than their singing, but which as it turned out cost twenty baht a throw. Dok spent more than Sombat and me put together; you figure it out.

In the morning, I could see that getting shot dead might not have been a bad move, the way I first thought. And Mu expressed some sentiments along the same lines, especially after I screamed at Granny, "Nothing! Nothing. Jesus Christ, oh dearie me. Nobody said anything."

I didn't mean to scream at her.

The best thing I could do, I thought, was go downtown and talk to Hippolyte. Maybe he could tell me what was what. And what to do. I was getting really edgy.

one way to cure a hangover

Selections from Arno Petty's Intelligencer and Weekly Gleaner

NO PROBLEM. Speaking less oracularly than is his wont, an elder statesman has said that Thais have no problem with mental illness. It is not on the increase in this country, no matter what is sometimes reported, praise the gods. (One prominent specialist has suggested that 44% of Bangkok's population is already loony.) People after all have their families, their communities, and their religion. That is the difference between the materialistic Western countries and this Buddhist society. But which people is he talking about? Surely it isn't just the 5% of the population who own 95% of the wealth who are 'Thais'? Are the rest merely labor and market?

GOOD NEWS/BAD NEWS. The bad news is that currently 40% of the population is below the poverty line. The good news? The Minister of Poverty has just bought a second Benz, and his wife is really pleased with the color.

STANDING IN FRONT OF ME on the bus there was a proper young Thai lady. She was doing a good job of filling a T-shirt that read I EAT PUSSY. Under this legend was painted a couple of fat red lips with a fuzzy pink kitten's tail dangling out from between them. This lady didn't know a lot of English, was my guess.

I had a sick hangover. A sticky thick sheen of sweat covered me, refusing to evaporate in the muggy closeness. I was standing on this old Isuzu bus, a wooden-floored relic of the pre-boom days, everything shaking and banging as we rocketed along in the bus lane, farting great blasts of black smoke in our wake, the driver under the misapprehension he was Jackie Stewart and this was a Lotus he was driving. He was horsing the Isuzu along, alternately

101

standing on the accelerator and then on the brake. And, just in case I was not uncomfortable enough already, he had some loud pop music on his tapedeck. We lurched back and forth and bounced up and down, packed in there like refugees, the Thais smiling at one another for some reason. Probably they had heard this was the Land of Smiles and, being conventional folk, they figured it was best to smile.

I was not smiling. I was too tall to see out the windows, and it was too crowded for me to crouch down to where I could peer out, so I could only guess at where I was. I crooked my neck slightly to avoid banging the ceiling and hand-rails with my head, which meant I was constantly getting a faceful of hair from the girl with the interesting T-shirt standing in front of me.

Sweat was oozing out all over me. The traffic fumes were unbelievable; I was breathing as shallowly as I could without passing out from lack of air. My head was throbbing. Why was it I never learned? Thai waiters kept your Mekhong topped up; you could never drink the glass down to the half-way mark before they were sneaking up behind you and slipping your glass away for a refill. A good waiter could do this so you never noticed; you just kept drinking and talking and thinking everything was okay until you tried to stand up.

I found I was a little on edge. To start with, as I said before, I had spent the night before drinking Mekhong with cousin Sombat and Dok the transvestite. Then I was awakened at daybreak by the flower children testing the Isarn flutes they were taking to the market to sell this day. This caused me to blow up at the whole assembly, which in turn had the effect of inciting Granny, who immediately took to hollering "*Arai na?* What?" in querulous tones and thereby putting everybody in a bad mood. Especially Mu was not happy; I was still not behaving like a proper Thai.

Nobody could behave like a proper Thai in this heat with a

hangover, or so I was telling myself.

The ticket-taker, an unhappy youth with an eighteen-inch metal cylinder full of coins and paper ticket-rolls, was squeezing his way through the passengers. He was snapping the lid of his cylinder open and shut so that it chattered like a set of joke dentures. I guessed somebody had to do the job, but why did he have to do it when I had this hangover? Then I felt a prod in my rib-cage and there was a sudden metallic snap-snap-snapping right under my nose. This caused me to swear horribly more or less under my breath and hand the guy two one-baht coins.

"You like to live dangerously, don't you?" I told him in English, smiling like a outlaw; this was the Land of Smiles, after all, and I should behave like a Thai.

"*Song baht,*" he replied, which meant "two baht."

We had been going along for some time already, and the bus was not stopping as often as you might have thought it should. I was getting the idea we were close to where I wanted to get off, but I couldn't see anything until I took advantage of a sudden lurch, shoving a few people down the way with my butt and performing a heroic kind of contortion so I could catch a glimpse of the street. "Holy shit," I said, and the girl with the pussy shirt smiled at me. We had just gone by my stop, however, and I didn't smile back.

With some amount of pushing and swearing and saying "Excuse me; *kaw thoht, krap,* Jesus Christ" I managed to get to the rear exit, where I stood down on the step and rang the little bell. I rang it and I rang it as we shot by the next stop as well. Sometimes Bangkok bus drivers do this — they get on a run, the traffic eases off for some reason, and maybe their bus is full anyway, so they don't stop. They don't stop to let people on and they don't stop to let them off. If you were in the right mood, you shook your head and you smiled ruefully, thinking "This is Bangkok; and this is a Bangkok bus driver." That was if you were in the right mood. Instead I tried smashing on the door frame with my fist, which had the effect of fucking up my hand and not stopping the bus.

The ticket taker came over to stand beside me, and he grinned at me. Possibly he was smiling, but I saw it as a grin, and I was not, as it happened, in the mood to shake my head and smile ruefully. What I did instead was I grabbed his change cylinder which, being chock full of change, was heavier than you might have thought, and I heaved it out into the road, cursing foully and by no means under my breath.

This surprised the ticket-taker somewhat. It surprised me too, come to that. But it had an immediate and gratifying effect — the cylinder exploded in a shower of money flying and rolling every which way, while the ticket-taker started screaming and blowing his whistle and, I was pretty sure, calling me a giant lizard, though my Thai wasn't that good. Best of all, the bus screeched to a halt, which was what my plan was in the first place; so I jumped out and took a powder. Before I disappeared up a side-street, moving like the wind, I had a glimpse of the driver piling off the front of the bus, shirt open, tattoos everywhere, a knobbed club in one hand, and I got the impression that this individual was disturbed about something. It could be that he and his ticket-taking associate would have liked to discuss matters with me, but I was already behind schedule and I had no time to hang around yapping. Besides, they had some work to do re-collecting their fares. I loped up the road and then took a detour through a market. Nobody paid much attention to me, since in this part of town they were used to seeing farangs, and farangs were often found doing silly things in the midday sun. Pretty soon I made myself scarce enough I could stop to catch my breath.

At first I swore some more, but then I started to laugh. This was not a typical thing I had done, just then; I was not the type to go around making a display of myself and causing people this kind of aggravation. But I was feeling better than I had since I woke up, and it seemed to have something to do with stopping the bus in this novel and dramatic way. Or maybe it was only all the running, I told myself. That must have been it. I made a mental note to get more exercise.

Though what I really wanted was a cigarette.

I walked the rest of the way to Shaky Jake's.

hippolyte

Selections from Arno Petty's Intelligencer and Weekly Gleaner

FORGE ON. Could it be that the girls at Lots O' Hots are buying their VD certificates from the same place Big Sammy Soo was getting his money printed? That would be nothing but a vicious rumor, were it not for the epidemic proportion of the complaints one hears from Lots O' Hots take-away customers.

WHERE IS HANS? Some of our readers like the girls in *Playboy Magazine* because they're often a bit top heavy. Well, we know Playboy is banned in this country because it is immoral, and we know that locally the ladies are generally only top heavy when they've got baskets of fruit or some such on their heads. Be that as it may, aficionados might drop around to have a look at the pair of barmaids Hans' wife Nid has working for her at the No Hans Bar. *Playboy* would need a fold-out annex to accommodate either pair.

"JACK, MY BOY," Hippolyte was telling me. "Jack, Jack, Jack."

I was getting the idea old Hip had something he wanted to say, and chances were it wasn't how much he admired my judgment. And I was right.

We were sitting in a back booth at Shaky Jake's, two beers and some peanuts on the table in front of us. I had just finished explaining why my hand was bleeding.

"Jack, you are too uptight. You know? Whoa. Slow down. You got to learn to relax."

"Relax? *Relax?* They shoot my typewriter. They almost shoot me. And the police figure I must be a drug smuggler, why else is everybody trying to kill me? So I have to make some contributions to a bunch of charitable causes, none of which to tell the truth I really care about. And I give the driver money or he loses his license; he wants me also to pay to fix all the holes in his cab. Mu needs money. Her cousins need money. Granny's got asthma. Our lane is full of tape vendors, the landlord says he's going to double our rent at the end of the year anyway. My best pipe gets shot, smashed to smithereens, and I'm going nuts; I need a smoke. And you tell me to relax? Hippolyte, give me a cigarette. Please."

Hip was a real friend, and he did not give me a smoke without first telling me I was a shithead, but he did give it to me, and I wolfed it down in about three drags, so he gave me another one as well.

Bald pate sunburned to the color of stained mahogany and fringed with a halo of graying hair, Hip wore dark granny glasses and habitually spoke in a soft mutter from the depths of a luxuriant white beard. He had been around since the Vietnam days — a bit of human flotsam come ashore in Bangkok, is how he put it. If you saw him sitting there and didn't know better, you would probably have figured he was blind. He worked at being deaf, as well, and you generally had to holler at him to get his attention. Though after that it was no problem; in fact he preferred to talk in undertones, and never actually had any problem understanding anybody.

Hippolyte Lafleur had this talent for self-effacement. He was like a *jinjok*, the house lizard that waits motionless on walls and ceilings, infinitely patient, waiting for a juicy insect to venture within range. Hip blended in with the woodwork of one low-life establishment or another, to all appearances, to the extent he could be said to appear at all, a burnt-out case waiting to die in his shabby jeans and sneakers and counterfeit Lacoste polo shirts, blind and deaf and acutely sensitive to everything that everybody did or said.

He ordered more beer. Also he got some colas for Boom and Mon, two of Shaky Jake's finest, who were sitting either side of him waiting to get their fortunes told. No matter how self-effacing he could be, Hip was not averse to having charming young ladies in skimpy costumes sit close to him. Only as a warm-up to reading their palms, most likely, and free of charge, he was also reading considerable areas of their bodies. Or maybe he was afraid the girls were cold, the air-conditioning going like a blizzard the way it was. But, like I said, Hip was a pal, and he unhanded these specimens for a minute and took hold of my own mitt instead.

Hip cast an expert eye over my palm and he said "One thing, yeah? I see you've never done a decent day's work in years, if ever. Whoa. That's right. And you don't want to go around hitting any *nak laeng*, any tough guys, or any buses either with this hand unless for some reason you want it broken. I also see it is a little damp. This is a natural reaction to recent events. It is a side effect of adrenaline anxiety, and is useful to our simian ancestors, since it lubricates their hands when they want to take a powder, swinging from branch to branch through the trees. This feature is less useful to us today. In fact, it causes us to feel clammy, and it gives people whose hands we shake the impression they are dealing with wimps. Yeah? People by no means think you are a wimp, of course. But generally speaking, you know?"

Hippolyte Lafleur was a fortune-teller and a notorious know-it-all. This latter accomplishment could be annoying since it often turned out that he did know it all. He was furthermore Izzy Scoop, the intrepid investigative reporter, though that was not something to bruit about. Hippolyte took his anonymity seriously. And well he might, if he wanted to live to continue being Izzy Scoop.

Izzy Scoop's real identity was one of the best-kept secrets in Bangkok — Hippolyte was the man behind some of the hardest-hitting, most fearless exposes of corruption and greed in high places to be found in the region. Izzy Scoop's stories were *tours de force* of investigative reporting. Everything carefully documented, these pieces actually said what had to be said, even when this couldn't be said according to anybody with any respect for their own well-being. Of course no local newspaper would touch the stuff, since no newspaper wanted to lose its license to print the news. But some of the big foreign newsmagazines ate it up with a spoon.

On the other hand, of course, you had Arno Petty's full-page column of wise-cracking news in review, wisdom, advice, and insider gossip that the *Bangkok Globe* ran every Saturday. I am Arno Petty; I have to admit it. Jack the Hack.

But I wrote other stuff, as well. Compared to Izzy, you could say I made up in versatility for what I lacked in journalistic muscle. Aside from gunman stories and reports on revolutions in Burma, which were selling like free beer at the moment, Arno had been known to write copy for a brochure or two, which was like stealing money compared to the return you got on newspaper and magazine stories. More like whoring than stealing, actually. And of course Arno Petty was the man behind Propriapist Publications' A-Z series of pornographic novels out of New York. We were up to "D," *A Dick for Dorothy.* Four thousand bucks apiece, though I was trying to negotiate a better deal.

"An alliterative exploration of the varieties of human sexual experience ..." Izzy Scoop had actually written the new blurb for the series. He was one of Arno Petty's biggest fans—you could say the only fan of Arno's I had ever met, since my novels weren't distributed in Thailand, being I guess too off-color for the local authorities. Hip was determined that when I got to "U," I would do *An Ungulate for Ulricke.* I told him he should probably stick to daring exposes, and leave the porno novels to Arno. He should also live so long, I would ever get to write my way to "U."

Hippolyte was loved, even held in awe, by the bargirls of the city. Not only was he a *maw doo,* a seer, of some repute, he took a personal interest in their problems. He had a way of reading their love-lives as though these chronicles were written all over their palms in thirty-point bold. It didn't matter that most of his predictions had to do with meeting nice foreign men and coming into sudden money. And of course it was uncanny how he would sometimes see illness in the family, when you considered that these up-country girls had more relatives than hard luck stories, which was saying something indeed, and statistically speaking one of them would just about have had to have been sick at any given time. On top of that, Hip's Thai was almost fluent and the girls would tell him all their gossip, so it might not have been surprising if every now and then he came up with a startlingly accurate piece of personal news for a client.

"But I don't need to read your palm to see you've got a problem, my friend. So what are you going to do about it?"

I told him what Mu had told me. She said I had been causing "influential people" and "dark influences" to lose face left and right. Chances were, if only you could believe her, half the contents of *Who's Who in Thailand* were gunning for me already. Listening to her go on about it, you might have even got the impression I was selling a lot of stories these days, the way I was managing to piss everybody off. But this would be a false impression, I assured him.

"I hate to tell you this, Jack," said Hip, "but with your attitude it could be just about anybody and everybody who is after your ass. Whoa. Maybe a whole bunch of people passed the hat and it's, like, a collective hit."

"For Christ's sake, this is no joke, Hip. Somebody's out to get me."

"Whoa. Calm down. Maybe it's a mistake. That's it. This could be one of those 'business conflicts' you're always reading about, and you look exactly like some guy who made a million bucks and somebody else figures it is really his million bucks."

"That's probably it — there's some rich Thai who's a dead ringer for me and who rides around in antique taxis selling antique typewriters so he can go to happy hour. Thanks, Hip. That's most likely it."

"Okay. Child labor. You did a series on child labor; but then again so has everyone else. And you did the pieces on Thai red-light districts — you couldn't hold still for the way politicians and editors claimed that Western writers, especially 'parachute journalists,' were 'casting Thailand in a bad light' and 'looking down on Thais.' You put it right up front: if anybody thought those stories were the dark side of Thailand, then they were dangerously naïve. Then there was the research you did on the police — remember that? You paid those Thai researchers, criminology students, to dig up all the funny stories about cops shooting innocent citizens and each other besides. Even though nobody would print it here. And the logging story?

"It could be anybody. Look, Jack; I'll tell you the truth; and you don't have to be a *maw doo* to see which way the wind is blowing. It doesn't have to be some bigshot with a grudge who does you in, you keep on like you are. You mess with the tape vendors, and now you throw the bus conductor's money all out in the street, even though this individual is only doing what bus conductors in Bangkok always do. Who are you to change the rules of the game?"

Hip got this look, the same look he put on when he was going to tell a fortune. His shades went even more opaque, don't ask me how that could happen, and he leaned closer. "As you know, Jack, our bodies and our minds move in rhythms. There are all kinds of influences that can affect our state of mind and our happiness. Nobody understands these things too good, and you get everyone from psychotherapists to astrologers trying to tell you what to do and why. But the fact remains, there are these cycles and things, and if you can get in tune with them, life goes better. That much is common knowledge."

It could have been news to his two charming companions,

111

though, the way they were hanging on his every word, understanding I would have said not more than a couple of these words, yet impressed by the sheer gravity of his manner.

"What some people don't know, is that some of these rhythms are part of culture. You get these ways of doing things set up by people living and working together over the years and the generations. Every culture has its own harmonies and rhythms, and these might not seem obvious to somebody from another background. That's right. They're often not obvious to the people in the culture either — no more noticeable than the beating of the blood in their own veins or the regular intake of oxygen and expulsion of carbon dioxide. Are you with me?

"Whoa. But then you put somebody from a different culture in there, and all of a sudden it's like you got someone doing the Funky Chicken in the middle of everybody's nice waltz. And that's you, Jack — you're doing the Funky Chicken when everybody around you is cheek to cheek."

"What is this Funky Chicken, Hip?" Sometimes I had to think there was a cultural gulf between Hip and me. "I can't do the Funky Chicken; I never even heard of this thing."

"*Hiew khow*," said Boom. "I'm hungry!"

"*Chahn duay*. Me too." Mon slid her hand inside Hip's shirt and told him "*Gai thawt, na?* You buy us fried chicken, okay?"

Whether it was the rumor of fried chicken or only the scent of cola, a likely looking lady named Ping chose this time to sit down next to me and start making nursing noises over my hand. Which did hurt like a son of a bitch, though I didn't want to say anything; and it felt okay to have it dabbed at with a cold towel.

Without a word, Hip handed Mon some money; and she went over to give it to the boy at the door, along with the order. Ping also got up to fetch her cola.

"You have the idea everything is out of synch," Hip went on.

"And it makes you mad. Wow. But everybody else figures you're out of synch; and who's right — you or everybody else? You toss somebody into the middle of another culture, and he doesn't try to adjust his behavior, you get a general grinding of cultural gears and gnashing of teeth on all sides. Two things can happen, now. One: the cultural intruder grinds away at his own cultural edges till he starts to mesh without too much friction. Two: he gets chewed up into bits and spat out. Yo, Arno. Which is it going to be with you?"

"Hip. Give me a break."

"I like you, Jack, or I don't ask you this: Are you sure you want to stay here in Thailand? It may be this country isn't too good for you, when all is said and done. You know?"

What was he trying to tell me? I had a girlfriend, here. I had a career as a writer I was trying to get off the ground; and he thought I should go back to the States where writers starved to death in job lots, even faster than they did here? I could sell one story in Bangkok, it was enough to pay the rent for a month; in New York City it wouldn't have covered my cab fare.

And I did try to adjust; what was he talking about? I was learning some Thai; I wasn't doing too bad, I had to say so myself. And I practiced my *jai yen*, my cool heart, all the time. I did these maintaining-my-cool exercises every day, not only to make Mu happy but also to bring my blood pressure down. There was no sense in having a brain hemorrhage at my age. It hurt me to hear my friend Hip talk this way, I had to admit it; so I told him to piss off. I wasn't leaving. Everybody else could leave. Or learn to do the Funky Chicken, if they wanted to do that, whatever that might be.

Mon got back with the chicken, and I realized I was hungry too. Ping had her cola; she insisted on clinking glasses *chok dee*, cheers, and then took to mopping my fevered brow with another cold towel.

Hip fixed me with his most opaque gaze, and spoke to me in his softest, profoundest tones. "Jack, Jack, Jack," he said. "You take my advice: calm down and think about what you're doing. You are cruising for a bruising, if you're not careful. Whoa. You don't have to be a fortune-teller to see that."

"Thanks, Hip. I will try to sidestep this bruising; and possibly even stop doing the Funky Chicken, once I figure out what it is."

As I got up to go, Ping asked me could I lend her 500 baht for just a week, or two, seeing as how her rent was due and she didn't have quite enough because her baby was sick and so was her uncle. Ping was a fine lady and everything, and she had always had a kind word for me when I dropped in at Shaky Jake's, but it wasn't as though we had something going, after all. So I told her how I was mostly broke myself, what with one thing and another, and here was 200 baht for her; I hoped it would help.

She seemed happy with this and maybe her rent wasn't that much, when it came right down to it. She leaned across Mon to give Hip a big hug, even though it was me who had covered her rent; and Mon told me Hip had said that Ping would come into some money that very day. Khun Hip was a maw doo among maw doos, it was plain to see.

He was ordering more drinks as I left.

a gentle warning

Selections from Arno Petty's Intelligencer and Weekly Gleaner

THE BETTER PART OF VALOR. Too often tourists take exception to the admittedly obnoxious touts on Patpong Road, and find themselves involved in fisticuffs. Be advised that anybody in these parts you asked would probably guess the Marquis de Queensbury was a new hotel. Locally, a fight is settled by *force majeure*, this being force of sheer numbers armed with instruments both blunt and sharp. It's far better to keep smiling, come what may, and remove your person from the area of aggravation. It's the Thai Way.

MUAY THAI. It is often said that Thai-style boxing is more deadly than any other martial art, and that a *muay thai* adept will make short work of karate experts and such-like. Be that as it may, one very real difference between these other schools of mayhem and muay thai is that muay thai is a full-contact sport, and there are about 50,000 practitioners of the art in the country at any given time—an impressive pool of hardened fighters, well seasoned by real combat.

I WAS WALKING along our little street wondering if I should pick up a bag of *somtam* or whether Mu had already bought some, when I noticed two guys leaning against the weathered teak and corrugated iron grocery shop up ahead. I got this feeling right away they were not merely hanging around waiting for dinner. They peeled off the wall and moved out into the street, exchanging looks and making some laughing remarks in Thai I didn't quite catch. Two young guys, probably in their early twenties. Dressed in T-shirts and jeans. I saw them kick off their rubber thongs as they moved out, loose limbed, fit looking. Purposeful.

I saw that it might be a good idea to walk the other way for awhile. Maybe even run; there's nothing like a good run before dinner. But when I turned around to start this new health regimen, what should I see but two more young men, and they were from the same cookie cutter as the other two, except for one of them who was wearing shoes and who had a mouthful of choppers like somebody tossed them in with a shovel. When I looked closer I could see he was also older than his buddies. He was grinning away like Dale Carnegie gone berserk, and he called softly to me: "You! You!" Then I heard the same thing from his buddies behind me.

My heart started pounding, and some other part of me was pumping adrenaline so hard I could feel it squirt. Things were happening too quickly for me to develop a tremble in the knees or any sick feeling in the gut. What the hell, I thought. I saw myself already dead; I felt only that I must first wreak some havoc, cause some pain, smash some flesh as my part in this scenario. I wondered if Mu was home yet. I tried taking a hard look at the guy with the mouthful of dirty ivory and I said, "*Arai, na?* What?" I even sneered a little, though this sneer tended to slide off my face when they came for me. They were going to use their feet. I knew that. Every Thai boy grows up with Thai boxing, kung fu movies, and *takraw*, this superathletic game that is much like volleyball, except you can only use your feet and head. Thais have intelligent feet.

I was vaguely aware of a gang of children huddled off to the side, gravely curious. Further along the lane there were a few adults; they were wearing expressions of distaste, even dismay. A monk stopped at the gate to the temple, and I saw him wince and draw his orange robes more tightly about his body as he stood there watching. All of these things I saw in the seconds I had left, and I saw no hope. Not even in the tae kwon do lessons I had taken two years before did I see any hope. Still, when the one on the right in front of me unleashed a kick I blocked it with a kick of my own, fists up to block Mr Front Left as I pivoted towards Mr Left Rear with another maneuver in mind — a sweep kick to take him off his feet in just the way my instructor had showed me back when. I prepared to do this, but instead I felt a sudden sickening pain spreading out from my kidney where Mr Right Rear had just planted a calloused foot of his own. A whole variety of unpleasant shocks and sensations followed, quickly blurring into one generalized sense of acute malaise.

My defense strategy amounted to curling up on the road like an armadillo, writing off my kidneys and head in favor of my testicles and face. My physical face, I mean. In other respects, of course, you might have called this situation a bad case of *naa tak* — what the Thais refer to as "broken face." Loss of face, acute embarrassment, whatever. And I was coughing; all this booting about of my person had started up my smoker's cough. In the mornings, sometimes, Mu would tell me I was killing myself. I told myself if I lived through this little contretemps, I would finally give up smoking for sure.

Actually, these gentlemen concentrated on my arms and legs, in the end, and most of the damage was in fact to my self-esteem. I was still conscious when one of them, the one with the teeth, bent down close to me and hissed in pretty terrible English, "You! *Farang*. My bot, the Big Bot, says to tell you 'Her-ro.' He says to tell you, you are dogshit. You make him an-glee, so he take *f'en* you, you raidy. Maybe he give back sometime. When he finish. *Kowchai?* Dogshit ... You! *Unnerstan?*"

I was afraid I did understand, and this made me try something foolish; I tried to remove all of this emissary's teeth with a backhanded fist. This resulted right away in an explosion of lights and darkness and I sank into a peaceful condition where there was nobody kicking me.

When I came to, the somtam lady was wiping my face with a

117

damp rag. I got to my feet with some help from this good Samaritan. I was a mess. My clothes were filthy from the street and all the kicking. I felt like puking. There was blood, as well, though I didn't know exactly where it came from. Some of it from my hand, I guess, from where I tried to remove the guy's teeth. Some more from my head and my face, I saw when Big Lek wiped at me again and wrung pink water out of her rag. I felt sick, and my head was splitting. The kids were still there, staring at me dispassionately, probably wondering what the farang was going to come up with next in the way of entertainment. I could hear the lunatic calliope of an ice-cream vendor down the road.

The somtam lady was speaking so slowly I could understand almost everything she was saying, for a change. "Some bad men; they come your house. They take one *phooying*, one girl you. She seem funny. Maybe drunk; something was wrong. Maybe they do bad things to her."

This news affected me more or less as though somebody had kicked me in the balls. I tried to say to the somtam lady "Get the police," but she didn't do anything. And she was speeding up to 78 rpm again, so I no longer had any idea what she was talking about. I couldn't run very well, with the pain in my kidneys and all, but I moved as fast as I could down to our little alley, and I pushed past some people standing out front of our place.

"Mu?" I called, not really expecting an answer, but calling again, "*Mu?*" I ran up the stairs, or at least hobbled pretty fast. The door to our apartment was open, and the living room was a mess. This was nothing new, of course, it was always a mess; but this mess was not standard. The telephone had been ripped out of the wall and flung into the fish box, which was smashed to smithereens and leaking loud swimsuits; you could see those golden arowanas had never been fated to make anybody's fortune no matter how you cut it. The coffee table had a broken leg, and it had dumped a pile of yellow silk roses down on the floor. A standing lamp had been knocked over. And for once there was nobody there. Or so at first I thought.

"*Arai na? Arai na?*" yelled Granny, as she came out of the bathroom. Then she saw who it was, and she evidently despaired of getting anything sensible out of me. "You! *Farang.* Aieeeeee!"

No matter this was the most extended bit of discourse I had ever had from the lady, it didn't much clarify matters in my mind. So I rushed from room to room falling over things and looking behind things for Mu. Or at least somebody. "Bia! I was saying. "Sombat, for Christ's sake! Hello?" To tell the truth I was not fully in control of the situation. My computer looked okay, but I didn't even turn it on to check, I was so upset. "Mu! Ah, Jesus. *Muuu.*"

"What?" Mu came in off the landing into the living room with an armful of bags. "What do you want?"

"*Arai na?*" Granny came out of the bedroom.

In about a minute, Sombat and Dok and Keeow and about a dozen other regulars were back and milling around. Rhot emerged from the bathroom with a bloody towel wrapped turban-fashion around his head. Before you knew it, things were back to their usual chaotic state, even worse, since everybody was trying to tell the story at the same time.

The gist of things, the common element in the wildly dramatized accounts we were getting from all sides, was that four men including a guy with a lot of teeth had come in and waved guns around while they fell all over everything. Eventually they went into our bedroom, where they found Bia, and they had taken her away. The only one who had done anything to try and stop them had been Rhot, and he had a headache and a flap of skin hanging off the side of his head for his efforts.

"Jack," said Mu, after the dust had settled and she had had a good think about matters. "No police — we must not bring the

119

police in on this. And Jack ... How much money do you have?"

There was a bad gash on my hand where I had tried to remove that guy's teeth. The same hand, I might add, that I had used to punch the bus. I had a pretty good headache, and I felt bruised all over, especially around my kidneys and my ribs. It hurt to breathe; I hoped nothing was broken. I was still sick in my stomach. I knew that the next day it would all hurt even more, and new pains would show up to surprise me. I noticed something else that depressed me—my wallet was gone.

"Mu," I answered her. "I'm busted flat."

I was starting to think Burma was going to have to have another revolution soon, or I was in trouble, the way all that easy money was evaporating. I spent about half an hour back out on the *soi* looking for my amulet, which had disappeared somewhere in the course of that day's proceedings. Many of the people in the neighborhood watched me all the while, waiting to see what this interesting farang would come up with next. I didn't find my amulet, but one kid came up to me and gave me my wallet, which was empty.

That night Rhot and Sombat and Dok and I went to the coffee shop down the road and drank all the Mekhong whiskey we could get our hands on, Dok paying the shot for once, and this turned out to be not much better for my system than having it beaten on by gangs of *nak laeng*.

120

a trip to the market

Selections from Arno Petty's Intelligencer and Weekly Gleaner

NO PROBLEM. According to reliable reports, more than 40% of Bangkok's citizenry is now on tranquillizers of one sort or another.

NO MORE LAND OF SMILES? What happens if officialdom ever decides to enforce the laws governing prescription drugs? What about all these people who have been simply going in and asking for their half-kilo of Valium or Librium whenever they need it? Maybe we can get a blanket pre-scription—all anybody would need would be a Bangkok address.

ALL OF EXISTENCE was one big chocolate mama's teat. My whole being was gumming and sucking and pulling at this liter carton of chocolate milk, the cold soothing sweet torrent smoothing the tur-bulence of my tormented soul. Oil on troubled waters.

"You have hangover?" Mu enquired, her voice conveying no sympathy whatsoever.

I drained the carton. Then I moaned softly as I rolled an almost frozen giant bottle of cola back and forth across my forehead. "Ahh, God," I said. Pain and ecstasy together shaped my visage into something you might have seen on a Shi'ite fanatic as he flogged himself through the streets with a cat o' nine tails. "This is what it was originally designed for, in the beginning, before any-body thought of drinking it."

Mu was paying me no heed, now. This was supposed to tell me she was not happy with me.

Having chilled my fevered brain somewhat, I unscrewed the cap and proceeded to gulp half the bottle straight from the neck. Ice-

121

cold cola gushed, blasting down my gullet, little diamond bubbles rasping out the gunge in my throat. I punctuated the half-way point with a resounding belch, and then drained the rest.

A remarkable tour de force of cola-drinking, it nevertheless went unremarked by Mu, who threw herself on the bed with a newspaper. I rolled over beside her, every bone in my body aching, every internal organ bruised, the cola and chocolate milk sloshing back and forth in my belly like a tidal wave. I rolled from side to side a couple of times in an experimental vein, listening to this phenomenon with surprise. "Hey!" I said. "Listen to that."

"Jack, you listen to me," Mu answered. "You have to be more careful. You can't go on doing the things you do. This is Thailand; you don't understand Thailand. It's not the same as your home."

This hurt me, seeing as how I had come to think of Thailand as home. Even this zoo I lived in, this apartment, felt like home to me; and here was Mu saying it was not my home. At the same time, I admit, I did not understand Thailand. That much didn't bother me, because it was true and there was no use my saying it wasn't. But I was learning. For example, I was learning, not for the first time, that waiters in Thai restaurants snuck up all the time and replenished your Mekhong soda from the trolley behind you, so if you didn't watch yourself you drank more whiskey than you knew what to do with; you stood up to leave and you found you had no legs to stand on. Rhot and Dok and I the night before, we had drunk more Mekhong than we knew what to do with. Then I had come back and punched a hole in the bedroom wall with my already in-fected hand, worried about Bia and wondering who was doing these things to us and why.

And now Mu was going to take me shopping.

*

Down by the river, near the Grand Palace and right in the heart of tourist Bangkok, there is a little market area much favored by

122

Thais. You can get anything you want in Tha Phra Chan. The average casual visitor to Tha Phra Chan never sees the really interesting part of things, though. Walk down one of the tiny lanes towards the river, and you discover a parallel universe running along the water: rickety plankways and noodle shops built out on wooden piers lapped at by boatwakes and the screams of the longtail taxis; stalls selling everything from amulets of rare provenance and power to dried lizards with forked tails and big tiger cowries in leather thong baskets. Bronze Buddhas stand beside portly Ganeshes and multi-limbed Shivas. Bug-eyed Cambodian figures cast in iron sit cross-legged, erect dicks in hand. Spiked brass knuckles and switchblade knives are laid out for those who prefer more workaday indemnities. Things more interesting still lurk hidden away beneath the counters, waiting for the passing aficionado. The main items of merchandise, however, are the amulets — tens of thousands of Buddha images and venerable monk images in every metal known to man, as well in tablets of clay mixed with various magical substances to lend added power. You can spend anywhere from five baht to 1.5 million baht on one of these things, depending on how potent the charm is and how badly you want it.

Mu had a favorite eating spot down here, I was distressed to find out. So there was nothing for it but we had to fortify ourselves before taking care of bisnet, never mind I was still awash in chocolate milk and cola and pain. Sitting across from Mu, the late morning sunlight glancing up off the river into my eyes, I was vaguely aware of her pique, one more thing making me uncomfortable on this hot morning in Bangkok. She was silent, at least, and for that I was grateful even though I was not supposed to be.

Mu had ordered a purplish mess of stuff she called *su-ki*, something that brought to mind a gut-shot toad in a bowl.

"You eat something," she told me.

"I think I'll have a beer."

She stabbed with chopsticks at the thing in her bowl. "You drink too much. Drink, drink, drink. You will make yourself sick."

This was no great insight, given the condition I was in already. The truth was, I didn't want a beer; I just wanted to feel better.

Now Mu was rooting around in her bag, the toad safely subdued for now, and she came up with a handful of little bottles and foil cards. I watched as she assembled a heap of capsules and tablets on the table. There was high-potency vitamin B complex, vitamin C, aspirin, Lomotil, which I didn't need, and Valium. Valium?

"Mu. What are you doing with Valium? Are you taking tranquillizers; what is this?"

I was shocked.

"This is not for me." Mu looked at me with some contempt. "It is for you. Jack, you are too hot, these days. You must cool down." She suddenly got all soft and sweet, and she said "Please. For me, Jack. It can't hurt; you take a couple of these every day till you feel better. Till you relax a bit."

Now I was really shocked. She wanted me to take tranquillizers. Me! I couldn't believe it.

"Mu. I am cool already. I am so cool I normally make Jesus Christ himself seem impulsive. But things have not been standard, these past few days, you know? There are some kinds of pressures on me, like for example people are shooting at me, when they are not instead kicking me and saying nasty things to me. And half the time I don't even know who these people are or why they wish these things should happen to me. And they tell me they kidnap my girlfriend, and they do kidnap your sister; and I can't even work at home any more because I don't know what's going to happen from minute to minute; we could all be shot dead or kidnapped. None of my editors are ever going to pay me; and we're almost broke. I can't write anything even with my new computer, I don't know how to operate it yet. I can't get near it; everybody else is using it to

124

learn touch-typing or spreadsheets. And you tell me I'm not cool? I'm practically a frigging saint, I'm so cool; let me tell you. Sitting here with a hangover besides, dying of the heat. Look, I'm going to order a beer, okay?"

I was sweating quite a bit, after all, what with the long reasoned argument I had just come up with. A man had to replace the bodily fluids, not to mention how was I supposed to swallow all these pills without something to drink?

Mu ordered me a lime juice and a bowl of *jok*. The waitress ignored my order for beer. Maybe she hadn't understood me. The juice, icy cold and flavored with both salt and sugar, was refreshing; I had to admit it. The jok — rice porridge with fresh ginger and garlic and shrimps and a raw egg stirred in — actually went some way towards making me feel human again. I was still sweating like a pig, even more than that, what with the hot porridge in me, but it almost felt good. Mu was more favorably disposed towards me, as well, now that she could see I was suitably impressed with her know-how when it came to this hard business of living. And the vitamins and aspirin were adding their fine placebo effect, though I wasn't about to take any tranquillizers, then or ever.

Though if you'd talked to me awhile later, I might have told you different. For about two hours after breakfast we went around this amulet market. Mu had long discussions in Thai I didn't understand one tenth of; and we got to check out probably ten billion placid little figures, ninety percent of which looked the same to me, though Mu assured me they weren't. And we had every amulet vendor in the place leering at me and trying to sell me *ai kik*, just because I was a farang. Phalluses carved out of wood, out of bone, out of ivory. Phalluses big enough to unman you; strings of phalluses like firecrackers. Phalluses with monkeys riding piggyback; phalluses with tigers. After a while I stopped leering back, and I said "Screw off" and things like that. This had the effect of causing

Mu to scowl, so then I'd smile at the vendor in the way I imagine snakes would smile at birds, if only they could smile.

Other people, Thais, were also going around staring at amulets. Some of them even had jewelers' loupes so they could stare harder. I was over hobnobbing with a group of these experts, wondering what they were looking for, when Mu called me back. "Jack. You hold this." Mu gave me a dirty bit of clay, about the size of a 50-satang coin. On it there was a stylized figure in bas-relief. It had its hands over its eyes.

"Do you feel it?"

"Um," I said. "Yes." Sure I felt it, as benumbed as I was by the morning's proceedings I still had my faculties about me, most of them. This was the right answer, in any case, because it meant our search was over. finally, Mu had found what she was looking for. To me it was much like most of the other doodads we had seen that day, but she assured me it was special. And it did make me feel better, I don't know why, having this thing around my neck. What I said to Mu, though, was this: "Why didn't we get a metal one? It would stand more chance of stopping bullets."

But Mu just got mad at me again; and she wouldn't talk to me till that night.

taking charge

Selections from Arno Petty's Intelligencer and Weekly Gleaner

THAT'LL TEACH HER. After all this time the oil-shares chit-fund scandal has resurfaced in the popular media. Mae Chamoy has been sentenced to 143,965 years in prison and fined 4 billion baht. It's safe to say she has managed somehow to irritate somebody.

MU WAS SITTING on the edge of the bed tapping her tooth.

I loved it, it always did something to me when Mu parted her gorgeous lips and tapped a front tooth with her fingernail in just that way. It never failed to give me a warm little buzz, no matter how much I knew this tapping was generally a prelude to some decision, and never mind I knew that decisions of this magnitude often complicated life in ways I wouldn't have chosen, had you given me the choice. And here was Mu tapping away, her soft brown eyes as hard as they ever got, and she was staring off into the distance where she generally found her good ideas.

"You still have money from those stories from Burma in your hiding place," she said to me, and I couldn't deny it. "And you get more next week. And you sell your computer. How much money is that?"

What she had in mind was the kidnappers might ask us for a ransom. If they didn't, then she said we would have to think about paying somebody to sort things out for us. She didn't know who yet, but she would find someone.

Mu had as many cousins as you had problems, and at least one of these cousins always knew someone who knew somebody who could fix you up, whatever what your problem was. So Mu asked a cousin what about this — who were these people who snatched her sister? And this cousin came up with someone who knew some-body who knew some nak laeng, a hard man who fixed things for people as a regular business. Before you knew it, in just a few days, this technician had a line on who took Bia, these unpleasant men who were working for the mysterious person who was trying to tell me something about his negative feelings towards me.

The fellow with the teeth was known on the street as Fun, meaning "teeth" in Thai, probably on account of all the teeth he had. He was known as a handy fellow to have around when you wanted to cause anybody some grief. He was dependable, compe-tent, and charged the standard rates plus a bit extra, just as a bonus for doing things right. What the consultant couldn't tell us was who had hired Fun and Co., where these kidnappers were now, or where Bia was either.

In the meantime, I had never seen Mu like this before. She was at least twice as businesslike as usual, and seemed pretty calm, ex-cept one night when she said to me: "This is your fault, Jack. I hate you." And then again later, after we'd gone to bed, when she turned to hug up against me and cry. "She's really only a little girl, Jack. What are they going to do to her?" And she cried for a long time; but she didn't say she hated me any more.

Maybe it was my fault. I wished I knew who was after me, and why.

The next morning, she was all business again. "And Jack. You be careful. Don't you do anything, do you hear me? You don't know the Thai Way, and you are going to get my sister killed. And you too. You don't know, okay? You are *dek rai saa*."

I was a babe in the woods.

*

Hip noticed my hand right away. He didn't approve of this new tendency to hammer on things with my fist, he wanted me to know. It was a bad policy.

"What else do I see? Whoa. Nicotine stains on your fingers. This tells me that you haven't stopped smoking. In fact, it could be you are neck and neck with a Bangkok city bus as a contributor to this rich atmosphere we get to enjoy here in the city. And you are chewing your fingernails. You are too old to be chewing fingernails, Jack.

"Oh, yeah. I see a lot, just taking a quick gander, here. For one more thing, I see the ring Mu gave you is missing. I am tempted to say you are having domestic problems, except I saw you and Mu only this morning having breakfast at Tip's, when all seemed as okay as usual. So what is the story?"

I was impressed with Hip's talents as a palmist. Also, I hadn't seen him that morning, so where was he when Mu and I were having breakfast?

And how could he be everywhere he had to be all at the same time? Sometimes I could see what the girls meant; there was something supernatural about Hip. But what I told him was this: "Mu figures if she is going to pawn her jewelry and furthermore tie up her rolling capital in fronting the money to hire some boys to look after business, then the least I can do is kick in my ring. And my computer, I guess. I've still got the old Royal, anyway.

"And I've got my ostrich amulet. I'm beginning to understand exactly how it feels; I want to cover my eyes and not look, my life's become that interesting lately."

Hip took a long look at my amulet, after I slipped the heavy metal chain over my head and held it out to him. He turned serious, and he said this was a good *phit taa*, a special one, and I should look after it. It would maybe look after me in return.

"But that's not enough, Jack."

From what he could see, Hip said, I had pissed off everybody from the tape vendor on my soi to the bus driver to half the business community of the country. "Jack, my boy, I would say just

129

about anybody and everybody wants to kick your ass."

I hadn't even told him about Noi, this bargirl I committed a kind of indiscretion with. Only once. Or twice; when I was drunk a bit. Nothing important. Only a minor slip. Or two. Now Noi was giving me the idea she wanted to kick my ass. And Mu would have taken out a contract on me herself, come to that, if she had had any idea.

Hip told me that however much mojo this amulet had working for it, it wouldn't be enough to keep me from getting well and truly dead if I didn't change my ways. "There are two things you've got to understand, here.

"On one hand, you don't want to criticize people, especially in public. What talking about shit at the dinner table is to Amy Vanderbilt, any kind of confrontation is to a Thai. Criticism is one type of conflict and, as such, it's bad form. The avoidance of conflict is behind half the stuff that goes down around here, you know what I mean? It explains half of what there is to know about Thai life. Remember this: for a Thai, it's best to walk away from anything that looks like a confrontation; but if that's not possible, then whoa. Your average Thai will kill somebody just to avoid a conflict with him.

"On the other hand, you don't want to cause somebody to lose face. Loss of face is a lot more than embarrassment. Losing face for a Thai is like losing part of yourself — you shrink in stature. And the best way to make up for a loss of face is to remove the agent of this loss, preferably in a way that tells the world that the account is squared.

"It's like this Mae Chamoy case that is back in the news. What do they finally give this poor lady, just for running her oil-share chit fund, which is after all only a pyramid money scheme? She is sentenced to 143,965 years, which even with time off for good behavior is a long time, and a 4-billion baht fine. Sure, she takes 16,200 people for their nest eggs, and supposedly she rips the public for a good deal of money. So what? You get these other dudes, pillars of the community, most of them, and they strip the forests, cover the beaches in shit, force the prices of land up to where your average Joe can't afford to live, and that's okay. No, what Mae Chamoy does wrong is she makes the wrong people look like dingbats. That's the one thing you want to watch around here. You don't want to make the wrong people look like dingbats.

"And that's what you do, I'm coming to think.

"You can't go doing things like that, Jack. Not with anybody, to be on the safe side, much less a tape vendor. Do you know how much money is involved in flogging pirate music tapes? Lots. And the boys that run these things, the guys who supply the street vendors, they are not going to sit by and let you interfere with commerce. They're not going to let anybody interfere."

"So what do I do now?"

Hip let me know that he was going to put out an all-points bulletin on his network. Half the city's bargirls, massage parlor ladies, and drivers would have their ears to the ground. "Don't worry, Jack. We'll find her."

That was nice to hear, I thought; but why then did Hip look so worried?

"And Jack — you just lie low, okay? Yo, Arno. You are something of a babe in the woods, I gotta say it. So don't do anything, okay?"

"Okay," I answered him.

But I wanted to say I was getting tired of everybody telling me what was what and how I was a babe in the woods. It was starting to make me mad, to tell the truth. On the way home I gave a couple of street dogs the eye, sizing them up for field goals, but they sloped off immediately, no doubt knowing all about the Thai Way. So I kicked a mango tree instead, which hurt and which fur-

131

thermore got me some strange looks from the sweet-corn vendor over by the temple wall.

Anyway, this wasn't a situation that called for kicking dogs, I decided. It was time to think about kicking some ass.

*

"Steve Davis!"

At first I hardly recognized the joint. The whole room was brightly lit. The busty blonde was hanging straight in her frame, and the tables had been re-covered in tangerine felt. Tangerine already liberally stained with other things. As for the rest, though, there was the same old smell of stale piss and beer and spittoons. The same cast of tattooed types were hanging about the place making me nervous, furthermore, and I still couldn't get a Kloster beer.

I never thought I would want to see Tommy and Willie again, after the last time. But under the circumstances it occurred to me they might have their uses. In fact it was exactly such resourceful individuals we were short of at this time. The problem was, the last time I had seen them, they were going like bats out of hell one way down the river and I was going the other. They didn't stop to leave a forwarding address, as it happened, and I didn't think I would find them in the telephone book, not even in the Yellow Pages under "Contractors." There was just one thing to do, I thought; so I did it.

"Steve Davis!" There was this joyous cry from the back of the room, and a man I recognized as my boat driver from last time was waving a cue at me. In no time, I had a glass of Mekhong cola in my hand, and I was being offered a game of snooker. "Five hundred baht, *na?* One game, 500 baht, okay?"

For people about to take on the world champion, they were too enthusiastic for my liking, so I changed the subject. "I'm looking for somebody," I said.

This didn't mean I wanted a lady, I had to explain, and it didn't mean I wanted a big-money game of snooker either. Not at all. "I have a kind of business conflict," I was trying to say, "this annoying problem in human relations ..." when the manager of the snooker room showed up.

"*Sawasdi krap.* Howdy," I told him, smiling in my most winning way. "The place looks really nice. Nice tables. Very classy."

He spat on the floor, missing the nearest spittoon by a yard or more and clearly not caring if he did. "We have to change our image," he said to me in passable English, "after you and your friends shoot the place up. Can you imagine that? And cops all around. Think of the money this cost us. You can't imagine."

And speaking of money, the next thing I knew there was a small matter of the outstanding bill for food and drink from my last visit here. It seemed Jean-Paul Somsak had not taken care of things after all, probably distracted by the press of events. As it stood, Somsak was spending some time in a local prison and was on a limited budget, the manager told me, one which did not extend to paying bills of this magnitude.

So I had to cover the whole tab for that other afternoon, not only the whiskey and the snacks, but also the holes in the door and the ceiling. And we should not forget the matter of the girl in the room upstairs; her customer ran out without paying, so she put in a claim for 200 baht as well. "We're not even going to talk about the fees I have to lay out to keep our public officials happy," says the manager.

Though really he was going to mention them, and he was just starting to spell it out when we were interrupted by an impatient gang of would-be contractors.

They had figured out what I was after, and it looked as though everybody in the place was ready to do the job, whatever that might be. But I told them I had to talk to my friends Tommy and Willie. Yes, I realized those boys were not standard and sometimes could be dangerous to the health of all and sundry, but friends were friends and what were they for if you didn't turn to them in times of need? And so on. But no one knew where Tommy and Willie had gotten to. After that interesting afternoon, it seems, they had kept a low profile.

Maybe it was because he remembered who my friends were, or it could be he was afraid of getting pushed into a tax bracket he couldn't handle, but the manager decided to waive the official fees and we settled the bill for 2,000 baht even, which was a bargain, as I had to admit, given the price of doors these days. As for the others, half of them wanted to give me their business cards or at least tell me I could find them there at the snooker room any time I had problems that needed ironing out. But none of them had Willie and Tommy's presence; they just didn't inspire confidence.

So there I was — another 2,000 baht down and no closer to a solution to our problems. It was enough to depress you.

a dinner invitation

Selections from Arno Petty's Intelligencer and Weekly Gleaner

GLUTTONY. Everybody's talking about runaway corruption, but exactly what is this thing? The Thais call being 'on the take' *kin*, which is the same as 'eat.' Now, it might be a mistake to confuse real corruption with *kin tham nam*, which is only the traditional 'eating,' where you offer public officials a kind of unofficial commission, say about 10% as a token of one's gratitude and respect. This is done. Real corruption is properly speaking only the rapacious *kin tuam nam*, where those in positions of power and authority start to take, take, take with no sense of proportion and no sense of responsibility towards those less advantaged. This is the behavior that has more and more Thai people questioning the direction national development has been taking lately.

NO COUPS IS GOOD NEWS. The government has announced that any rumors of an imminent coup are entirely without foundation, and it is only people who want to manipulate the stock market for their own dark ends who keep spreading this nonsense. Okay?

FAT FAT was dressed in an Aloha shirt with palm trees on it, maybe three acres of palm trees and they still didn't cover his belly. He was pissed off at me, though he was smiling a lot.

Mr Hung Fat, or "Fat Fat" as he was more often called, though not within his hearing, was sitting at a table with a couple of smaller and more self-effacing fat Chinese men. The smallest of the three was obviously the second in command. His voice was a husky wheeze, and his English was good.

"You annoy Mr Fat," he told me.

135

I took out a cigarette and lit it, but Fatman No.1 said, "No. No smoking." He snatched it out of my mouth and threw it into the spittoon under the table, leaving me to inhale the toke I'd managed off the match straight down to my toes. And that only made it worse. Now I really wanted a cigarette.

"Fat Fat doesn't like smoking. He always says your body is a temple; why do you want to poison it?"

Fat Fat smirked at me self-righteously.

At another table, over against the wall, sat four goons — the same four who had done a dance on me the other day. Fun kept showing me all his teeth. Possibly he was smiling; it was hard to say.

There was also a fat Chinese maitre d' and so many skinny Chinese waiters buzzing around the table you might have thought there was somebody important around the joint, or maybe the food critic from the *New York Times*.

Fat Fat had asked me to join him there in the New Great Wall Restaurant, he told me, because he had something he wanted to discuss. He especially wanted me to join him; in fact, he even sent me his car and driver. So when I got back from the snooker parlor that evening, and I had gotten out of the cab at the mouth of our *soi*, thinking to pick up some beer on the way home, I was approached by three men. Two of them had guns pointed at me; the third just grinned at me with his big mouthful of dirty teeth. We had met before.

I'll tell the truth: I would rather have been lying dead under a bus than go for a ride with these gentlemen, but I didn't tell them this since they might have been offended, and I could see it was best not to offend people such as these. In the car my careful inquiries regarding the purpose of this nice drive were received with shakes of the head. When I persisted in reasonable tones, my voice hardly shaking at all, a fourth man, the driver, said "You no talk!"

and Fun shoved his automatic pistol up against my ribcage hard enough it hurt, this ribcage being the same one he had earlier used for place-kicking practice. *"Farang* dogshit," he said by way of explanation. So I decided to stop persisting.

And now I found myself in the back room of the New Great Wall Restaurant. Fat Fat was eating with gusto. If only he had a Jewish grandmother, it would have done her heart good to see how he ate. Eyes hooded behind fat eyelids, he was concentrating on getting rid of as much food and drink as he could as fast as possible, fingers and chopsticks darting and snatching and tearing and flipping bits of food back into his greasy maw. Sweat glistened all over his face and his bald head and he kept wiping at himself with a damp cloth. He never stopped chewing, even when he had something to say, which was quite often; and once in a while he barked at the maitre d', who then barked at the waiters.

Not always fast enough, though, did the maitre d' bark. Fat Fat banged the ice bucket on the table a few times so water and some ice sloshed over onto the floor. He wanted fresh ice. The big bottle of Chivas on the table was still three-quarters full, and he waved some eager waiters away from it as he topped up first his glass and then those of his buddies. A regular potentate he was, dispensing favors on all sides. He fished up some pieces of squid and dropped them on his friends' plates, yapping away in Chinese, stuff flying from his fat lips, a gob of something stuck amid the beads of sweat on one jowl. Then he remembered me, and he dropped some squid on my plate too. His shirt was pulled up so the air could get at the sweat on his vast belly.

There was a mobile telephone on the trolley, and every so often it yelped for attention. Whenever this happened a waiter would bring the machine to the guy I thought of as Fat Man No.2, who would then answer it. He would say a few things into the phone, and then say a few things to Fat, who would then bark, and the lesser fat man would bark in a similar way back into the phone and hang up. This happened two or three times, and once Fat himself, first wiping his hands carefully on the tablecloth, took the phone and barked like an enraged dog for a while into the mouthpiece. This time he handed the phone back to his assistant, who hung it up and passed the machine back to the waiter.

"I get a complaint." Fat Fat suddenly turned his attention to me. "My people bring me a problem."

Fat Fat seemed fairly humorless, on the whole, but every now and then, apropos of nothing I could see, his belly started to shake and he had a quick fit of giggling. He would grab his whiskey glass and spin the ice round and round before he belted the drink back and then topped it up again. It was always him that poured the whiskey; he kept the bottle handy beside him.

He smacked his lips as he ate, smacks of self-satisfaction and appetite. He sucked his teeth loudly, and then he sucked on a little rib bone. He held it to his mouth and chewed at it and sucked it and then popped the whole thing in and gnawed away for a minute before leaning down and spitting it with a clang into the spittoon under the table. He followed this by inhaling sharply, clearing his nose and expelling a great luscious gob.

Then he nodded to Fatman No.1, saying "Tell him the problem."

"Some of our people have this tape business," the lesser fatman told me in wheezy but idiomatic English. "They sell cheap tapes to anybody with a taste for music; it's like a public service, you think how expensive tapes can be in the big stores. Many smaller businessmen work for our people; they take the merchandise out into the streets where the public can see what they got. One of these employees, then, has a problem. He bothers no one, minds his own business and makes a living for his family. You know what I'm saying?"

138

I had a feeling I did, though I didn't say anything. It turned out, as the story unfolded, this small businessman was complaining that a farang was poking his nose in and telling him he couldn't sell tapes no matter how hungry his family was, just because this farang didn't like music.

Both of the lesser fatmen were giving me hard looks now, as though I was something unpleasant sitting there at the table. And when I thought about it, the two smaller sidekicks didn't seem so small any more, and they didn't seem so self-effacing. The way they looked at me, in fact, you got the idea they wanted me to think life was a dangerous practice, and maybe I had some nerve enjoying this thing at the same table as them. Fat Fat, on the other hand, turned twice as genial as he was before, and it was clear there was nothing he wouldn't do to make me happy. He giggled and shook and emptied his glass. Then he flung some bits of stuff from a dish onto my plate and said "Eat." And so I did. It was tasty.

Did I know what I was eating? Fat wanted to know.

As far as I was concerned, this was something you didn't ask when you were eating Chinese food. But this guy was my host, and he was asking me a polite question, so I answered him truthfully. "I don't know," I said.

He and his henchmen tittered and shook like a trio of agitated blowfish on a line.

"This is pig's — what you call it? — uterus. You know? Pig's uterus. Where they keep the baby. Hee, hee."

This was actually something of a relief to me; and I don't mind saying I didn't give a shit if this was a pig's uterus or not, since I knew the Chinese would cook anything they could get in a pot, and I could think of many things worse to eat than a pig's uterus. This particular one was quite tasty, actually, and caused me no grief to eat whether I knew it was where they kept the baby or not.

Still, it was funny, but I had to fight off this impulse to pretend this dish shocked me only because that was what Fat wanted. Nevertheless, what I said was "Really? Pig's uterus? My, my; how nice."

"You. You drink whiskey. Chivas." He poured me a whole tumblerful, and just when I got around to wondering where I was going to put the ice and, I wished, some water, he reached over and dropped a handful of ice right in there on top of the booze so it poured out over the sides and onto the table with all the other slop. He wiped his hand on his shirt-front, and then he wiped it across his forehead.

I was thinking I didn't want to drink this neat whiskey, I didn't care how much Fat Fat wished me well; but he and his buddies were watching me expectantly, and there was an uncomfortable silence going on. Then I thought, Fat Fat was so casual this had to be an informal affair, and I was probably making a mistake by getting too uptight, so I grabbed a bottle of water off the trolley and I dumped it right in on top of the ice, so even more whiskey went all over the table. I kept pouring till it looked about right. Then I picked up the glass and smiled and wished everybody a long life.

There was whiskey and water all over the place now, and it was running down into the lap of one of the minor deities, Fatman No.2, not the one who was responsible for translating Fat Fat's thoughts into English. This individual shifted his chair and looked at Fat Fat; then he looked at me; then he looked back and forth again between Fat Fat and me. He reminded me of a Doberman, if only Dobermans were fat and Chinese, a Doberman begging to be let off the leash. I gave him a big smile and tried another toast, this one in Thai. "*Chok dee,*" I said.

"In Chinese," Fat Fat told me, "we say '*yam sing.*' When we say yam sing, everybody goes bottoms up." He giggled and said "Yam sing," chugging his glass to show me how. Everybody looked at me for a while, and I looked at them. Then I gulped my whiskey down. I reached for the water bottle, but a lesser fatman slapped my hand away. Fat Fat smiled at me some more as he poured the whiskey.

So this tape vendor, Fat Fat's mouthpiece continued, was unhappy with this other person who wanted to stand in the way of commerce, and he told his superiors that he wanted this person taken care of. In fact he would like to see him dead, and not too painlessly at that.

This was not a problem, but then a question arose: did the gunman get a bonus because this was a farang he was going to hit, or not? (Fatman No.1 told me he forgot to say, this was a farang we were talking about.) Not, was what his bosses had to say about it. Why would anybody pay a bonus just to hit some penny-ante farang scribe, nobody had ever heard of him? And he couldn't even get the business of being a farang straight; there he was living on Soi Boondocks in some dump with a Thai *mia* who was moreover from the Isarn and not even beautiful; everybody knew all the women from the Northeast had skin dark as a rice farmer. No, forget it. The fee was 10,000 baht, take it or leave it.

So the gunman put in a grievance. The gunman said that the hit was a farang, and even if he was a nobody he was a farang nobody, and there should be a bonus. Before long Fat himself happened to catch wind of this. Since he was the boss of all bosses in this organization, the "bot of all bots," he said they would do it his way. What he decided was that Fun — for it was none other — should get his bonus. But he should get it not to kill the farang, exactly. That was too good for the likes of a pain in the neck of this caliber, and dead reporters were not so much fun as live ones could be anyway.

"I don't like farang, you know?" Fat interrupted, smiling at me some more and pouring whiskey into my glass, even though it was already full. I poured more water on top of it, and got a look from the fatmen. "And I hate reporters."

Fat had a certain prejudice in this regard, as he let me know. He

141

didn't care if they were farang reporters or Thai reporters. They were always going around writing about things they had no business writing about, as well as about other things they didn't understand. So he didn't mind paying some money to make some reporter's life uncomfortable. He told Fun merely to teach the farang a lesson — take his girlfriend, and boot the reporter around some. But he should make sure he didn't break any fingers in the process because they wanted this writer to be in good working order when they needed him. Same with the girlfriend. She had to be in good working condition for when they needed her. "Hee, hee." Everybody at the table laughed at this, when Fat Fat repeated it in Chinese and in Thai as well, so the punks at the other table could also enjoy the joke.

"I guess it is me who is this farang," I told Fat Fat, and he beamed at me as though he was proud of my precociousness. "But you have made a mistake ..."

Fat Fat stopped beaming. Everybody else immediately stopped smiling as well. "*Farang*. It is *you* who make mistake."

"You make the mistake, *farang*. Why you write bad things about me?" Fat Fat was smiling again, though not reassuringly. "Eh? *Why?*" He poured another drink.

What bad things? I had never written anything about Fat Fat. Not a single thing that I could think of.

"These things are not your business," said the interpreter. "Why you want to make Khun Fat look bad? You don't know him. 'Izzy Scoop.' You don't even use your real name. Why? You afraid? This stupid nickname you give Mr Fat. This doesn't make him happy. No. You call him a gangster; and you don't do it with respect. You talk about Khun Sa and these other punks — these 'warlords' and these 'kingpins.' But you only call Mr Fat stupid names."

"Wait a minute," I was beginning to get an idea of what was what. "I'm not Izzy Scoop. You've got the wrong man here. I'm

Arno Petty. I never said anything bad about you. Like you say, I don't even know you."

"You're not Izzy Scoop? Our people tell us it is you who are this farang reporter who should be dead, for sure. It must be. If it isn't, then who is? Who is Izzy Scoop? You tell us."

"I don't know," I tell him. "I only know it isn't me. You ask at the *Bangkok Globe*; they'll tell you — I'm Arno Petty."

"Arno Petty in Thailand; Izzy Scoop in Hong Kong — that's right? You think you can say anything, hide behind this stupid name. You are Izzy Scoop."

"Is-sey. Is-sey *shit*," added Fun from the other table, where the boys were getting bored. Probably it was because they got to drink nothing but tea and water and no whiskey, imported or otherwise.

"So this is what we're going to do," said Fatman No.1. "Mr Fat sees he's getting this bad press, and it makes him unhappy. He has been talking with his advisors, and he decides he needs to pay more attention to public relations. Here he is, he likes kids, he is concerned about the environment and Thai youth and rural development and everything, and what does he get? He gets called criminal. How can he be a criminal? He is rich. He has many friends, big people in this country. He gives money to many charities. And you are going to help him."

"You," Fat Fat told me. "You work for me now. Unnerstan'?"

I didn't like the sound of this. "Sorry," I answered him. "I don't understand. What do you mean I work for you?"

"You work for Khun Fat any way he tells you to work for him," said the interpreter.

"*Farang* dogshit." Fun added a comment from the next table.

"Shut up!" This was directed at Fun from Fatman No.1.

"I still don't understand ..." I began.

"Shut up!" the other minor fatman said to me, the first English I had heard from him.

"But why did you try to have me killed?" I asked Fat Fat. "It is not easy to write nice things about you or about anybody else either, when a writer is dead. And there you had those guys shooting at me in the taxi. My best pipe is totally ruined."

"Kill you?" Fat Fat acted surprised. "Why? I kill you, you don't know I'm pissed off. No, no. This better policy, what happens to you now."

Fatman No.1 laughed, and he told me it must have been somebody else shooting at me in taxis. It looked like I had lots of friends. If Mr Fat wanted me shot in a taxi, he could promise me, then I would never be found sitting around talking about this to anybody afterwards. Did I get the message?

I got it. Suddenly I also got another message. I was making a big mistake in trying to convince them I wasn't Izzy Scoop. If they realized now that I was only Jack Shackaway, nemesis of the tape vendors, and not really the great writer Izzy Scoop, then I was for sure a dead man.

Then Fatman No.1 gave me my first assignment. It was easy, he said. And I would be paid. Hung Fat was building a luxury condominium and office tower, and he wanted a brochure, one that would tell all the investors what a good deal this was and what kind of class they were looking at. I would write this brochure, and I would do a good job. Why would I do a good job? Because if I didn't, then I wasn't a good writer; and if I wasn't a good writer, they would have no further need for me. If they had no need for me, then the last place on Earth either me or anybody else would ever want to be was in my shoes. They would cut off my hands, to begin with, while they thought of where to go from there, possibly leaving me my feet so I had something to stand in my own shoes with, but not necessarily for long. Did I understand?

I understood, I told him, even though I didn't, not entirely.

Then, after they had looked at this brochure, which I would

bring to our very next meeting, they would tell me what my next assignment was.

What about the girl? I asked. What about Bia?

"Beer?" Fat Fat looked confused.

"The girl."

"*Gurh-f'en* you? I keep some time."

"Insurance," Fatman No.1 elaborated, "in case you decide you can get along with no hands, figuring you can type with your nose, for example. Then we still got your girl. Though I don't know why you should care."

This got Fat Fat wheezing and giggling and fluttering his hands around. In fact, all the fatmen giggled together and shook and fluttered and flapped as though somebody had just inflated a gaggle of geese with laughing gas.

You write the brochure, I was told. We would talk about the girl next time. And that was that. Fatman No.1 flopped back into his chair; and Fat Fat looked pleased.

"You won't do anything to hurt the girl?" I asked. "If I do a good job, you'll let her go? You won't hurt her?"

"Shut up!" said Fatman No.2, thereby probably exhausting his entire repertoire in English, and maybe in Chinese too, who knows.

"*Farang* dogshit!" added Fun from the other table.

"Shut up!" said Fatman No.1, either to me or else to Fun, I couldn't tell which.

Fat Fat ordered tea and cookies and splashed noisily in his finger bowl. Then he smoked. It was okay for him to smoke, I learned. Only it wasn't tobacco. It was Thai stick, the sweet smell of ganja slightly nauseating to me. I wanted a cigarette. He sipped from a tortoise-shell holder that he held like a candle, expelling the smoke in tiny blue curls from his nose, occasionally hawking and spitting into the brass vessel under the table.

"You do what we tell you," said Fat Fat, at one point.

145

"Then we see about your 'girlfriend.'" Fatman No.1 sneered.

The place had closed up, and we were the only people still there, except for the maitre d' and the half dozen waiters. The door was locked and the curtains drawn across the windows. Nice and cozy.

Fat Fat was making a big production of checking through the bill, which was about two yards long. Every now and then he barked at the maitre d' and stabbed at some item with a pudgy finger, but whatever answers he was getting left him happy, I guess, because each time he just grunted and continued on.

It was funny; I was so blown away I was having trouble focusing, but Fat Fat seemed dead sober now, except that he was all flushed. Dead serious and sober. After he had checked the addition, he slapped a bunch of 500 baht notes on the silver tray the waiter brought. I didn't know how much it was, but Fat Fat waved it away contemptuously, and the staff started *wai*-ing and groveling and smiling like they were in great pain, they were so grateful.

He called one of the waiters over, then. A little one, his face squeezed tight with fear. Fat Fat barked, and the waiter shriveled up some more and started to motormouth in a low voice, all of it Chinese, and he might as well have been speaking Greek as far as I was concerned. Fat Fat barked again, and the waiter bent to get the spittoon from under the table. He held it out to Fat Fat, who proceeded to pour a bottle of soda water into it. Then, without further ado, the waiter hoisted the thing and began gulping away. Only for a gulp or two, actually. At that point he started upchucking into the spittoon, puking till he had the dry heaves. One of the lesser fatmen said something to the waiter, and he took another swig from the brass vessel, immediately spewing it back again. Fat giggled.

I was sitting there trying not to spew, myself. My dinner companions started to leave the table, Fat Fat first. Fun and friends had taken up positions by the door like proper heavies, eyeing me as though I might turn into a howitzer or something. As the minor deities ballooned to their feet in drunken defiance of gravity, the interpreter picked up the half-empty bottle of whiskey remaining and leaned over to pour it into my glass. All of it. Then he poured a large bottle of water into it as well, with the result I was fairly wet from the runoff. He stared into my face for a few seconds and then smiled. "You work for Mr Fat," he wheezed.

Fat Fat had one more giggling fit and then made his exit, his entourage behind him. I just sat there for a while in my puddle, thinking about things and feeling sorry for the little waiter, who was shaking so badly he was having a hard time finding his chin with a towel, trying to wipe the mess off. The maitre d' told me they were closed, and I left.

good help is hard to find these days

Selections from Arno Petty's Intelligencer and Weekly Gleaner

KEEPING UP. Old men are often moved to appreciate younger women. In spirit, at least, they are often so moved — the flesh sometimes needs kick-starting. To this end an enormous trade in everything from ginseng to snake bile to deer antler and rhino horn flourishes all over Asia. Such is the demand for this magic that rhinos have everywhere become endangered species. In fact, or so my guru tells me, it is all in the mind. Basically, if you feel like it and you think you can, then you can. So leave the rhinos alone, okay?

WHEN I GOT HOME I found Mu in conference with Rhot and two men I had never seen before. It turned out these dudes were a couple of Mr Fix-its the friend of a friend of her cousin's had come up with. They reminded me of the guys that did me in the lane, not Fun, but the others. I looked at them hard to see if they reminded me of that face on the motorcycle, the one behind the muzzle of that 11mm pistol, but it was no dice.

They gave me some hard looks of their own, and then were surprised when it turned out this was my joint and they were my guests, though I personally would never have invited them in.

And Mu looked me over as though I was a bill collector; then she sniffed at me. I was still wet with whiskey.

"Where were you?" she said to me, speaking in a way designed to tell me that, wherever it was, I could have stayed there, for all she cared. "You've been drinking."

I could hear this tone in her voice, like, "Here we've been living together almost a year, and you always told me you were a Presbyterian teetotaler, yet now look at you."

148

"Mu," I replied. "I have been to see Fat Fat. And he made me drink; I didn't want to. Although to tell the truth I could use a glass of something now."

I still had a bottle of Black Label whiskey stashed away, all that was left from the payment for the story on Thai drinking habits, the one for the magazine which then discovered they had no money to pay their writers, so they had to draw on their barter accounts with advertisers. They had just enough real money for the printers and advertising sales staff and so on. And for the editors, of course. It wasn't as though the writers were in any way vital to the production of a magazine, after all. But the bad habits of editors everywhere were neither here nor there, under the circumstances; and I was merely feeling sorry for myself. I poured myself a generous shot and then did the same for Rhot and the two hoods.

"Jack, can I see you for a minute in the bedroom?" Mu obviously had something on her mind. She closed the door behind us.

"Jack, you write crazy things about dangerous people and you get yourself banged up, that's okay, I guess, though you are my man and I don't need you banged up. But then you get my only sister kidnapped and I don't know what is going to happen to her. And then you go out and get drunk and leave me alone here. I don't know where you are; maybe you're finally dead after all …"

"Jai yen yen," I started to tell her, seeing she was overwrought, and thinking she would calm down when I told her what the real story was. So I was surprised when Mu slapped me right in the head, this being the same head that was already bruised from various other attacks on it by people who meant me no good. But to have my own woman doing her bit to add to my discomfort was too much. This not only surprised me, Mu never having carried on in just this way before, it hurt my feelings. And then she also punched me in the shoulder.

"Mu. Please do not hit me. I am sore enough already."

So Mu grabbed me in a hug, not trying to cave in my rib cage, I guess, though it did hurt like hell, but mainly to say she was sorry. "I was so scared. I thought they killed you. Why didn't you phone?"

"I did not come home and I did not phone because I was kidnapped. I have been to see Fat Fat, the man who has Bia."

No, I had not seen Bia, but these were the people who had her. This was the man who had Fun do a job on me, though he said he had never had anybody shoot at me, yet. He knew all about who I was, except he had me figured for the wrong writer. Which was just as well, since I would have been dead if he hadn't thought I was Izzy Scoop, and not merely some farang who hassled tape vendors. Though of course the bad news was they still might kill me, if I wasn't careful, only I didn't tell Mu this. And Fat Fat also knew who my girlfriend was, only he was wrong because he was holding my girlfriend's sister, no matter what he thought.

I had to explain everything again, after we went out from the bedroom, and as soon as I got to the part where I said it was Fat Fat who was the problem, Mu's hard men suddenly remembered they had cakes in the oven and their mommies were calling and everything. They finished their drinks in a hurry and said to Mu there wasn't enough money in this whole neighborhood to finance a hit on Hung Fat, and thanks for the drinks they were going home.

Wrong-Way Willie was right. It was hard to find good help, these days.

I was feeling a little weary and more than a little wired at the same time, and I asked Mu if we could just go to bed. We would have to think about things in the morning, okay?

What I needed was some loving. I tried telling Mu a couple of long jokes about farangs and Thais, but she didn't laugh and I didn't blame her. Even when I described to her what was Thai

Heaven and what was Thai reality. A Thai editor told me this one. It seemed that Thai Heaven was living in an English house, eating Chinese food, drawing an American salary, and having a Japanese wife. The reality of things, which was not too dissimilar to Hell, he said, was living in a Japanese house, eating English food, drawing a Chinese salary, and having an American wife. By the time I explained why this was supposed to be funny and that, no, I didn't want to live with a Japanese woman instead of her, I didn't find it very funny myself.

Then I put her panties on my head, but my heart wasn't in it; I only felt kind of silly.

And I could tell Mu was also feeling not so hot, so finally we just cuddled up and waited for sleep, which was okay. It helped me relax as I drifted in and out, troubled dreams gibbering away on the fringes of consciousness like rumors of bad news.

a quiet sunday at home

Selections from Arno Petty's Intelligencer and Weekly Gleaner

SCORE CARD. There have been 16 elections in Thailand since the Revolution of 1932. During the same time, there have been 14 coups—and that's only counting the success-ful ones. Meanwhile the man in the street's reaction to new governments, no matter where they come from: One's as good (or bad) as the other. *Mai pen rai*; never mind.

IS NOTHING SACRED? The government has threatened to crack down on these people, whoever they are, who keep spreading rumors of a coup. This is bad for Business, and offenders will be dealt with severely.

THE NEXT MORNING I was dreaming about helicopters. I could hear them coming in over the rooftops, and I had to get away; only I couldn't seem to run, no matter how hard I tried.

I awoke to the deafening throb-throb of helicopters everywhere like giant angry insects. A deafening, a totally insane racket.

"Jesus Christ, Mu! They've got helicopters." And sure enough, the first thing that leapt to mind, as I lay there wide-eyed but still half dreaming, was that Fat Fat had come for me. Or else some-body had decided to do the Thai version of *Apocalypse Now* right there just for our benefit. They had taken to dive-bombing our apartment with martial music and strong words in Thai that I couldn't understand blaring from PA systems. What with the music and the Doppler effect as they dived in and out on us, all I could get was that they wanted us outside. But I wasn't about to go out there, not without a bunch of anti-aircraft guns that I didn't hap-pen to have on hand at that moment.

I jumped out of bed and ran into the living room, where I found half a dozen cousins or so milling around all agog and grinning, prepared to be festive, no doubt, but not yet sure what the occasion was. And for once Granny probably got to hear something, only she wasn't sure what it was either. Her mouth was opening and closing like a querulous fish, and, even though I couldn't hear her, I knew she was screeching "*Arai na?*"

As I ran back into the bedroom, one of the choppers came in so close it rattled the windows in their frames, the music at an unbelievable pitch. It was terrifying; and here Mu was laughing. "Jesus Christ, Mu!" I yelled.

She was saying something to me, but I couldn't hear it because another helicopter had come in on us. I was waiting for the machine guns and rockets when our visitors backed off a bit and I could hear Mu telling me "Jack. It's okay, Jack. It's the walkathon."

"Mu! Mu, for Christ's sake, what is this? Is this a coup?"

One of the helicopters swung in so close I was waiting to see its props slice in through the walls. From the window I caught glimpses of the aircraft, and made out there were at least three of them. Though they were gradually moving off, now, heading over towards the river, the noise was still incredible.

Mu finally explained to me that this was merely a special holiday, and the Army was exhorting all good citizens to get out there and join a public walkathon. This was everybody's chance to help raise money for children's charities. It wasn't the end of the world or anything like that. She found the whole thing hilarious. It was so funny that she pulled me down on the bed and made fairly passionate love to me; I don't know how she managed it in the middle of the bedlam. I don't know how I managed it, come to that.

After a while, we were left with nothing but the usual ambient noise — three different pop songs going at the same time, Granny interrogating everybody and everything, Dok being a girl, sewing machines pumping, chopping boards clattering, mortar and pestle pok-pokking — merely the homey sounds of your typical Sunday morning, something that I had to admit seemed almost peaceful after the aerial attack we had just sustained. I was taking the opportunity to do my breathing exercises, practicing what the local types call "mindfulness." *Rising; falling … Rising; falling …* It's better to breathe out long, it helps to concentrate your attention.

Suddenly a loud hammering at the front door intruded on all this. The next thing, everything went silent outside the bedroom, quieter than it had ever been around there, in my experience.

"*Arai na?*" hollered Granny.

There was a knock on our door, and then Rhot's voice: "*Puens*, friends you, Jack; they come." Just then I heard a crash, and for a minute I thought Bia was back. And in fact it was somebody stumbling over a bundle of sugar cane, only it wasn't Bia — it was Tommy. Tommy Two-Toes.

"Tommy!" I said, as I came out of the bedroom, the delight in my voice not unmixed with apprehension, given that Tommy was broadcasting the Look in all directions. I understood him to be saying he was not happy to be stumbling over miscellaneous stock and cousins of Mu in this shambles I called home.

"*Farang*, our friend!" said Willie, who only then appeared in the door to the stairway. He was tucking in his shirt, and you got the idea there was something smaller than an M-16 also tucked into his pants, though not much smaller. Being of a cautious nature, he wasn't inclined to rush headlong into situations as obviously non-standard as this one was. "Hey. You live here?" He bent down to pick up his mobile phone. Willie with a mobile phone. This was what the world was coming to.

They had heard I had been at the snooker parlor looking for them. It was a simple matter, then, to find the taxi driver who had taken me back to my soi and find out where he had dropped me.

What hadn't been so easy was getting from the mouth of the soi to my apartment.

"The somtam woman out there, she isn't about to tell us anything." Willie shook his head in admiration. "*Na?* Not even when I tell her we are undercover cops. Not even when Tommy here gives her a quick flash of the Look."

It was only when they walked in as far as the tape vendor and asked him if there was a farang living in the area that they got anywhere. He told them right away. "Is he a friend of yours?" Willie wanted to know.

Everybody in the joint was impressed no end with my buddies. My stock had risen considerably in their estimation, nobody ever suspecting I might be so well connected. And these two gentlemen did have an undeniable presence. So impressive were they, in fact, that I had a hard time convincing Mu that they were not some more men out to kill me and possibly anybody else connected with me, sisters of girlfriends and suchlike for only two examples.

Mu asked if she could see me in the bedroom for a minute. I excused myself, telling Keeow to see what my visitors wanted to drink and to give them something to eat.

"Jack. You are crazy. *Ba-ba baw-baw.*" Mu was speaking in calm, level tones of sweet reason. "I want you to go home; go back to America. Get away from Thailand before you get killed. Get away from me before I get killed, and everybody in my family too. But first you get these men out of this house."

"What's wrong?" I asked her.

"Who are these men, Jack? What have you brought into my house? These men are dangerous. Oh, Jack; what have you done?"

Now, I knew Mu was under some strain. Weren't we all? But I was getting sick of everybody always telling me what a rube I was, and how I didn't know my ass from my elbow, much less from the Thai Way; and I figured it was about time to set things straight. I was a big boy, after all.

"Mu," I told her. "What we need right now are dangerous men. We are dealing with dangerous people; and when you fight fire, you use fire."

I could see that had a nice ring to it, in her mind; she always was a sucker for neat turns of phrase that sounded like the wisdom of the ages. Still, she looked doubtful. "But if they are as good as you say, then we can't afford them anyway."

"Let me look after that, Mu. I think we can get a special price."

Mu sent everybody except Granny and Rhot out to find the walkathon. We needed peace and quiet and privacy to discuss the kind of things we had to discuss this fine Sunday morning.

Willie and Tommy were sorry to hear about our troubles; it was never pleasant to have mysterious people shooting at you or snatching your sisters either. On the other hand, they were delighted that we could finally do some business, and they hoped we realized that we couldn't have done better than come to them.

Business had not been all it might have been, these past months. Even if you overlooked the cops, who everywhere were still of the opinion that Willie and Tommy were persona non grata on this earth, the whole economy was going through a period of consolidation; did I know what they meant?

To Tommy he said this in Thai: "*Tommy, what do you think; we can do our friend a favor and take care of Fat Fat?*"

Tommy looked grave, and poured some more Black Label. "*This is good whiskey,*" he said. And then he grinned. "*Why not? Let's do him. I hate this hia, this giant lizard who is at the same time a fat mangda. 'Boss of bosses.' Huh! Fat Fat dies. This is very good whiskey.*"

Willie thought on the matter for the space of one large glass of this good whiskey. Then he told us it would be your classic half-million-baht job. Doing somebody like Fat Fat was no piece of cake, after all; some people might go so far as to call a person sui-

156

cidal to think about it, even.

"Half a million!" I said. Then I said it again: "*Half a million!*" After that I breathed deeply and concentrated on keeping my eyebrows from migrating up into my hairline. This was US$20,000 we were talking, here. You could call it only five more books for Propriapist Publications. Or, hey, no problem: I could pay it off with about 250 articles for the *Bangkok Globe* instead. No problem. Jesus Christ.

Willie noticed I was having trouble with this sum, I guess, because he immediately said that since there was no agent, of course, in this case we could knock off fifteen percent right there — and 425,000 baht was not so much, when it came right down to it, given the cost of living these days and all. Even as he said this, however, his eyes surveyed my abode and he looked distinctly less happy. "We can call it an even 400,000 baht," he said with an air of finality. "Only 200,000 baht down, the rest in easy payments," he added, seeing I was still in danger of losing my eyebrows.

"Willie," I said, "Fat Fat doesn't have to be dead. All we want is to get Bia back safe and sound. Soon. We have to convince Fat Fat to give her back. Or else we need to find out where she is, and then get her out."

"In the first place, Fat Fat doesn't give the girl up. Or if he does, you don't recognize her when he does. I know Fat Fat. On the other hand, we take the girl back, and Fat Fat isn't dead, then you are on borrowed time — you, your girlfriend, the girl, everybody. Even Tommy and me, unless we turn around and do something about it then. Hey. You think somebody like Fat Fat says 'Geez, they really get the best of me that time' and then goes away shaking his head? You want that girl back, you have to finish Fat Fat off. Completely. That way you got the girl and you got a life too. You follow me? Also Tommy and me. *Na?* We got a life too."

Tommy sat there dropping his switchblade down between his

feet, sticking it into the wooden floorboards and muttering to himself.

"I know this Fat Fat in Hong Kong, many years ago," Willie went on. "He is a fat *mangda* same as now. Only he is no big deal those days, just a pimp. Not a nice one. You might wonder why nobody kills him way back then and saves this world a lot of trouble now. Funny thing, I also know him in Vietnam.

"I ever tell you I am in Vietnam two years? I drive cars for people, sometimes the Americans. I do other things too, and sometimes I make quite a bit of money. Fat Fat, though, he is a wheel in the black market those days, not to mention whorehouses. But he doesn't have too many friends; I for one won't piss on him if he is on fire. And from what I hear I feel the same way about him today, only more so. Still and all, he is a very big score, *na?* And Tommy and I, we have to hire a few people ourselves on this one, so we have to charge some money or the whole operation doesn't make much sense from the point of view of business."

"*Chai, chai,*" Tommy added. "*Bisnet.*"

Mu told me to sit back and relax. She wanted to talk to my friends. She didn't look so worried anymore. In fact, she had that look on her face you might think that Willie and Tommy were the ones that had to watch out. Except of course Willie and Tommy weren't scared of anything.

Our telephone was still out of order, and I asked Willie if I could use his mobile phone; I had to call an editor. Willie looked embarrassed and told me his wasn't working either. Then why was he carrying it around, then? I inquired. Image, he said.

I told everybody I wanted to stretch my legs. I was going to go down to the telephone booth on the corner. I could pick up some beer at the same time.

*

When I came back I found most of Mu's cousins had returned,

158

having done all the walking for charity they could handle for one day, and they were sitting out on the stairway making paper orchids with the kids, who for once didn't try to sell me anything. I had to tap on the door three times and tell Mu it was me before I could go in.

The whole assembly was smiling at each other and it could have been somebody's birthday party, everybody looked so happy with things. And Mu had discovered that Tommy was charming. *Nah rahk* is how she put it — "cute," if you can believe that. Tommy, for his part, was mightily impressed with Mu who, according to what Willie told me, was the spitting image of Tommy's first wife, Mrs Two-Toes Number 1. And now that Mu had gotten over her initial apprehension, she and Willie were getting along like a house on fire. I never realized before what kind of ladies' man Willie really was, when he wasn't busy being a gunman and everything.

And we had a deal. We were going to pay 150,000 baht in cash for the services of these paladins — 75,000 now and 75,000 when we could. On top of that, Mu would cut them in on a business deal she had cooking — something to do with construction materials; I hated to ask what, exactly. In any case, it seemed as though this was a notoriously popular game, these days, and competition sometimes got more than a little fierce. So Tommy and Willie were going to provide security services. "These are hard times," said Willie, with an air of satisfaction. "It's best not to keep all your eggs in a basket." He looked at his mobile telephone as though he wished it would ring. "Hey. We can do business."

"*Bisnet*," said Tommy. "*Chai, chai. Yes.*" He turned to Cousin Keeow, who poured him another drink and smiled shyly. She was obviously impressed with this skinny gimp who was grinning at her and shifting around so the 11mm pistol in his waistband didn't pinch. No question, Tommy had a way with women, who knows why.

You never saw such a turnaround — one minute Willie and Tommy were the craziest move I ever came up with, and that was saying something, and the next they were "Uncle Willie" and "Uncle Tommy," almost, except that Willie refused to let the kids see his new Uzi, and now Tommy was in the corner with Keeow and he was looking at her in a way uncles should try not to look at their nieces.

Willie said not to worry. They would have a plan for us in no time; and everything would be fine. "We have the master plan in place by tomorrow afternoon," he told us; and you could see this was no end of comfort to Mu. Rhot was nodding approvingly, as well; he could see that our money was already well spent if there was going to be a master plan and everything. Probably a task force, as well, and then we'd be saved for sure. That's it — we'd simply organize a crack-down on all this kidnapping and carrying on. I didn't know why I hadn't thought of that. Or better still, we could declare the whole area a Hassle-Free Zone and live happily ever after.

Now that events had been put in motion, though, Mu was more like her old self. Of course, she did spend part of that night leaking tears on the bed till I had to turn off the fan, afraid I was going to freeze to death. You could see she was still worried about Bia. On the other hand, we were no longer just waiting around; and she had decided that my friends might indeed be exactly what the doctor had ordered, after all.

But the truth is, though I recognized that Tommy and Willie were not your run-of-the-mill torpedoes, I also knew enough to suspect their plans did not always go entirely as planned. It was not going to surprise me if we had surprises in store down the road; and I don't mind saying I was actually a bit nervous.

fat fat is a mangda

Selections from Arno Petty's Intelligencer and Weekly Gleaner

COME SOON, VOICE-OPERATED WORD PROCESSORS. I heard some people talking, and they said one prominent fatcat has promised to have the hands of a certain reporter who has been indiscreet about how the above-mentioned fatcat got so fat. The scoop in question, it seems, was an Izzy Scoop, and more than one person would like to know who this nosy and loose-lipped individual really is.

"HUNG FAT?" said Hip. "Whoa. The McDonald's Hamburgers of whorehouses. Yeah, I know him."

Hip and I were having a drink in Shaky Jake's, which was by no means the McDonald's Hamburgers of Bangkok bars. Hip was bracketed by Boom and Oo, Jake's newest girl. I was only sitting beside Awn, the skinny one with the longest legs in Thailand, because she was Boom's best friend and it wouldn't be nice for Boom to have somebody to sit beside, and colas to drink, while her best friend had nobody and nothing.

That morning Hip had phoned to say he'd found out who sicced Fun on me. And for once in this life I managed to surprise Hip.

"Hip, I will bet you all the beer I can drink at happy hour I know what you're going to tell me." And I did know, and for once Hip was nonplused. So here I was drinking all the beer I could drink. I was also explaining to Hip how Fat Fat was some kind of a philanthropist.

Fat Fat and his friends had told me about his reforestation projects, for example, where at considerable trouble and expense he was planting thousands and thousands of trees on land that he had cleared of "degraded forest." Of course, you had seen insinuations in the press to the effect that these forests weren't as degraded as they might have been, prior to being razed to the ground. But where was the evidence of that? After all. And then there was Fat Fat's program to use displaced youngsters to do the planting, doing his part to create jobs for the needy youth of the nation. He even built accommodations for them and fed them.

"That's right," said Hip. "I've heard about his 'bunkhouses.' He looks after these kids real good. Each one of these bunkhouses has a bar and lots of food, and there are these armed guards everywhere to protect the new trees and the young boys and girls from harm. And these establishments get a lot of visitors, mostly older men, many of whom like the facilities so much they stay half the night. Yes, our friend Fat is a real humanitarian. That is common knowledge.

"But he is also a pimp of no mean proportions; and Fat Fat wants to have the government legalize prostitution, mostly because he's only got the best interests of his girls at heart. It's best for them, and it's best for the country, too, because they will have to pay taxes and license fees and also get regular medical checkups, which is good for tourism. So this slimebag even gets to meet with deputy cabinet ministers in five-star hotels to discuss these matters, and somehow everybody forgets prostitution is illegal; and everything is 'My, what a fine public benefactor we have on our hands here.'" Needless to say, these were not Hip's own sentiments; and, even if they had been, he would have been speaking only figuratively, since he already had both hands full, one of them with Boom, who was snuggled up tight, she was so cold what with all this air-conditioning and practically no clothes on, and the other with Oo, who was a bottomless pit when it came to colas; you had to wonder how she could get so thirsty in a climate this frigid. But Hip was a generous man, and didn't ask too many questions.

Awn had the grace to be sipping at her one cola, and she didn't

162

care whether I kept her warm or not.

"Fat Fat's into everything," Hip said. "Drugs, prostitution, gambling, pirate music, logging, loan-sharking … You name it. What a businessman. He likes to combine operations; it cuts down on costs. For example, he exports Thai women to Japan."

I would have sworn the ladies hadn't been following a word of the conversation; but as soon as they heard mention of Japan, they perked right up.

"I go Japan," said Boom. "Maybe neks year. I need money for sponsor, Hip, dah-*ling*. What my hand say — have money or no; go Japan or no?"

No, he told her after the briefest glance at her palm. You had to figure this news was set out there with two-inch headlines.

"What happens with some of these girls, they pay his people 30,000 baht so they can go get one of these great jobs as a waitress or tour guide in Japan. He sends them in on phony passports; and, once they get delivered to the yakuza, the girls are informed their sponsors never actually coughed up, their passports are lifted, and they are put into brothels to recoup the fee they already in fact paid. Only with the interest on the outstanding debt, they never pay it off, and they work till they aren't fit for anything but deportation back to Thailand."

"Yakuza" had also gotten a response from the girls, and now they took to rattling away among themselves in Thai, and you could hear *ya-ku-zaa* recur more than a couple of times.

"Other women, before they leave Thailand, he stuffs them with condoms full of heroin, makes the girls swallow them, mostly. So Fat Fat makes his money selling the girls and selling the drugs both. Which is only sound business practice, some people argue, though others take exception to it. Then he has what you might call legitimate interests in stuff like construction and banking. Yeah; you could say he's big, all right."

163

Fat Fat was bucking for *chao por*. "Godfather" status. He wanted to go around getting hugged in public by bigshots, never mind there was a crackdown on at the time, so influential figures and dark influences were in the process of being suppressed. But he had an image problem.

"I did a piece on him for *Asian Document* some months ago. And there's another article coming out next week in *Far East Panorama*. I really do a job on him this time. Oh, yeah. Izzy Scoop rips the lid right off that *mangda*."

Another article on Fat Fat? Oh, boy. Hip had written another article on Fat Fat. I dragged most of my cigarette down in one go. "Tell me, Hip. Did you actually call Fat Fat a mangda in this story?"

"Did I just. Whoa, I mean to say. And more."

Oh, good. Now I was dead. I lit another cigarette off the one I had been smoking, and then noticed I had still another one already burning in the ashtray. This whole operation amused the ladies no end. So they left off gossiping about the yakuza and took up their favorite daytime occupation, which was commenting on the foibles of the farang punters. Jake's new girl, whose name as I said before was Oo though I never found out why, left off giggling and chugging colas and offered to help me smoke these cigarettes.

"Hip. Tell me it isn't so," I said. "Tell me you didn't do this thing; especially tell me you didn't do it under the name of Izzy Scoop."

"Of course Izzy wrote it. What's the matter with you, Jack? You think Hippolyte Lafleur is going to put his byline on something like this? Sure; the same way you're going to put Jack Shackaway on *A Bunch of Boobies for Betsy*. Whoa. Get serious."

"Hip. You just signed my death warrant. I didn't tell you this yet, but Fat Fat thinks I am Izzy Scoop."

I figured Tommy and Willie now had about two weeks to get to

Fat Fat or I was a goner. Hip told me not to dramatize things.

luckyland dead show

Selections from Arno Petty's Intelligencer and Weekly Gleaner

APROPOS OF NOTHING. Ambrose Bierce, in his *Devil's Dictionary*, defined wealth as impunity.

THEM AND US. One high public official says that the recent raid on the biggest illegal casino ever discovered in the city was a waste of time. Thai people like gambling, he says, and no amount of police raids is going to change that. What's the harm anyway, he asks? Most of the people the cops grab in these raids aren't criminals. They're 'rich people.' Enough said.

"YOU. *FARANG* DOGSHIT. Khun Fat say you come."

This time Fun and his helpers actually invaded my apartment. Just another quiet Sunday at home. One of them stayed with the car out on the soi, while Fun and the other pair walked into the lane to come up and bang on the door. I was sleeping when they arrived, and they pushed right into the bedroom to get me.

Mu was screaming at them, and I was screaming at her to relax — it was okay. Mr Fat and I merely had some stuff to discuss. Granny was screeching queries at everybody the same as usual, while the girls were all screaming in sympathy with Mu, though I'm pretty sure none of them had any idea what was going on. And Dok, of course, loved any opportunity to shriek in a high-pitched voice. All in all, it was no way to wake up from an afternoon nap.

Probably figuring that as long as there was going to be hysteria, people might as well have something to be hysterical about, one of Fun's helpers grabbed Rhot on our way out, walked him into a corner and pistol-whipped him till his face was torn and bloody.

Fun meanwhile held another gun on me, grinning away like a busted piano with too many keys. None of this helped Mu relax.

We had to come back upstairs once more to get the brochure copy I had written, after I explained to Fun that Fat Fat would be unhappy if we didn't bring it. Rhot was in the kitchen getting cleaned up. He looked pretty bad, and the girls looked at me as though the whole thing were my fault. And maybe it was at that.

Outside, I smiled at Big Lek the somtam lady, telling her "No problem" as we went by, Fun and friend hanging onto either side of me; but she just stared at me and the rest of these proceedings in amazement. They threw me into the back seat of the car, a big black Benz with smoked glass windows and gold trim on the grill and everywhere, and put a bag over my head. Hip had told me the article wouldn't come out till the following week for sure. I hoped he knew what he was talking about. I really hoped so.

It was a long ride, much of it spent stuck in traffic. I tried to keep a sense of direction, but soon gave that up as a lost cause. So what I did instead, I did my breathing exercises, trying to get my heart-rate down to three figures and concentrating on what clues I could pick up, which were none. One thing: the practice of mindfulness in this case proved to be no problem; in fact it was difficult to be unmindful of the situation I was in, which was by no means a good one. The air-conditioning was cranked up to the point I was freezing to death, moreover, which of course explained why I was shaking just a little.

Fun whiled away the time by poking at me with his gun or else nattering on a car phone to what could have been a bunch of girlfriends, only that didn't seem right to me: who would want to hang out with this disaster, if he wasn't actually holding a gun on you? When Fun wasn't on the phone, the guys in the front seat were playing Carabao tapes at top volume. I figured they probably wanted to soften me up for whatever other tortures were on the agenda. At least it wasn't Milli Vanilli.

Finally I had this feeling we were traveling along some more or less quiet residential streets, and then we slowed right down and did an abrupt turn uphill. There being no hills in Bangkok, I figured this for a driveway, and I was right. Fun opened a window and said something to somebody, and then a big metal gate opened up, clanging shut behind us as we drove through. Then it happened again and, since I didn't think we had turned around and gone out again already, I figured there were two big gates, and possibly two walls to go with them as well.

We got out of the car and I was led stumbling up some steps into a building. Only when the first door closed behind us did they remove the hood. Then we were admitted through three more heavy doors, solid steel they looked like, with locks and crossbars and guards on each one. This gave me the idea that maybe Fat Fat was on the run from some babe back in Taiwan. But this notion might have been due to some mild hysteria on my part; and on the whole I was not too light-hearted about the way things were going this right at this time.

The room I finally found myself in was ordinary enough, if you overlooked the absence of windows. You had the standard quarter-life-size teak elephants by the entrance plus the bigger-than-life-size bronze storks that flanked the sweeping stairway to a second floor. Even the ten-foot-high copy of a Reubens in its ornate gilt frame could have been typical, the way things were going in this boom economy and what with this new middle class going around fixing up places to live in. White plaster statuary, neo-classical maybe, held what looked like street lamps and stood guard everywhere there were no elephants or birds and all the way up the stairs too. Just to make everything perfect, there was fusion jazz emanating from speakers stashed in the corners somewhere.

I noticed that I was sweating despite the arctic air-conditioning, this testament to the good times we lived in. Big ceiling fans with kitschy lamps attached hung from the ceiling, though in this class of place nobody ever used fans because you weren't anybody unless you could turn your guests blue with the air-conditioning. Though I didn't spend much time thinking about these aspects of the matter just at that time.

All I would be able to tell Willie so far was that I'd been taken to a big house located an hour and a half away from my apartment in moderately heavy traffic and parked, I suspected, behind two walls of indeterminate height equipped with iron gates. There were men, I didn't know how many, at each gate; there were more men in an anteroom with video screens off the main hallway. And there were elephants and big birds in the vestibule, not to mention some huge pink ladies in a gold frame and elevator music everywhere. Something told me that wouldn't be enough information to go on.

Fun and his boys took me upstairs and down a corridor to a room where they had to knock three times. A ceiling-mounted video camera swiveled towards us and stared a moment before we were admitted.

"Where is Mr Fat?" he asked one of the two men with submachine guns who greeted us.

"Khun Fat is late," the guard answered. "The traffic is terrible."

"You. *Farang*. Sit." Fun showed me his teeth.

Three more men, all of them armed, sat at a long table, and I joined them. They'd been monitoring the banks of twenty video screens that were mounted on two of the walls. Now they took a break to leer at me and say "You! You!"

"Yeah, yeah," I answered them. "You." I checked them out, but none of them looked like the guy who tried to shoot me in the taxi. The elevator music was everywhere.

On the banks of monitors I could make out a variety of scenes — one of them an enormous high-ceilinged room with crystal

169

chandeliers and a sizeable crowd of people, at least for a Sunday afternoon, milling around a vast array of gaming tables. Another afforded a look into a smaller room where about twenty lovely girls sat naked on bleachers behind a glass wall, each of them with a different number stuck to her shoulder like prizes at a dog show. Between the camera and the tank, a few men sat on divans sipping drinks and enjoying the scenery. On another screen, a man was doing something with a woman that he probably didn't realize was a public performance. At least he wasn't showing many inhibitions.

Fun walked over to an elaborate control consol and adjusted something. The view on the screen zoomed in closer, and the girl looked directly into the camera and stifled a yawn. Chances were the john didn't know about the camera either.

Other monitors were covering a variety of doors and gates. One screen blinked regularly, alternately displaying what seemed to be at least three, and probably four, guard towers. These were the only outside views, and they told me nothing about where we were. Some of the screens were blank. The room itself was windowless.

Just then there was a triple knock at the door, and one of the screens showed three fat men at a door, the three fat men in question being Fat Fat and the two lesser fats, and the door being the very one that now was opening on the room in which we sat.

"*Farang*. Is-sey," Fat Fat said. "I am happy to see you."

Right away, I could see something was wrong. He floated into the room with his buddies, a trio of weather balloons on short leashes.

Fat Fat did almost look as though he was glad to see me, at that; and his two henchmen appeared as benign as I'd seen them. They came to rest at the table, Fat Fat settling beside me, on my side of the table. Hardly had the trio ceased to billow when two waitresses wheeling a trolley of food were also admitted to the room. Cute waitresses with no clothes on except for little lace aprons that cov-

170

ered a bit of their fronts and that was all. One of them was slim and fair-skinned. Her breasts were firm nubbins tipped with soft pink aureoles, the nipples erect with public attention and air-conditioning. When she stood between myself and Fat Fat to serve him, I noticed goose pimples and the fine downy hair, almost invisible, that covered her back. Not to mention some fine, crisscrossing stripes of what looked like scar tissue, also almost invisible. She looked about sixteen, tops. There was a tiny blue and red and yellow butterfly tattooed on one buttock. The other waitress was a ripe little berry, brown-skinned and full-breasted; she was no older and maybe even younger than her friend. She had what could have been a merry sort of face, except that now she looked mostly scared.

The taller, slimmer one started feeding morsels of this and that to Fat Fat, first tasting each dish herself but not because she was hungry. The Brown Berry wiped at his face and then his arms with a cold towel. Then she ran another cloth up under Fat Fat's shirt, doing his belly in big swipes just as though she were washing a Volkswagen. He chomped and slurped at a large mouthful of noodles, and pulled at his crotch, mightily pleased with life it was plain to see.

I had to wipe my own face. My towel reeked of cheap cologne, and it burned my eyelids. I wanted to ask about Bia, though on the other hand I didn't want to.

The three fatmen had been on a weekend meditation retreat, or so Fatman No.1 informed me.

"You. *Farang.* You must slow down. Learn the way; the Middle Way," Fat Fat said. "Hee, hee," he added, in a more inscrutable vein still. "All the time *jai yen yen.* Cool heart, *na?*"

His underlings meanwhile bobbed away in the background on their clouds of good karma, not saying anything, but clearly having lots to say if only words could tell. All three of them kept moving

171

very carefully, floating around in slow motion as though they didn't want to let any of that karma spill over.

Then Fat Fat slapped the waitress's hand away, impatient with this tedious succession of morsels no matter how blissed out he might be. He shoveled a bowl full of food for himself and dug in with a will. "You," he said to me. "Eat." But I wasn't very hungry. Then Fat Fat lifted the tall girl's apron. "You. *Farang*. Eat!" Fat Fat poked at her. "Here. Is good! No? You no like? Hee, hee."

The girl blushed from her hairline down to her apron string, and looked away into a corner. I noticed that she was slightly pigeon-toed, though that was a minor flaw in an otherwise perfectly set-up young creature. Aside from a few goose pimples and scars, of course. The butterfly was nice.

All the fatmen and Fun as well laughed and said maybe the farang doesn't like Thai food, plus other comments in a similar vein. It seemed there was some inside joke going on, though I didn't know what it was. Fat Fat slapped the tall waitress on her bottom, leaving a greasy spot. Then he took to an avid fondling of the Brown Berry, weighing each breast in turn and leering at me. "Is virgin," he said.

Fat Fat wanted to demonstrate his toys.

There must have been fifty video cameras installed around the place and, as I said, about twenty screens just in this one room alone. He had his technicians show me the dogs that patrolled the grounds. These were Dobermans and they were kept hungry, or so I was told and I had no reason to doubt it. A thicket of punji stakes, of a type you wouldn't want to fall on if you were climbing in or trying to climb out either, were arrayed inside the outer wall. But this was nothing compared to what else Fat Fat had stashed between the walls. I was going to have lots to tell Willie, and none of it was what you would have called good news.

"Closer," Fat Fat said in Thai; and a technician zoomed in on one of the crocodiles. An ugly, prehistoric beast which, as though it sensed our attention, chose that moment to slide off the bank into the moat, its V-shaped wake joining those of several more denizens of the perimeter defenses. They looked big, and more than a little intimidating, supposing you were of a mind to climb in over this wall after hours. Or out. "Fun! Show farang the cloco-die."

All of a sudden Fun was really and truly a crocodile, just as ugly and even toothier. He leaned over the table towards the waitress, rolling his body and grunting and gnashing his ivories. He was a man of many talents, I could see that. He sat back laughing heartily, well pleased at how his performance had been received. Fat Fat sent the Brown Berry around the table to wipe Fun off.

The guard towers, according to what the video screens had told me, were on the fourth wall, the inside one. I didn't see anything else of note except what looked like the neighborhood's first condominium project, only the structural steel so far, just beyond the outer wall. It was probably the wall to the west, judging by the angle of the sun. A billboard hung on the side of it said ONOCO: BUILDING A FUTURE FOR YOU. I repeated this to myself a few times, hoping it would stay with me. Maybe it would help us find this place afterwards. The trouble with going around always writing everything down in notebooks is that finally your brain, or at least my brain, thinks it's okay to stoap remembering anything that isn't written down.

"You see these people?" Fatman No.1 was pointing to the casino screen. "They are Mr Fat's clients. You think they look like criminals? So they are gambling. Thais like to gamble. Everybody likes to gamble. The police are never going to stop that. And these people — look down there — these are rich people. Important people. How can they be criminals?"

Within the same walled compound, there was also the Luckyland Shaking Heaven Massage Parlor and Bowling Alley, which we had already had a glimpse of on the video screens. The building we were in was known as Luckyland One.

Screens No.12 through 18 monitored the Luckyland Casino — the main gambling hall plus the smaller rooms. There was a card game going on in a private room, just a quiet affair with five players, one of whom would have given me a story with two-inch headlines. That's if the newspapers could have printed it, which they couldn't have; and if I would have written it, which I wouldn't have.

Screens No.8 through 11 were giving insights into life in the Shaking Heaven Therapeutic Massage Parlor and Bowling Alley. Screen No.11 of course was the fishtank, where the clients got to inspect the girls through one-way glass.

"And you see here?" Fatman No.1 continued. "Here are some more people enjoying Mr Fat's hospitality. And you are going to call Mr Fat a criminal because he does what he can to make life good for these rich people? That's not right."

He punched some keys on the control panel, and one of the screens started flipping from bedroom to bedroom, revealing these citizens engaged in a variety of therapeutic activities, some of them quite imaginative and not necessarily beneficial to health.

"You see here?" he went on. "These are important men. These men get respect; they are honored by society. But you see their bottoms?" He zoomed in on one such article in particular. "They are big and ugly and they go up and down exactly like yours or mine.

"What it is, it is image. Public image. You must present yourself the way you want people to see you. You must tell people who you are and what you are. If you don't, then they won't know. They will think you are just some guy."

Fat Fat said something to the lesser fatmen, and Fatman No.1 translated it for me: "'Do good work, but don't stand out.' That is always Mr Fat's policy. But where does it get him? People call him bad names and talk about only some of his business dealings, and never mention the good work he does in the community."

Fat Fat was following all of this with great interest, as though he could understand everything, and he looked very happy with things. "Write. *Farang*, you write this down, *na?* Yeah. You write."

"Good idea," said Fatman No.1. "Maybe you should get this stuff down; you can use it in your stories."

"That is a good idea," I answered him. "But don't worry; I have a retentive memory."

"You write," he said.

So I wrote some stuff in my pocket diary.

"*Farang*," Fat Fat suddenly asked me. "Where you get that pen?"

This confused me. I held up my stick pen, which had cost 3.5 baht, and I said "This one?"

"Is nerd pen."

"*Nud* pen?" I replied, thinking I really should do something about learning more Thai. "*Noed* pen …? What the hell? I don't know. I think it's mine …"

"Nerd," Fat Fat yapped. "Nerd. *Nerd*." He said something to Fatman No.1 in Chinese. Now his hands were fluttering, and he was going to need another dose of meditation to keep him on the Middle Path, at this rate.

"Mr Fat says you have a nerd pen," Fatman No.1 advised me. "He says, 'Do you have no respect for yourself?' What kind of reporter writes with a pen such as that one?

"You work for Mr Fat now. Here; you take this." And Fatman No.1 handed me a gold-plated ballpoint pen of the type I hate, with a skinny barrel that gets slippery with sweat even before I am well started. "Mr Fat deals with top people only. You work for Mr Fat, you are part of his face. Your job is to let the public know how much face he really has.

175

"And remember this: you write these good things about Mr Fat, and you do it soon, or Mr Fat cuts your hands off. Understand?"

I did understand. Fatman No.1's English was excellent, and he had a succinct way of putting things. I could see it would be quite hard to write anything either complimentary or uncomplimentary about Fat Fat, or about anybody else either, if I had no hands. So I said no problem; I will write what you want.

At the same time I said this, I noticed I was making scribbling motions in my diary with my new pen. Maybe I was a nerd at that, I thought to myself, and I put the pen away.

Fatman No.1 had been going through the brochure copy I had brought with me, frowning with concentration. "This is good," he said to Fat Fat in Chinese. I knew this was what he said because he repeated it in Thai for Fun, who didn't care if it was good or not, as far as I could see.

To me, however, Fatman No.1 said this: "Why you don't say this is the best condominium? Or that it is "exquisite"? And you don't say here how it is in parkland, with trees all around even though it is in the heart of the city. Why don't you say these things? Other condominium brochures say these things; you want people to think we are not as good as these other places? You will change this."

"Sure," I said right away. Once you actually steel yourself to the prospect of writing a brochure, any concern for the facts of the matter or the ethics of it either is kind of misplaced. It's like a hooker agreeing on her price, climbing into the sack, and then refusing to screw unless she's certain it means something to both parties.

Fat Fat was happy again, sitting there in the center of his control room full of windows on his world. And, still brimming with spiritual goodness, my host barked only softly at Fatman No.2, who in turn barked softly for a while into the mobile phone. Fat

Fat then had his technicians bring up an indoor shooting range on one monitor.

"*Farang*," he told me in his kindliest voice. "You look this."

Seven lanes were divided one from the other by long partitions; they extended from the shooting stand towards a wall of both fixed and moveable targets. Just three men, one of them with an automatic pistol and the other two with revolvers, stood ready at three of the lanes. The camera looked down from a vantage point above and behind the stand, so we had a good view of proceedings when a door to the left of the range opened, down by the targets, and a young man came stumbling out. The door closed behind him. He threw himself against it, but it was obviously built to handle such contingencies. The shooter on the left fired once downrange and the guy started to sprint for the other side. In doing so, he had to cross the fields of fire of the other two marksmen who, I noticed, were only firing from the hip; they didn't seem too bothered about hitting anything. The target got to the other side and whammed into the wall, spinning on the rebound and heading back the way he had come, legs pumping like Ben Johnson on jet fuel, his hands and arms just a blur by his sides.

I noticed Fat Fat had grabbed the skinny waitress, and he was telling her "Look, look!" even though she didn't want to look. She was crying. The Berry, on the other hand, was gazing down at her feet, face hidden behind her hair.

The men with the guns, the ones who were now laughing and firing way over the head of the target and laughing some more, were business associates of Mr Fat, I was told. Two Japanese gentlemen and a Thai. Two Japanese businessmen, actually, and a police captain.

One of Fat Fat's interests, mostly a hobby, was running this shooting gallery, which was a popular feature of Luckyland One, maybe because they sometimes used live targets. Usually these targets were people Fat Fat was displeased with in some way. Sometimes the yakuza would bring their own pigeons, people they were displeased with in some way.

"You. *Farang*," said Fatman No.1. "You see? This person does not make Mr Fat happy. In fact he pisses him off. So Mr Fat says he must run three times across the range. That is bad for him. But it is not shooting fish in a barrel. Not at all. The rules say you have to hit a hand first, and then a foot. After that you can shoot to kill.

"Sometimes you only have to run once, or twice. That is if Mr Fat is pissed off just a little bit."

Fat Fat's gallery was the most popular one in Thailand, on the whole, or so he told me, and I saw no reason to doubt this, looking around at the happy faces on the gunmen. It was especially popular with the yakuza, it seemed, who had a tough time getting enough target practice in Japan. They also liked the support facilities.

The guy who pissed Fat Fat off had made two runs and he hadn't been touched, though, as I said before, it didn't look as though the shooters were really trying. And this was the case, because on the last lap the first gun caught him in the hand, throwing him off stride for a second and causing him some shock and pain, by the look of it. The next gun got him in the foot; and he went down immediately, spun off balance and now in some more shock and pain. Running on his bad foot was probably out of the question, so he tried to crawl the rest of the way. As he came into the last gun's line of fire, he took a slug in the side, which left him flopping around on the floor. The three sportsmen got together at that and tossed a coin. Then one of them, the guy whose lane it was anyway, took quick aim and fired once more and the man stopped moving.

"Dead Show!" exclaimed Fat Fat with delight, throwing up his hands and going hee, hee, hee. "*Dead Show.*"

I had this funny feeling in my stomach, as though I had eaten

178

something bad, except I hadn't eaten anything at all, so that couldn't have been it.

"Mr Fat calls this the Dead Show," the lesser fatman told me, just as though Fat Fat was Oscar Wilde and this was a witty thing he liked to say.

"Not same live show." Fat Fat was giggling and shaking like a big glop of jelly escaped the mold, and the lesser fats were shaking and giggling right along with him. Fun was showing his teeth and everybody was having a hell of a time, except for the waitresses. And me, of course.

"We see live show now," Fat Fat informed us, looking very pleased with life indeed. "Pum-pum too much. *Farang* reporter — now we also see your *fen*, guhr-fen you. Hee, hee."

He spoke to one of the control-room technicians, who fiddled at his panel for a moment, and then my attention was directed to screen number ten. It was a dressing room. Several girls, most of them wrapped in towels, but a couple of them wrapped in nothing, seemed to be applying body makeup to themselves or to one another. Some of them were doing stretching exercises and suchlike instead. Others were just sitting around. I couldn't see Bia anywhere.

One in particular was applying some cream or jelly to an intimate part of her person, and Fat Fat had his men zero in on this operation with the camera. He made some comment and the whole room, except for me, who didn't understand it, and the waitresses, who I guess didn't find it funny, burst out laughing.

Meanwhile, on the other screen, the one with the shooting range, two boys were at work with a hose and a mop. You had to figure these guys for the Jean-Paul Somsak type — who else were they going to get to screw around at the business end of the Dead Show? Not me, that was for sure. No way.

The tall waitress and the Brown Berry wheeled the trolley out, while Fun and the fatmen made motions as if to go. I got up and was halfway to the door when there was a loud whoop-whooping as though we were getting depth-charged. But no one appeared in any way alarmed.

"Wait. Look," Fat Fat said. "Number 15."

"Laser-beam alarm system," Fatman No.1 told me, the pride in his voice making you think maybe it was none other than him who first invented the laser. "Laser beams along the tops of the walls, and electric eyes everywhere. That is security."

Screen No.15 was offering a view of the crocodile moat. The camera was aimed down along the inner wall, and a guy at the top of a ladder was wrestling a bag of something the rest of the way over the wall, over the spikes and broken glass. Feeding time at the zoo. The crocodiles had no doubt about what was in the sack, given the way they homed in on it as soon as it dropped onto the grassy bank. They waddled straight at it in the way crocodiles do when they have pressing business, fat scaly tails thrashing from side to side as they converged.

And Fat Fat decided he had one more scene for me. This came up on Screen 18. It was a simple room, much like a Holiday Inn, and sitting there on the edge of the bed in denim skirt and blouse was Bia. She was holding her bangs up and looking into a hand mirror, opening her eyes as wide as they would go, again and again.

*

No matter what an innocent bystander might have thought, this was not primarily a display of naked flesh. It was a display of naked power, and Fat Fat was the star of the show.

The stage was enormous, and would have sufficed for a pornographic half-time at the Rose Bowl. On the ceiling, a good fifteen feet from the stage floor, a big stained-glass rosette, softly backlit by the dying light of day through the skylight behind, nicely accented this cathedral of evil. Broad planked terraces with tables and chairs for the spectators rose from the stage, amphitheater style. This afternoon's presentation, however, was merely an intimate affair for a few privileged guests who got to sit at three tables right up front, stage center. Fat Fat apologized, indicating that his shows were often much better than the modest effort this impromptu matinee represented. Aside from Fun and his boys, there were the two Japanese marksmen and the police captain, the three fatmen, Bia, and myself. Plus the performers and waitresses, of course. I got to sit with Fun and Fatman No.1.

The live show reminded me in some ways of a Sunday school pageant, the way the girls, all of them very young, kept smiling shyly and blushing at the applause, clearly modest about their accomplishments but nevertheless pleased someone appreciated them. They took turns, helping each other where assistance was needed, getting up on the stage and doing various things that I didn't think were erotic, just ridiculous. And sad, even though most of them seemed to be performing these acts with what you could only call a large measure of innocence.

Bia had to stand beside Fat Fat the whole while, and she and I weren't allowed to talk. Bia was dressed in a short skirt and blouse. The girl on the other side of Fat Fat was entirely naked. Her main job was that of wiping Fat Fat's arms and belly with cold towels. Bia was protected from much of this and from the show, I suspected, by the fact her bangs hung down over her eyes and she probably couldn't see anything. Her legs had blue and yellow bruises all over them, of course; but this was nothing new.

"Bia. Are you okay?" I said, thinking at the same time that this was a fairly stupid question.

"You, *farang*. Shut up!" This from Fatman No.2.

"*Farang* dogshit!" Fun chipped in.

"Shut up!" was Fatman No.1's contribution, though it was hard to say who he was addressing.

"Jack," Bia told me in a calm voice. She was, after all, Mu's sister. "When can I go home? I'm scared."

Fat Fat was pinching the towel girl's nipples, one and then the other, rolling and twisting them between his fingers till she gasped in pain. Then he stabbed her in the bellybutton with a greasy forefinger.

"*Farang*. You like? Eh? Maybe you have this one, okay? I take *fen* you. Okay? Hee, hee." He pushed the girl away from him, towards me. He put one hand on Bia's bottom and scooped a handful of nuts with the other, firing them into his mouth and chewing avidly, bits of food dribbling from his lips as he giggled and groped and chomped and shook.

I smiled at the towel girl in what I hoped was a reassuring manner, and she smiled back. But she went to stand beside Fat Fat again, looking confused and fearful.

Up on the stage, meanwhile, the ping-pong girl kept missing the beer glass on the floor between her legs. She would laugh sheepishly and shake her head in a way that told you she had got it right at rehearsals, but now look. Another girl, a elfin thing with a fragile, bird-like frame, was the official ball-girl, and she would run to collect the ping-pong balls which missed. She was wiping them off and keeping them in a big bowl full of Vaseline. At one point she started to reload her friend; but the police captain volunteered to take over this duty instead, looking more avuncular than you would have thought he could. Fun and his sidekicks took to placing bets on each shot.

A variety of acts followed this one, most of them routine examples of the standard Bangkok live show, from what I knew of these things.

We had to witness a series of tricks with bottles of cola and marker pens and cigarettes. The latter artiste flirted with brand-new varieties of cancer, and I found myself lusting for a smoke. It seemed unreasonable that she could have a cigarette and I couldn't; but that's the way it was. Then we came to the blowgun girl, a lanky Indian-Thai girl with buck teeth and long jet-black hair. The Japanese men and the police captain at the next table and me, we had to hold big balloons. The blowgun specialist squatted on the stage and then leaned way back on one hand, while with the other hand she steadied the blowgun and raised her hips high, drawing a bead on a balloon. Then she'd abruptly drop her pelvis, propelling the missile unerringly to its target, never once missing except when it came to me.

I was last, and I was sitting there with this big yellow balloon held well away from my face, though not far enough away, because Annie Oakley planted the dart right in the middle of my forehead and I yelled "Jesus Christ. Ow!", which proved to the hit of the whole evening. I couldn't understand him very well, but I think Fatman No.2 was telling Fat Fat we should do it once more and get it on video. To tell the truth, I didn't believe it was an accident, and it wouldn't have surprised me to find the dart was tipped with curare, though I didn't die. It stung like crazy, though. What a way to get AIDS, I have to admit crossed my mind.

And as though that wasn't enough, we had to have snakes. A dark beauty, one considerably older than the other performers we had seen, came out and danced naked with a twelve-foot python. The beautifully colored and patterned creature coiled and twisted about its mistress, its scales glistening, its thick muscular body squeezing and caressing every part of her. For a finale, the python's head reared up from between her legs and gaped toothy jaws at the audience. After the applause had died down, two assistants brought out a heavy wicker basket and set it on the stage, one of them flipping the lid off and then backing away in a hurry. Within seconds a big king cobra reared high, flaring its hood. There followed a genuinely spell-binding, incredibly controlled contest of

183

reflexes, the snake always striking just past the dancer's face, past her hands, the woman then pretending to strike back, darting her head forward, feinting and stabbing her tongue at the snake. finally, she grabbed the cobra behind the head — one lightning quick snatch — and then took its body in her other hand. She brought it down off the stage and carried it to Fat Fat, who examined the creature with great interest, sliding lewd fingers up and down a length of its body, and insisting that his attendants touch it as well, even though they were whimpering with terror, the Brown Berry barely stifling a scream. Bia, on the other hand, remained entirely impassive. It could have been a piece of hose, for all she showed any concern.

While Fat Fat tormented the girls with the snake, an old man was brought into the room wheeling a small metal trolley. He drove right up to Fat Fat's table and set about a physical examination, lifting Fat Fat's eyelids and nodding sagely, poking at armpits and looking down Fat Fat's throat using a tongue depressor. Now Fat Fat was the star of the show. The snake lady stood to one side, still holding the snake, which now and then convulsed in long quick sinuous ripples. The snake handler brought her charge closer and held it over a plastic tray that had been placed on the floor. The old man reached with a razor and slashed the snake its length, moving the tray the better to catch the drip of blood. Then he cut deeper, tugging the flesh aside, the snake writhing in slow great contortions. Pulling free a dark gobbet of something, he flipped it into an empty glass into which he then also shook out a small foil packet of powder. He handed the glass to Fat Fat, who promptly added a measure of Chivas, stirred it around, and chugged it back with much smacking and sighs of satisfaction, looking all around to gauge our reactions. He belched delicately and pulled the Berry closer to him.

I had seen this before, the time I did a piece for the *Globe* on

Lumphini Park. One of this park's many colorful attractions was the street vendor who sold snake blood and gall bladders mixed with whiskey. His clients were mostly old Chinese men — men who believed this habit would add potent years to their lives.

The cobra blood was mixed with more whiskey and then dispensed to the rest of the audience. It tasted just like whiskey.

There was one more act to go. A lady who was at least twice as old as any other we'd seen that day came out and danced nude. Her body was long past the point she should have wanted to display it in public, though she moved with some grace. It the course of her dance, she started to pull a metallic tinsel streamer out of herself, wrapping herself in it like a Christmas tree. She came down off the stage and offered the free end to Fat Fat; but he declined, sending her instead over to me. I was embarrassed, but she was smiling so nicely and was so obviously eager to please that I accepted the streamer. What I did, I tied it to the table leg, smiling and giving her the thumbs-up as she danced away here and there and then up on the stage dispensing, as she went, miles of tinsel streamer. Finally, it came to an end.

After the performance, Fat Fat called her over. He slapped her tired old dugs back and forth, watching them swing and making some laughing remark to the assembly. You could see she was hurt; but she was probably used to it, because she just jiggled her boobs some more and leered at Fat Fat in what might have been a fond manner. He rewarded her by stuffing 100-baht notes up where the tinsel had come from. Given her capacity for tinsel streamers, you could see this might set him back a pretty penny, but before long he got bored with it and told her to move along.

The stage lights were finally turned off and Fat Fat's guards cleared the room of audience, the Japanese and the Thais *wai*-ing their deep thanks and pleasure as they went out. Bia and Fat Fat's three attendants were also taken away, the ping-pong girl's tiny assistant having taken over their duties for the time being.

The fatmen and I had business to discuss.

"We will now give you your second assignment. Mr Fat would like you to write a nice article for that same magazine, and for the newspapers too, explaining how many of the things you said about him in the other story were the result of wrong information. Then you will say about the good things Mr Fat does all the time."

"But I can't. The magazine won't ..."

"Yes they will. You write it. Understand?"

"Okay."

"And after that, we have a special job for you. We will pay you well. Mr Fat has his fifth-cycle birthday in a few months. He is a Goat. This is an auspicious occasion, and he wants to publish his biography, the story of how he comes to be such an important man today. This you will also write."

"My, my," I said to Fat Fat, thinking I would make him feel good. "You don't look sixty years old. I must say I am surprised."

Fat Fat giggled at this, and seemed very pleased indeed. He fluttered his pudgy hands at me and told me this: "Eat good food; drink good drink; make pum-pum every night. Stay young. Hee, hee."

Fatman No.1 elaborated on this for me. "Mr Fat, he fuck a different girl every night. All of them virgins."

"Hee, hee," Fat Fat added. "No sick. Pum-pum alla time, and no sick."

So virgins kept him young and healthy; and he was indeed an old goat. You had to think the Chinese horoscope of twelve-year cycles, each cycle associated with a different animal, might know something about what was what after all.

Fat Fat said something to the girl on his knee, the ping-pong girl's assistant, running a hand down her arm and then along the back of her thigh to her knee. She shuddered and looked towards

Fatman No.2 as though for help. He leered at her. She looked all around, though she wouldn't meet my eye; I think she was afraid of me because I was a farang. Seeing no hope, she leaned in against Fat Fat, stiff with fear and loathing.

I couldn't keep a certain amount of similar feeling off my face.

"Hey, *farang*," said Fatman No.1. "You gay?"

They had determined that my girlfriend was a virgin. Bia, that is. From what Fatman No.1 went on to tell me, this was all that had saved her from a number of unpleasant experiences, including that of appearing in the little show they had had performed for our entertainment this very evening. For one thing, they were now keeping her pure for Fat Fat's birthday celebrations. He liked her. And he wondered what kind of man this farang reporter was, living with such a girl and she was still a virgin. Maybe he liked boys instead?

I was surprised to hear Bia was a virgin, actually, even if Mu had always said she was a good girl. For sure that had to be the only part of her that had remained inviolate, given her talent for banging about through life.

Fat Fat worked a hand in between the ballgirl's legs and squeezed, mostly for my benefit, I guess, because he giggled at the same time and said to me, "First time; first time. Is good, first time."

The girl twisted away from him, reconsidered, and then turned back with a grimace that might have been a smile.

impressive erections

Selections from Arno Petty's Intelligencer and Weekly Gleaner

EAT YOUR HEART OUT, SINGAPORE. Various interests have announced plans to build what will be four of the world's ten tallest buildings right here in Bangkok, all of them scheduled to go up in the coming year.

DESIGNS ON NIC-HOOD. Bangkok is at once sprawling ever wider and soaring ever higher as NIC-hood approaches. The prospect of Newly Industrialized Country status has among other things inspired a dog's breakfast of neo-classical antebellum mansions riding piggyback on utilitarian blocks tricked out in Doric columns and other nice stuff. Unless you're looking for a laugh, there are really only two interesting kinds of architecture in the city — the traditional temples, in all their variety and charm; and those modern temples to Mammon, the banks.

MU HAD RECEIVED ASTROLOGICAL ADVICE that this was an auspicious period in which to embark on major plans. Which was truly fortunate, in view of the fact I had not much time before I was going to have a choice between doing a few laps in the Dead Show or else finally fingering Hip. Or I could pull a vanishing act, no doubt showing up in Peoria or some other hotspot to write the obituaries for the community rag.

Willie, Tommy, Mu, and Hip were there to listen to my report — the whole Working Committee present and accounted for. I didn't get much to go on, I told them. I was kept hooded the whole way there, and there were no windows or anything. I did manage to figure out a few things by clever observation and deduction, however. I got no further than the part about crocodiles and casinos before Willie stopped me. "Oh, yeah," he said. "Luckyland. They're keeping her at Luckyland."

"Of all the joints we have to bust into, it would have to be Luckyland," said Hip, shaking his head sorrowfully. "Isn't that just dandy."

I waited for Mu to say "Oh, yeah, Luckyland" too, and wondered why I was the only person in the country who had never heard of this place before. But she didn't.

"Hey," I said. "Why did these jokers keep a hood on me the whole way if the location of Luckyland is common knowledge on the street?"

"It's a good practice, any time you do a snatch," said Willie. "You don't have to do it always, but if you make it a habit, then you won't screw up when it's important. It's professional."

"*Chai, chai,*" said Tommy, grinning at me. "*Plo-feson-ur. Is good.*"

"They probably just wanted to hassle you, Jack," was Hip's opinion.

I gave them everything I knew about numbers of men, layout of the three main buildings, the perimeter defenses, and the central monitoring room. Aside from Fun, who seemed to have taken over as head bodyguard and general factotum, there was a small army of goons and guards. There was one building that was the casino, complete with restaurant, bars, and gaming rooms, both private and open. Another building was a brothel decorated with massive potted plants and gigantic wood carvings. Besides the service staff, these two establishments reputedly were infested mainly with solid citizens. A third building was Luckyland One, and this one was off-limits except to Fat Fat and special guests.

"What about alarm systems?" asked Willie.

"Laser trip-beams along the tops of the walls and inside the grounds," I told them. "And there's more — Fat Fat likes to brag

189

about his security systems. The two steel gates have electronic locking mechanisms and are designed to stand up to bulldozers. The laser beams and electric eyes are just in case all the other defenses don't discourage intruders. The lesser fatman informed me they weren't much use, really, other than to tell people inside when they should rush to the video room and see the intruders get torn to shreds by the rest of the system. Indeed, one way Fat Fat brightens up a slow afternoon is to tell somebody they are home-free if they can break out. The fun comes when Fat Fat brings guests into the video room and they bet on how far this lucky stiff will get. Only one person has ever even made it past the dogs, I'm told, and that made the crocodiles real happy. If someone somehow ever made it past the moat, he'd be shot from the guard towers anyway. There are video cameras everywhere."

Now that I'd listened to myself outline the problem, I really got depressed.

"That's one game that won't go on much longer, anyway," said Hip. "Fat Fat is building the tallest building in that part of the city right beside Luckyland. He'll have to be more discreet, what with thirty-seven floors of offices and condos peering down into his compound."

Suddenly I realized this was the condominium I had written the brochure for — I had known where Luckyland was all along. But I decided not to tell anybody about this. Reporters are generally supposed to be able to put two and two together.

Hip told me he'd talked to Far East Panorama about holding his story till later, but they had said it had already gone to press. It wouldn't be economically feasible to hold the issue back now, even if it was to save a writer's life. The advertisers would scream bloody murder. But there were still several days before I had to worry.

It was decided I would have to go back to Luckyland, as soon as I got the chance, and get some more information. I should try to find out exactly where they were keeping Bia. And I had to get more on their security procedures, the number and disposition of employees, and more on the general layout of the premises. I should try to see what hardware his men were carrying. If I didn't know exactly what a particular weapon was, at least I should remember how to describe it, and Willie could work out roughly what kind of firepower we were up against. They would need anything I could get.

Sombat was delegated to contact the cousin who worked on a crocodile farm and learn what there was to know about consorting with crocodiles in the middle of the night, Willie and Tommy having admitted to little experience of crocodiles as it stood. They were better on Dobermans, though all they knew about it told them to stay clear of such animals as much as possible.

Other than that, Willie allowed, we would have to sleep on the problem. This was a challenge.

Tommy and Hip were deep in conversation; I couldn't follow more than five percent of the Thai. Mu and Willie also started up in Thai, and I was left feeling like a fifth wheel.

*

That night I told Mu they still thought Bia was my girlfriend, and how they were surprised she was a virgin. I also had to tell her that Fat Fat had in mind correcting this oversight on my part at an early opportunity, that occasion being his birthday, which wasn't far away. It was a good idea to get her out of there as soon as possible, was the way I saw it; and Mu said yes, that was a good idea.

I wanted to tell Mu about seeing a man shot dead for sport. And how it felt to have these men tell me they would cut my hands off. I wanted to tell her about the kids who were forced to degrade body and spirit to satisfy the whims of a bunch of assholes. But what I told her instead was "Bia is fine; if we get to her soon, she'll be okay. I'll be okay, too. They only want to do some writing for

191

them. Some PR."

"PR?" Mu said. "Not PR? Oh, Jack. I'm so sorry."

She could see I was not doing too good on the high spirits front. So she did a lot of playing around and laughing and so on, even though she was probably as depressed as I was. And I loved her for it. But I had to say this: "Mu, I'm sorry. I can't."

This was a big surprise to both of us, though Mu didn't say anything.

In the morning, she told me I should find a friend to stay with someplace the other side of town.

"You want me to do this?" I asked Mu.

"Yes," she told me. "There's nothing you can do. You go in there, you don't know these people; you don't know the Thai Way. You will get yourself killed and Bia too. You have done enough already."

This hurt me.

thinking it over

BUT DON'T HOLD YOUR BREATH. Tests show there are now three more intersections in the city where it is a good idea not to breathe. Not to worry, though: in ten years or so the planners hope things might improve a little and we will all be able to take a sip of air to see how things are going.

GOOD NEWS OR BAD NEWS? Pollution has been democratized. Now that Bangkok has become a 'heat island,' the hot air rises and carries pollutants up to where even the occupants of penthouses are exposed to the noxious gases that can penetrate air-conditioning systems.

WHAT'S THAT YOU SAY? What do Bangkok traffic cops and dogs have in common? They can't hear a dog-whistle. Recent tests have shown that 23% of our traffic policemen have suffered significant hearing loss; this is blamed mostly on the masses of unmuffled two-stroke motorcycles scrambling at the intersections. Meanwhile, it has been determined that Bangkok dogs don't come when you blow a dog-whistle. Why? They're deaf to the higher frequencies.

BAD COUPS IS GOOD NEWS. While we wait to see whether we go deaf or die of a lung disease first, there are these rumors of a coup. Of course there are always rumors of a coup in Thailand; but this rumor is one supported by Izzy Scoop, and that makes me nervous. Mind you, such things can be good for business if you are a freelance writer.

FOR ONCE my newspaper got to me before somebody turned it into artificial roses or take-away bags for pork satay.

But then I didn't know whether this was a good thing after all.

193

It was nothing but the usual: rumors of coups, predictions of floods, everybody accusing everybody else of being corrupt, and the price of beer was going up again.

And if ever I got tired of worrying about the news, then I could always read my mail.

The phone bill included seven calls to Satun and twelve to Udon Thani. What the hell was anybody doing calling Udon Thani? Where the hell *was* Udon Thani, come to that? Worse than phone bills, there was this letter from Esther, my old childhood affliction back in Peoria, a lady who had been some part of the reason I left the States in the first place.

"I've been talking to your mother, Jack, and she thinks it's a good idea if we come to Bangkok to see you." This came right after where she told me how much she missed me, why didn't I write, and wasn't it awfully hot over there in Thailand?

"This girl Esther, Jack — why does she still write to you?" Mu wanted to know. She was tapping a front tooth and gazing away into the distance.

"Mu," I said, "that's all over with. I don't know why she still writes to me. Maybe my mother makes her do it. My mother wants me to marry her."

Mu gave one last decisive, clearly audible tap and said this: "You should go back to this girl, Jack. I want you to leave. Go back to her. Go home."

All this was delivered in a flat, hard voice. Her face was turned away from me. I reached to touch her hair. "Look at me, Mu." I held her chin and turned her face towards me to see tears in her eyes.

"Go home, Jack. You don't belong here."

This came as a shock to me, even though I didn't believe Mu really meant it. It was just that she was under a lot of pressure.

*

194

You want to think, you need to unwind, the thing to do is take a long walk. You want to do these things, the place not to do them is this big market area down the river from where I lived, one of the most densely populated places on the planet. But I guess I was testing myself. Testing and training myself both. For Mu. And for me. She could have been right—it might have been I needed to change my ways. Maybe just a little. If I wanted to live and prosper in Thailand, that is.

But persuasive circumstances were arguing it was time to take my leave of the country altogether. For one thing, it was hard not to get this feeling that lately I was stumbling along always one step away from sudden death or worse. I didn't even know for sure just who all were gunning for me, which I admit was preying on my mind somewhat. Meanwhile both my girlfriend and my good buddy Hip kept telling me I was basically a moron when it came to getting along in this life. And now Mu was also telling me she didn't want me around the joint; I should go back to the U.S. of A. and marry one good reason I left that country.

On top of that, and even if some of this was to blow over, finally, things had gotten to the stage where I would have to make up my mind what I was going to do about Mu. Marriage to Mu. Now that was something to think about. Mu with the cousins beyond number. Mu whose business dealings, if they didn't land us all in jail, could some day leave her bigger than General Motors. Mu who had strong, I won't say dogmatic, ideas about the way any man of hers should behave, what was correct conduct and so on. Mu who believed in ghosts everywhere, who laid out more on astrologers every month than I spent on Camembert cheese only so she could figure out whether it was an auspicious time to pay the bills or not.

It could be Mu was right. Maybe I didn't belong here. It could be nobody belonged in Bangkok, the way things were going. But I had a choice. Didn't I? I could go back to the States and start over again. Why not? On the other hand, Mu had said this whole business, Bia getting snatched and all, was my fault. Maybe it was at that; and if it was, then you could say I had a responsibility to help fix things. Even if it wasn't really my fault, it could be I had this responsibility.

I was trying to breathe deeply and regularly, something which is hard to do when, one, you are pissed off and, two, you are trying to minimize your intake of exhaust fumes from the slow torrent of buses, cars, and tuk-tuks crawling the street. I was counting each inhalation and exhalation, trying to turn my attention in on the simple business of respiration, in on the odd numbers and out on the even. Mindfulness.

An incredible mass of humanity spilled off the sidewalks onto the road; people moved every which way, eddying around the traffic and the innumerable street stalls. There were vendors selling fruit, selling clothes, selling watches, costume jewelry, cleaning sponges, toothpicks, and second-hand shoes. There was food — all manner of tasty things steaming and sizzling and boiling and smoking, aromas and stinks and scents and, suddenly, a burst of fragrance from a klatch of girls sitting on the pavement stringing garlands of jasmine buds. The vendors were stacked three deep across the sidewalks, so you couldn't make much headway there. If you were in a hurry you had to walk on the street, except that the street was so jammed with other people in a hurry you could hardly move. So there was no place for the cars, of which there would already have been too many even without any people. You could say it was crowded.

The blind street band on the corner was going full blast, the faces of the musicians filled with a quiet intensity, an innocence and vulnerability, a sweetness of expression found only in saints and the blind. Their instruments and amplifiers were set up right in the middle of this hubbub, an unholy clamor of drums and guitars and electric organ and some love song squalled into microphones fifty feet from where a tape vendor was playing classical Pink Floyd at maximum volume. Not for the first time, I wondered if the blind band weren't also deaf. They used to get twenty baht a week off me, on average, till I learned they were run by petty hoods who probably skimmed off most of my contributions for themselves.

A pickup truck full of rambutans was meanwhile blaring the day's prices from a PA system mounted atop the cab; and a kid was hawking blue jeans using an electric bullhorn. Right in my ear, he was doing this.

"Do not feel pissed off," I told myself. "*Jai yen yen*. Be cool." I breathed in and out and counted. "Do not be pissed off." And I strode on, pissed off.

I strode into a gaggle of ladies who stopped right in front of me to have a chat. "Excuse me, please; holy shit," I muttered as I squeezed through. "*Kaw thoht, krap*; Jesus Christ."

Thais amble. Furthermore there is no pedestrian traffic pattern whatsoever. Everybody moves with this timeless kind of deliberation, much like upcountry oxcarts, managing nevertheless to be right in front of me no matter where it is I am going. The problem was, I couldn't get the hang of ambling. Even in the heat and humidity, I couldn't amble. My standard procedure was to look ahead, choose a trajectory, and steam on. That was the way things were done, back in America. And no amount of mindfulness or regular breathing seemed to do anything to lessen the habit. And when people veered directly in front of me or stopped abruptly to mill about in impromptu roadblocks I got pissed off. I couldn't help it. Though I realized I shouldn't do this thing.

"Don't get angry," Mu would tell me. "If you act like that, you give power over yourself to others. The way to do is hold back and watch. You see what the other is doing and why. And you show

197

none of yourself. You wait. Never act from emotion, especially with Thai people. Watch and see, and then do what you decide they want to see or what you want them to see. Don't show yourself."

If you weren't in control of your own temper, then you were never in control of the situation, whatever it might be. So getting angry was only hurting yourself, leaving yourself open to trouble. Second, I had to ask myself sometimes: Why the hurry? Take this day, for example — all I was doing was going for a walk to straighten out my thinking on a few matters. What difference did it make how far I got and how fast? I wasn't going anywhere; I was just going. So why not relax and enjoy it? Third, this was Thailand, as Mu kept pointing out, and these people were Thais, walking in the Thai Way. They were right, and I was wrong. If I wanted to walk in my way and not find every sidewalk and street an obstacle course, then I should go and walk in Peoria or someplace. This was probably part of what Hip meant when he said I was always doing the Funky Chicken in the middle of the Thai waltz.

So I tried to slow down. I counted and I breathed. And I swore under my breath and sweated. Not for the first time, it occurred to me that maybe Mu was right. And Hip. Maybe I wasn't cut out for life in Asia. At that instant, a phalanx of uniformed schoolgirls materialized in front of me, causing me to swerve to the side. And as I did do, I was brought to a sudden halt by a stab of acute pain. I had swerved right into this metal street sign that was mounted too low to take account of tall farangs. The corner of the sign had grazed my head, edge-on, just enough to almost lobotomize me.

"You! You!" A couple of the passers-by were addressing me.

I felt a trickle of what turned out to be blood run down from my scalp. I smiled at everybody, showing none of myself, and I said "*Mai pen rai*. For Christ's sake. Hey, no problem." Some looked relieved and others looked disappointed, and none of them paid any more attention, except for the pineapple vendor who offered

198

me a wad of tissue paper. I strode on, dabbing at my crown and wondering if I needed a tetanus shot.

Back in the States I could walk around and never think that my blood pressure, never mind any street sign, was about to lift the top of my head off. Nobody back there was threatening to kill me, kidnapping me and my friends every time I turned around. And it wasn't so hot. And you could go for walks without your chest starting to hurt, the way mine was now; if this air got any worse, we'd soon all be dead already and the gunmen could go to the beach and relax.

It was no doubt harder to make a living as a writer back in the States. But what was I writing here, when it came down to it? I was flirting with terminal hack-writerdom. And to make things worse, I was now on Fat Fat's payroll.

Mu had found a white hair on me only the week before. I was too young for white hairs, she told me, and she was right. This was from writing brochures, I claimed. Though I had to admit it: Fat Fat and his crew scared me silly, and possibly it was them turning my hair white as well. Any thought of going back to Luckyland filled me with very bad feelings indeed.

It might be best for all concerned, I had to think, if I split. If I wasn't around to piss Fat Fat off, maybe he would just let Bia go. She hadn't done anything to him, after all. And he had no reason to hurt Mu or anybody else.

I wasn't much use to Mu or anybody anyway. She was the one doing all the planning with Willie and Tommy and even Hip. They could speak Thai in a way I couldn't, for one thing.

"Anyway," I told myself aloud, getting some interested glances from the passers-by, "You're only a babe in the woods." I didn't understand the Thai Way; I was going to get us all killed. It was better if I left Thailand and let the experts get on with it.

And the pollution. Here I had been walking for less that half an

199

hour, and there was this tightness in my chest. Though whether this was air pollution or intimations of still more acute forms of lead poisoning it was hard to say.

So I bought a pack of cigarettes. I smoked as I walked. I smoked and thought about radioactive isotopes and how I had read that hydrocarbons from exhaust emissions settle on the glowing end of a cigarette and turn into radioactive isotopes that accumulate in your lungs and throat and eventually give you cancer. And ever since my pipe got shot I had been smoking cigarettes like a demon. Even if you didn't smoke, you inhaled the equivalent crap of two or three packs a day, with this traffic. So what the hell. So *mai pen rai*, right?

I was oppressed by more than the tightness in my chest, though. There was the crassness, the constant throb of greed and carelessness in the air. Driven by Singapore penis envy, the construction boom had concrete and glass monstrosities thrusting up on all sides, the cranes like huge metal stick insects come down to earth to refashion the environment according to some alien ideal of what is appropriate.

There was this constant element of impermanence; you never knew what the city was going to look like from one week to the next. And over there across the road was that great big supermarket. They broke every article in the building code putting that up. Now it sold rotting vegetables, stale eggs and stale bread yet at the same time charged higher prices than anywhere in town. The open market had had far fresher produce at better prices, but as of a few months before it had been removed to make way for the multistorey parking garage that was needed to service the new supermarket and the adjoining department store. This was what you called progress.

Buildings kept rising on all sides higher and higher till there was no breeze left to blow away the smog, and the concrete and glass had already turned Bangkok into a simmering heat island three degrees hotter than its surroundings. Meanwhile the old community life in the streets — the sidewalk restaurants and shops open on the street — were being progressively closed off by the air-conditioned malls and boutiques and the traffic. Land kept doubling in value every year, appreciating so fast you could sometimes feel it shudder with delight right under your feet. Rents were going up to the point ordinary people had nowhere to live anymore. And the background to everything was the noise, the incredible noise.

Of course that time I went back to the States for a visit, I had missed it all. The streets had seemed like sets from some science-fiction movie where the city had been evacuated. It was so quiet it gave me the creeps; and it had taken me two weeks to start feeling homesick for Bangkok. You figure it out.

*

I felt calmer when I got home. Or maybe I was only tired.

The opinion of the working committee was now that I should instead lie low until the master plan was ready. It might simply complicate matters to have me in Luckyland before they knew how we were going to proceed. Though it could turn out, if Hip's sources couldn't come up with the information we needed, I'd have go back to Luckyland and case the joint a bit more. For now, however, it was best to hide out at Hip's place.

Mu, on the other hand, wanted me to go to ground till the whole thing was over. She didn't think I ought to get involved with things any more than I was already, being a babe in the woods the way I was. "Go back home. Go to the United States and live with Esther," is what she told me.

And I had to think this might not be such a bad plan, except the part where I got to live with Esther; though I knew Mu didn't really mean it.

But I never had a chance to run for the States; I never got to lie low. I never even managed to hear any of the Plan. That very evening I was walking back to the apartment to get some clothes so I could move in with Hip for awhile, when I saw Big Lek the somtam lady waving and carrying on in the soi. When I got close enough to see what was up, I realized she had been trying to tell me to run for it.

Fun and Co. were waiting to take me for another ride. This time they didn't bother putting a bag on my head, which gave me the idea they didn't care if I knew where I was going or not, which in turn gave me the idea I might be in some trouble.

And I was right.

live show

GOURMET ALERT! The government has issued a warning: don't buy fried grasshoppers from street vendors. It seems people upcountry are netting the grasshoppers in their tens of thousands and then spraying them with large quantities of insecticide. This is not intended as a garnish; it is merely a convenient means of subduing the creatures before they are shipped to buyers in the city.

SALT OF THE EARTH. Notoriously, the people of the Northeast will eat anything that moves, not to mention quite a few things that don't. Now reports have it that many children have taken to eating clay. Some theory has it that the earth has beneficial effects on the digestion, and these kids instinctively recognize this. A more likely hypothesis: You'll eat anything if you're hungry enough. Unsuccessfully supporting one third of the country's population, the Northeast enjoys only a pitiful proportion of the national income. The land has been denuded of forest, and as a result is now alternately plagued with drought and flooding. Many of the children of the Northeast have no recourse but to leave for the south, often to go into prostitution, there being too few jobs of a more respectable type, even in the booming construction industry.

FORTUNATELY THERE ARE LOTS MORE WORKERS. After traffic accidents, construction mishaps are the biggest killer in the country. In the rush to build more and taller buildings everywhere they can, many people are cutting corners, often with disastrous results. Increasingly, buildings are collapsing even before they are completed, which one would think is just plain bad business. Meanwhile, installing safety nets on the sides of buildings under construction is simply too expensive, or so we're told. The tendency for heavy bits of things to drop off and fall crashing to the street, sometimes even through the roofs of neighboring buildings, tends to be written off as one more unfortunate cost of progress. Anyway, when your number's up it's up, whether there are safety nets or not. So there you are.

"YOU. FARANG. EAT." Fat Fat was at his most solicitous. "This is nice Thai dish. I order it special."

I concentrated on the taste, which was too not bad at that, and I concentrated on not thinking about what the *mangda*s looked like before they were mashed into the purplish sauce into which I was dipping bits of raw vegetable. This was a selective mindfulness, and it showed my meditation practice had been having some effect. *Nam phrik gapi mangda* has a pleasing aroma anyway, an unspecifiable taste that is reputedly at its best when the beetle is in heat. It has something to do with its sex glands. Though I was trying not to think about these matters as I ate.

In fact I was pretty hungry, seeing as how I had just been kept locked in a room for three days with no food. No food, no tobacco, nobody to talk to, not once, and fusion jazz about fourteen hours a day. I tell you. Nothing to do but practice my mindfulness exercises, and these exercises kept making me mindful of things I didn't want to think about.

All in all, as I said, it was a tasty sauce; and I ate it up with what could have passed for relish, if you didn't examine my attitude too closely. But then Fat Fat had the waitress bring the *pièce de résistance*. She set down a large bowl, and in the bowl were some whole mangdas, big flat beetles scrabbling to get up the sides and no doubt away from anything that looked like a Thai chef. Each was at least three inches long.

"Is-sey, my fen'," Fat Fat smiled at me. "You eat."

I told him I was kind of full already.

"You eat, or you run. Dead Show."

Fun and his aides perked right up, and they stationed themselves either side of me in what I could see was a hopeful manner.

I'd eaten fried grasshoppers, which weren't too bad on the whole. I'd eaten fermented fish that smelled worse than old socks. I'd even eaten Mu's attempt at chili con carne, once. But nothing I'd eaten compared with the experience of eating a live mangda. Life's rich pageant. You wouldn't have believed how strong the legs on those critters were, pushing away trying to get my mouth open again so they could leave. I managed to duck under the table and grab the cuspidor before I puked, and only then remembered the Chinese waiter at that first meal with Fat Fat. But Fat Fat had other plans for me.

I was getting the idea Fat Fat already knew about Izzy's article. And I was right again.

"Farang," said Fat Fat. "Now you know something about mangda; maybe you go write story about them now, *na?*"

"You will write Mr Fat a story tomorrow," Fatman No.1 elaborated. "You will explain how everything you said before was a mistake, and how Mr Fat has many good sides. You will sleep here tonight. Tomorrow you will write a story like you never write before. If this story is not such a story—if Mr Fat is not one hundred percent happy with this story and possibly more than that, then you will be in the Dead Show. You will run until you die. Your ladyfriend will shoot you. We will hurt her until she sees she must shoot you. Do you understand what I am saying, farang?"

I waited for Fun to punctuate this proposal with "Farang dogshit," but he only grinned hugely and showed me his gun. Everybody seemed to be in very good spirits, on the whole, and this assembly could have made a fine Land of Smiles poster for the Tourism Authority. So I grinned back, wiped some puke from my chin, and I said "I understand," which was all any reasonable person could have said under the circumstances.

205

Still and all, I wasn't as cool as that, not entirely. I was actually thinking it would be nice not to die just yet; and I was busy thinking of ways out of this mess, only nothing was coming to mind. But I could see there was a very good chance indeed that I was going to die. Quite soon, I was going to do this thing, if I was any judge of which way the wind was blowing. I could write all the Izzy Scoop stories I wanted, for one thing, and nobody was going to publish them. Hip and his magazines were going to have to help me out on this one, if I ever got to leave Luckyland again; and I didn't care how much the advertisers would be unhappy.

With any luck, I would survive a couple of days, though I wouldn't have made book on that. And I didn't even know when Willie and the others were going to make their move, much less what that move might be.

*

"Now we see live show," Fat Fat said.

This one was to be a special show, you could see that right away. Not like the modest affair we had witnessed last time.

For one thing, we were seated at cafe tables with white linen and vases with orchids. Waitresses, some more young girls in lacy wee G-strings, tottered about on high-heels taking orders for food and drink, taut little buns going every which way. There was an audience of about twenty men and no women.

Fat Fat was being the perfect host with his important guests and Fatman No.2, while I was at a table with Fatman No.1, who clearly resented this, and Fun, who clearly did not. From the wolfish grins he kept turning on me, I had the feeling he was relishing proceedings more than just somewhat. Then I got an idea why.

"You. Farang dogshit. Raidy you come now. Now raidy Khun Fat." Fun showed me all his teeth. "You no pum-pum, Mr Fat pum-pum, no ploblem."

From stage left appeared a wedding procession. first came a

double file of girls, carrying baskets and naked but for long diaphanous white wedding veils in their hair. They were strewing orchid blossoms in the path of the two grooms, one an enormous Arabic-looking individual with bushy mustaches and a barely tumescent dick that hung halfway to his knees, the other an average sort of Thai guy who slouched along looking sheepish. Their bride was the same elfin creature who had been the ping-pong person's ball girl last time. Carrying the train of her elaborate wedding dress came Bia.

At first I didn't recognize her; she looked different. Then I saw what they had done to her. The bastards. They'd cut her bangs.

The bride threw her wedding bouquet in Fat Fat's general direction, and one of his men picked it up and brought it to his table. Smiling and giggling like a bashful big toad at this flattering attention, Fat Fat then motioned for Bia to come and join him, holding the flowers out to her with some ceremony. I tried not to notice how fetching Bia's little breasts were, or how nicely set up her bottom was, framed that way in its lacy blue and white G-string. I had wondered about these matters, from time to time, seeing Bia around the apartment in a towel and so on. Of course all the bruises tended to detract from her youthful charm.

"Raidy you melly Khun Fat next time, sure. Hee, hee." Fun poked me companionably in the temple with his pistol, and I gave him a big smile.

It was worse, I found, when the person was someone dear to you. This shouldn't have surprised me, if I'd thought about it. It also shouldn't have surprised me to find that Bia was pretty dear to me. But she was, and it did. And it hurt me considerably to have her in any way connected with this affair.

Maybe it was karma, and I shouldn't have been writing porno novels for Propriapist Publications no matter how much I needed the money and no matter how much I claimed it was okay as long

207

as I kept my tongue in my cheek. Mu had told me again and again that didn't make it any better, and I had to learn to show more respect for myself. Could be she was right, like I said; and I mused along these lines as I sat there. All things considered, I was on a real downer. For lack of anything better to do, I fingered my amulet and thought about how, if I lived through this interesting experience, it could be I'd go back to the States and see what was what in that part of the world for awhile. I even thought about Esther, and about what life with her might be like once you got used to it.

So there I was, thinking this and thinking that and getting so depressed, to tell the truth, I just about wanted to cry. I looked over at Bia, and she was trying to look anywhere except at the stage, or at the naked waitresses, or at the girl under Fat Fat's table who was ministering to his needs in that area. Now Bia was trying to look over at me, but Fat Fat kept grabbing her by her neck and twisting her around so she could see what was happening.

"Look, *look*. See?" he was exclaiming with delight.

After the consummation of the marriage, we were treated to a full program of fleshly delights. The audience were having the time of their lives, drinking and cheering and expressing disbelief at what groups of human beings were able to do to themselves and to one another, if it was required of them. They kept drinking toasts to Fat Fat, who kept beaming and nodding and fluttering. He was quite flushed with the success of his evening, not to mention whiskey and sexual arousal.

They brought out two boys, and Fun really loved this one, calling over to me "You like? Farang dogshit. You like? Pum-pum *phoochai*, yeah?"

After the boys went skipping off, a woman came out and started pushing needles through her nipples, which were unusually long and strangely pendulous. This procedure held everyone rapt; even Bia was spellbound.

Fat Fat got so interested he forgot to eat for a couple of minutes. He banged his hand on the table, upsetting a bowl of soup in the process, and called: "You. Come here."

The woman shielded her eyes against the footlights and looked out at us, scared. But she came, of course. Before she climbed off the stage she began to take out the needles, but Fat Fat barked at her and she left them there.

Fat Fat was curious. He pulled at a needle experimentally, sliding it back and forth a bit. It was surprising; there was no blood. In an experimental vein, then, he pinched two of the needles together. The woman smiled desperately over at me and at Fun, perhaps seeing something benign in that mess of teeth, and then she looked away to a corner of the room where there was no one. Fat Fat twisted until she gave a sharp gasp and said, "*Garuna*. Please." He slid one needle all the way out at that, and poked it at the tender flesh a few times as the woman tried to hold still. finally he pulled the nipple out to its full extension and pushed the needle right through. The woman yelped and bit her lip, blood welling and dripping, but only from her nipple. It ran in a dark line down her belly and into her pubic bush.

Fat Fat giggled, patently satisfied that this body had finally decided to behave in a standard manner, and waved her away. He said something to Fatman No.2, who stopped the Human Pincushion and gave her money, first reaching to tug at the needles himself, bemused. Some men at other tables then called her over so they could take a closer look as well. This puzzle was the highlight of the evening thus far.

Our host took a fork and stabbed gently at his towel girl's nipples and then at her crotch, merry as could be; and she gave him a big smile, you could see how fond she was of him. She swiped at his face with a towel and patted his stomach.

Fat Fat was in a rare mood, this evening. Everybody was laughing and carrying on and having a grand old time; and it was almost difficult to remember that I was going to be dead shortly if I wasn't careful.

In the meantime, some stagehands had been at work, and two girls of about Bia's age had taken to writhing around together naked in a huge champagne goblet bubble bath. They looked a lot like the waitresses from my first visit to the Luckyland One. Clean young flesh was getting pressed up against the glass in ways that spoke directly to Fat Fat's soul, judging by the amount of giggling and shaking going on. He kept squeezing Bia's bottom and stroking her legs, but he went no further than that. You needed discipline to be Boss of Bosses around here, and he wasn't about to spoil his birthday present before time.

"Dead Show." Fat Fat hollered at me, but he didn't elaborate.

I was feeling not too pleased with things as they stood. So it was a surprise and something of a relief to get the message from the marker-pen girl. She come out on the stage and squatted down over a big sheet of paper, performing her peculiarly graceful contortions as she moved crabwise across the page. first she wrote something in Thai, and all the Thais applauded enthusiastically and beamed at Fat Fat. Then she wrote some more, on another piece of paper; she stood and held the scrawl up for everyone to see:

WE HIP. NOT TO FRET

She looked in my direction and smiled.

Now how had Hip ever managed that? I wondered, feeling some of the awe his legions of demimondaine admirers generally expressed for his powers. It did wonders for my morale, anyway; and I started to think maybe I wasn't a dead man after all.

Fat Fat didn't get the message, of course. He didn't get any message, and this irritated him. He barked at Fun, who went up and slapped the girl a couple of times across the head and then returned to his seat. This time she wrote something in Japanese, and the Japanese contingent erupted into pleased smiles and applause.

Bia had been busy trying to keep her face pointed at the ceiling through most of the show. For one thing, of course, Bia didn't like people to see her eyes. More importantly, you had to suspect, the ceiling was the only place not full of naked girls and leering perverts.

Or so it seemed until the ceiling, to Bia's and pretty well everybody else's dumbfoundment, suddenly began to open. The stained-glass rosette slid into a recess and, fifteen feet in diameter, a hole gaped at us. The assembly was spellbound as the lights went down and strobes started to flick their baleful hysteria around the room.

Abruptly a motorcycle started revving. No ordinary motorcycle, this one belonged to some malevolent biker god. The deafening cough and roar and throb vibrated in the marrow of your bones. The revving of the engine was taken up and reinforced by an electric guitar, blasting us with a tidal wave of rock'n'roll sufficient to turn a tape vendor impotent. It was hallucinogenic. The first thing that came to my mind was we were all going to have to go on a walkathon. But that was not in fact the case.

While the music raged to a triumphant pitch, a mass of chrome and steel began to descend through the ceiling aperture. A gleaming Harley-Davidson 1200 lowered into sight, swinging slowly around its cable. As it emerged, you had to notice a bunch of bare feet — four of them, to be exact. And these feet were attached, two apiece, to a man and woman. These young people were astride the bike, the woman furthermore astride the man, who wore only a Nazi helmet, spiked armlets, and spurs. What a weird individual was Mr Fat, was all I had to say, which was safe enough to say since for sure no one could hear me through that din.

There was nowhere for Bia to look away to now, even if, under

211

the circumstances, she had had the presence of mind to look away. The champagne glass had been spirited away while we were mesmerized by the noise and lights and feet. But now the stage was a frenzied phantasmagoria of jerky blue-white figures in carnal knots of two to four, with the couple on the motorcycle the centerpiece.

Eventually things wound down, and everyone took a bow, a nice curtain call. The biker picked up the girl from where she lay on the floor, slung her over his shoulder, and everybody trooped off stage right through a door. The motorcycle itself ascended through the storm of hard rock and strobes and disappeared once more into the ceiling, which closed behind it.

The Japanese gentlemen were still applauding enthusiastically, and I was wondering what could ever follow such an exhibition, when there was the muffled sound of an explosion from somewhere outside. A big explosion, audible through a break in the rock'n'roll. Then another. And another.

Fat Fat turned towards our table and barked interrogatively at Fatman No.1. You could see from his face he wasn't in the mood for explosions right at that moment, especially explosions he knew nothing about. Fatman No.1 then barked in a similar vein at Fun, who told sent some of his pals to check things out. Fun himself stuck to minding me for the time being.

The rosette had closed up once more, and Bia was looking at the ceiling again — careless of how this ceiling had already betrayed her once before. Suddenly there was an almighty crash, louder than the music even, followed almost immediately by another, and a huge metal object, as big as a bank vault, came smashing through the ceiling — right through the rosette and down onto stage center, coming to rest in a pile of splintered flooring and glass and bits of Harley-Davidson. What a showstopper.

My, my, I was thinking. Fat Fat was certainly sparing no expense for this one. What was going to crawl out of the bucket, I wondered. A couple of fucking elephants? No matter how depressed I was, I had to admit this act had caught my attention.

Even though I didn't have the faintest idea what the hell was evolving here, I had to admit it was impressive. It had style. Willie and Tommy were just never going to stand accused of being standard, not if they had anything to do with it. And this monstrous metal bucket sitting there on the stage was a masterpiece, especially with the strobes still flicking away. The music had stopped, which somehow lent this *objet* even more of a presence.

So that's how it stood for the space of several seconds. We all sat there stupefied with admiration and various other emotions, while the bucket sat there and stared mutely back. Neither elephants nor anything else issued from it to relieve the suspense.

One of the Japanese, the drunkest one, started to clap again, but that died down in a hurry once he and his buddies started to see which way the wind was blowing.

Fat Fat stood up and started screaming and fluttering frantically. His fly was wide open, but I felt this was neither the time nor the place to point it out. The lesser fatmen, plus all the hard boys who were still with us, also got up to make their departure. Fun grabbed me and indicated I should join the exodus, underlining this idea by ramming the muzzle of his pistol up under my jaw.

Bia and the waitresses, not to mention the performers who were huddled at stage right and the audience, who were showing signs of confusion, were being left behind to ponder the enigma of the bucket by themselves. I looked back and tried to smile reassuringly at Bia, feeling that she was too young and had led, until recently, too sheltered a life to be left alone with situations such as this one. But it was almost impossible to smile reassuringly with the gun shoved up under my chin, and I could see Mu's sister was upset despite my best efforts. As we went out, all the girls were huddled together in a fetching way that would no doubt have done Fat Fat's

213

heart good to see. Some Japanese meanwhile had taken to huddling together under a table, a delayed reflex probably instilled by lifetimes spent waiting for earthquakes.

We went directly to the control room, where the alarms were whooping away, and where Fat Fat screamed at a technician to turn them off, leaving only the sound of elevator jazz and heavy breathing. The twenty screens were ablaze with action. What a program. This was all hell breaking loose, and I had a pretty good notion who was responsible.

On one screen, you could see that the walls on one side of the compound had been smashed in. Now we knew what the explosions had been.

There was a stream of people fleeing the casino — a regular Who's Who of the society pages, you had to imagine, though I personally recognized no more than one or two of them. The majority were trying to get out through the breach in the walls. This was in preference to trying the front entrance. According to other monitors, there were a small army of policemen out that way, some of them hammering on the big metal gate, to no effect whatsoever. One had a bullhorn to his mouth.

Under the circumstances, wealth, you could say, had lost some of its faith in its own impunity.

Over at the Shaking Heaven, there was also all kinds of action. Most of it involved girls and johns in various states of undress rushing around like they were in a Buster Keaton movie. Only one guy was determined to get his money's worth, forget about how much his attendant thrashed about like someone who had pressing business elsewhere.

Meanwhile Fat Fat's large staff of dangerous people were hustling around waving guns at everything in sight. All in all, this was the most interesting television I had ever seen anywhere.

The Dobermans were snapping at the crocodiles, while the

snakes were mostly busy trying to stay out of everyone's way, though a couple were obviously pissed off, reared up and hoods spread, swaying back and forth and looking for an opening. I didn't know where the snakes had come from; nobody had said anything about snakes. The next thing you knew, one Doberman was dragging itself in circles, a nine-foot cobra attached to a hindquarter, while another dog had a different cobra in its jaws and was snapping it back and forth in a frenzy. I even saw one pillar of the community try kicking a dog, which turned out to be a bad policy under these circumstances, since we then also had a rich person, who was of course by no means a criminal, nevertheless trying to get over the remnants of a wall with a Doberman attached to his ass. The crocodiles, on the whole, were trying to keep a low profile. For the most part, though, it was a fine inter-specific donnybrook, one that would have defied the powers of a Howard Cosell commentary.

The sight of these community pillars up to their assholes in crocodiles and snakes and Dobermans was indeed an edifying thing. It probably would have been a relief to most of these citizens to have some police around by this time, only the police appeared to be up to their own assholes in Fat Fat's defense system on the other side of the compound.

The two lesser fatmen were busy on telephones and walkie-talkies, barking at various minions while they stabbed fat fingers at video screens. Fat Fat himself sat in the center of things, staring wildly all around, scowling at his lieutenants and wolfing fried rice from a big plate someone had brought him. Even though the room was air-conditioned to the point I could have used a sweater, Fat Fat was sweating. Sweating and snorting as he shoveled in great spoonfuls of rice, smacking and whining away to himself as he tried to make sense of the spectacle unfolding on his monitors.

Then he stopped. And so did the lesser fatmen. On Screen

No.8, where the giant bucket had up till then been sitting like the Enigma of the Ages, things were happening. Beings were emerging from the vessel, and the first of these beings was none other than Mu's cousin Rhot, who was carrying an M-16 assault rifle. His face was still a mess from the pistol-whipping.

I suddenly remembered Rhot's boozy stories about patrol duty with the Rangers down on the Malaysian border, and it occurred to me that perhaps it hadn't been total bullshit after all.

"Rhot!" I said, which was not a smart thing to say just at that time. But maybe nobody had heard me, I thought.

He swung first one leg over the side and then the other, balanced for a second and then dropped down, crouching and moving to take cover behind the far side of the stage.

The next face to appear did not surprise me half as much, this particular space cadet being none other than the noted layer-waste-of-all-things-obstructionist Wrong-Way Willie Wong. Willie had blood streaming down the side of his head. With Rhot providing covering fire if needed, Willie also first disembarked and then dismounted the stage, taking up a strategic position with his Uzi.

"Who are these people?" Fat Fat was stabbing his finger at Screen No.8 and turning purple.

The next face to appear I could have made money on, if anybody had wanted to bet with me. Tommy Two-Toes must have landed harder than anybody else, though, because he looked totally fed up. Even with translation into electronic signals and transmission through camera and wires and video monitor, the Look had force, and there wasn't anybody in the control room, including Fat Fat himself, who didn't flinch.

Tommy had locked onto the video camera. He raised his 11mm pistol, sighted in on us, and the screen went blank.

There was an excited gabble, as everybody forgot about the other screens and stared at the space where Tommy had only re-

216

cently been.

"You! Farang." Fat Fat indicated he wanted to talk to me. Fun still had his gun on me. He shoved me over towards the table.

"You sit!" Fat Fat's eyes were hooded.

I sat down across the little table from him.

"Who is 'Rhot'?"

"Doesn't that mean 'car,' in Thai?" I asked. In fact, Rhot was named 'Rhot' because he had been born in the back seat of a car.

Fat Fat told me to stand up and lean over closer. He told me to do this in a tone of voice I didn't want to argue with, especially when Fun rammed the barrel of his automatic into the back of my head. The lesser fatmen had come over to stand either side of me, now, and I was getting this twinge of claustrophobia. It didn't help that I was starving to death and needed a smoke so bad my lungs ached.

Fun said something to Fat Fat, and even without understanding what he said I could read in Fat's face that Fun had recognized Rhot.

Fat Fat half rose to meet me, still chewing a mouthful of rice. He grabbed the chain on my amulet and twisted it up in his fist till it cut into my neck. He was barking in my face in Thai and Chinese and none of it did I understand. Meanwhile Fun kept ramming the gun into the back of my head, which made me uncomfortable; and I was leaning over so far I was afraid that any minute I was going to take a dive into Fat Fat's plate of rice. Fatman No.1 told me Fat Fat wanted to know what I knew about these interesting events.

"Nothing," I answered. "I thought this was all part of the show."

"Farang dogshit!" said Fun, and drove his gun into my kidney, I guess for a change.

Fatman No.2 grabbed my hair in one hand and drew a knife gently across my throat with the other. The keen smarting and a tickle of blood running down inside my shirt told me I had been cut. I was starting to think the timing of Willie's raid had gone seriously haywire, at least from my point of view.

"You will answer Mr Fat's questions now, farang," Fatman No.1 informed me.

Fat Fat himself was screaming at me at a range of about four inches, bits of rice and spittle flying into my face and making me sick. He twisted and yanked on my chain till the blood roared in my ears and I couldn't have told him *jai yen yen* even if I'd thought that was a good idea. Abruptly he released me and fell back into his chair. "One minute, farang. One minute and then you tell me. Or you die." He scooped a big spoonful of rice and tossed it back like you stoke a boiler, snorting and chewing mightily.

This was not good, I thought. This would be a poor time to die, with help so close at hand. Come on Willie, Tommy, I thought. Move it.

I reached for my amulet, thinking maybe its power had finally worn off after all, probably drained by my bad karma. But there was no amulet. The chain was still there, but the little clay figure was gone.

I had just started to put two and two together, and I was running my eye over the table, when Fat Fat started to choke. He rose from his seat, clutching at his throat, gagging and trying to gasp and turning purple.

The fatmen and Fun and the others all gathered around as Fat Fat subsided to the floor, choking on my amulet. You might have expected somebody to start pounding him on the back or something. After all, these were supposed to be his buddies. It could be they suffered the same inhibition that allowed commoners to stand by as royalty drowned, it being a capital crime, in the old days here in Thailand, to lay hands on a member of the royal family.

I had learned about the Heimlich maneuver and that stuff way back when. But to tell the truth I wasn't so keen on seeing Fat Fat in good health. Anyway, I noticed that Fun put his gun down for a minute so he could try to pull Fat Fat up off the floor. It really is a disgrace, I agree with Willie, what professional standards have come to these days.

At the same time I went for the pistol, I snapped a piston kick right at Fun's arse, which was conveniently turned towards me as he bent over. Gun in hand, I yelled "Reach for the sky, assholes!" Most of the people present were able to figure out what I was after, given my general manner and tone of voice, but two of the hard boys were plainly confused by my choice of idiom. "Put your hands up!" I elaborated. "Up, *up.*"

Fun got back to his feet and merely grinned, though not too happily, seeing as how I had launched him nose-first into the floor and, adding insult to injury, swiped his arsenal besides.

"Farang. You no shoot. Cannot."

"Oh, yeah?" I said, thinking that probably I could if I had to. I was no killer, okay; but Fun was a special case, in my mind.

"Cannot shoot. Safety. No safety." He was smiling and gesturing helpfully towards the gun.

I knew he was trying to bluff me. The trouble was, I was not one-hundred percent sure where the safety catch was, much less whether it was off or on. I could see Fun sizing me up for a tackle. And the fatmen were making moves that smacked of going for their guns.

So I tested it. I pulled the trigger.

This had the consequence of making a loud noise and blowing away the video monitor that had been showing the lack of progress the police had made coming in through the northern defenses. Fun stopped smiling, and everybody except Fatman No.2 stopped going for their guns.

The latter individual I shot.

219

Wyatt Earp I'm not, needless to say, not even knowing which is the safety catch and which is the clutch. Nevertheless, as it happened I hit No.2 right in the gun. He went over backwards, what with the impact of an 11mm slug whanging him in the gun and then glancing off to put a hole in his armpit.

I got a solid two-handed grip on the pistol and sighted in on Fun's teeth next, imagining the shower of ivory and blood, and I wondered how many bullets this gun had in it. I was also wondering how to say "Put your guns down and turn to the wall" in Thai.

I was wondering a lot of things. Things such as where the hell were Willie and Tommy and what was I paying them for anyway?

I was also thinking what a hard thing it was to shoot a man in the mouth, even this man and this mouth, when I noticed Fatman No.1 reaching down and then raising something towards me. At the same time I swung the barrel of my pistol towards him, I was aware of Fun lunging towards me. And at that moment Fun's face did explode, and there probably were teeth all over the joint, though I didn't stop to check. Everybody in the room hit the floor, including me, as we tried to duck the incredible storm of bullets that followed. I had my nose pressed flat against the floor, my hands over my head, and for once I wasn't thinking anything. Nothing at all. I was only waiting to see what existence had in store, always supposing there was going to be any further existence in which to store things.

Eventually, the shooting stopped, and I heard a voice say "Jack."

I opened my eyes and looked up to see Hip bending anxiously towards me.

"Hip!" I said. "Thank God. Give me a cigarette."

*

So there we were, standing by the door to the control room having a talk just like we hadn't seen each other in years. Willie was jacking another magazine into his Uzi and telling me we had to hurry; Tommy was already on his way back to the theater to rejoin Rhot, who had been left behind look after the girls. "I see they cut your throat," said Hip in a conversational tone, as though this was something that happened to most people from time to time. "Your shirt is a mess."

"Yeah," I answered him.

And then I blasted Fatman No.1 in the face, which I admit was just a lucky shot, seeing as how I didn't even know where the safety catch was on one of these pistols and I had smoke in my eyes as well. Fat Fat's chief lieutenant had appeared over the edge of the table with a gun and an unpleasant expression pointed at Hip's back.

"Yo, Arno. Thanks for that." And Hip did look grateful, once he saw what the score was and why I was going around shooting off guns and scaring the shit out of people.

"Good job, farang. You, I mean. Jack." Willie was clearly in his element. He looked ten years younger, and moved with a confidence that was entirely inspiring. He turned, just before we left the control room, and used his Uzi to hose down the few remaining monitors and a couple of the guards who might have still been moving.

The rest of it went like clockwork, sort of. Tommy and Rhot were waiting for us in the showroom with Bia and the rest of them. The audience had split, that part of it which wasn't lying around dead, and they were out there taking their chances with the dogs and crocodiles and suchlike. None of the girls who had elected to go with us had much more than a stitch on, so we wrapped them up in some linen tablecloths and lifted them aboard.

You can say anything you like about men who go around making a living by shooting and otherwise hassling people, but Tommy and Willie were real gentlemen. Not only did they wrap all the girls

221

in tablecloths, they put them in the bucket first. Only then did the rest of us climb aboard.

Willie turned to Tommy so his partner could get at the little khaki pack he had on his back. Producing a stubby pistol with a bore like a toilet roll, Tommy reached up and fired a flare through the hole in the ceiling. About ten seconds later we were on our way. We briefly got hooked up with some parts of the roof on our way out, and for a second I feared we might have to go out through the interesting times in the compound instead. But whoever was operating the crane could have been an old trout fisherman, the way he played our getaway conveyance, and in a second or two we were away, soaring high into the night sky.

High into a night sky that was all lit up red and also seemed to be full of flying bullets, judging by the constant ringing and whanging on our bucket. You had to wonder for a minute if the alternative route might not have been best after all. We could also see spotlights were playing on the cable and on the clouds of smog above us, but nobody was in the mood to try looking over the side to try shooting them out.

"Tommy," Willie said. "You bring flares with parachutes on them. This is a bad policy, I have to think."

"*Chai*," answered Tommy. "Yes."

Anyway, it didn't matter so much about the parachute on the flare, because it was only a moment later that the fireworks went off. You could hear the pop-popping and some bangs and there was probably lots more than we got to see since, looking out through the top of the bucket, all we could make out were the rocket-bursts. It was pretty, though.

"I make him about twelve minutes late with the fireworks show," said Hip. "How could he screw up that badly?"

"You just can't find good help these days," Willie suggested.

The fireworks display had the effect of distracting the ladies from their attempts to out-scream each other, which was nice. And the shooting seemed to have let up, though of course by now we had been swung way around to the other side of the condo.

"Hip. Where are we going now?" I was pleased to hear how steady my voice was.

"Yo, Arno. Don't worry."

"*Mai pen rai*, Jack," added Willie. "We have a truck waiting."

At that instant we stopped. We hung there swinging for a few seconds, then we dropped fast enough to leave my stomach somewhere up there in the night sky above us. The ladies took to screaming again as we crashed through the roof of some place, coming to rest in a brightly lit room full of other people who were screaming. They didn't build things to last in Bangkok, was my impression; but I could understand that, since anything you built was going to be torn down to make way for a condominium anyway.

There we were, a pile of people all mashed down in the bottom of our bucket, listening to the sound of unhappy voices expressing emotions in a way Thais were not supposed to express their feelings in public. And a sudden swirl of frigid air carried with it the smell of hamburgers and french fries, which was just about enough to drive me crazy. I hadn't had anything to eat for three days, after all; the *nam phrik gapi mangda*, which I'd heaved anyway, didn't count.

When I pulled myself up and peeked over the rim of our spacecraft, I saw that we were in an A&W. Could you believe it? Way out here in the suburbs, and the aliens had invaded even before we got there. As far as I could make out, we hadn't landed on any people, but we were blocking the stairway to the ground floor, and a small crowd of local fast-food freaks were massed over behind the counter with the staff, everybody totally forgetting to maintain their jai yen. I thought about asking someone to toss me a hamburger or two, but my Thai is a disgrace. By the time I doped out what I had to say, the bucket had started to ascend again.

And I was yelling "No, no."

Tommy and Willie, on the other hand, were yelling "*Mai chai; mai chai,*" which is about the same thing, while Rhot and Hip were not saying much of anything, only trying to calm the girls down. These individuals were all making shrill noises, which created an unfavorable atmosphere if you were trying to think what to do in a situation such as this one.

We had caught the edge of the ceiling on the way out, and there was a great rending and screeching of building materials that failed to cover the sounds of more screaming from somewhere below us.

Then we were swinging free, and we were thinking thank God for this, when suddenly we swung way around and dropped again. This time we didn't go through any roof. Instead, we first slammed into the side of something — another building, as it turned out — so that we were all in a heap in the bottom again; and then we landed with a horrible crunching sound and tilted sixty degrees to the side, which was enough that we could crawl out and stand down on the street, not too much the worse for wear, all things considered.

Under the bucket was a Mitsubishi pickup truck, well flattened. And wasn't that something, Rhot told us, because this very pickup truck had been our getaway vehicle. How did Sombat do this thing, sitting in the cockpit of the crane way up there about two hundred feet above us in the dark?

"Sombat is a real artist," was Hip's opinion, and this was the first I knew that Sombat had been our pilot on this interesting trip.

It would have been a poor idea to hail a taxi, what with a bunch of girls wrapped in tablecloths and all the guys rodded up to the earlobes, looking like the Dirty Dozen on crack. But we couldn't stand around here forever. If Fat's men didn't get to us, then the cops would, and that could have been inconvenient under the circumstances. So Tommy and Hip hot-wired one of the Benzes parked along the street, getting past the door lock, wheel lock, and any other lines of defense faster than most people could have done it using the keys.

"Something I picked up in Vietnam," Hip said to me.

The number of people we crammed into that car might have got us a mention in the *Guinness Book of Records*. And I was surprised to hear Mu's voice in the back seat saying "Bia, are you okay?"

"Mu?" I asked her. "What the hell are you doing here?"

"Bia is my sister. You are my man. I was waiting with the pickup truck."

"Jesus Christ, Mu," I said. And that's all I said because everybody was trying to talk at once, and Willie finally yelled, "Shut up! I have to drive this car."

the master plan revisited

Selections from Arno Petty's Intelligencer and Weekly Gleaner

LOOKING GOOD. Have you heard how the authorities are going to solve Bangkok's traffic problems for the big upcoming international pow-wow on industry and the environment? First, they're going to declare a two-day national holiday, just to keep commuters off the streets. This way, the international delegates may be able to get to their nice meetings before the conference is over. But just in case this isn't enough, those in charge are also in the process of organizing any number of festivals and things upcountry, hoping that half the city will leave for the long weekend, thereby giving our guests more elbow-room still. Meanwhile, aesthetic considerations are leading them to build high walls around all the slums that lie within eyeshot of the conference center.

THE BEST-LAID PLANS. The Meteorological Office is telling us that about the time of the big conference Bangkok may be in for record floods. Predictions are that exceptionally high tides could well coincide with a cyclone coming at the end of what has been a very wet rainy season. Not to mention the fact that the city of Bangkok has subsided another nine centimeters this past year at the same time sea levels have continued to rise with the melting of the polar ice-caps. Expect to see offers to trade condos for arks.

THE PLAN had been worked out to the last detail, a masterpiece of subtlety and forethought. Rube Goldberg couldn't have done any better.

They blew the east walls with a rocket attack, using a few missiles somebody had diverted from a shipment that had been on its way from Cambodia to the Karen rebels in Burma. These were

226

launched from a pest-control panel truck arranged by a ladyfriend of Willie's, a dispatcher for Bug-I-Cide. Timed to go off at the same time had been both the phony police raid on the front gate of Luckyland and a display of fireworks to be launched from a schoolyard half a mile away.

As though this weren't enough, there was to be one more diversion, this one designed to draw the local police away from the entire area for a time, giving the boys some elbow room to work. The idea had been to start a small fire in a warehouse, which warehouse happened to belong to Fat Fat, and at the same time trip burglar alarms in a couple of neighboring buildings. Tommy had set this one up. Despite his expert input, however, things got a bit out of control in the actual execution. The warehouse, a roller-skating rink, and an entire department store belonging in part to the local chief of police, though that wasn't common knowledge, went up in flames. Nobody was killed, given the lateness of the hour, but it did for sure distract the local authorities.

The key element, of course, had been as simple as they come. Sombat and the main task force infiltrated the condominium project next door, which had only a few security guards looking after it on the night shift anyway. Then, while the fake police force stormed the front gate to distract Fat Fat's guards, Sombat had started up the crane, gently swinging the bucket, complete with task force, high in over the walls.

The original idea had been to set the bucket down gently on the roof, whereupon Willie, Tommy, Rhot, and Hip were to have gone in through the ventilation system. The marker-pen girl, who was part of Hip's network, had earlier smuggled fairly detailed plans of this system out with the laundry truck driver. The plan was then to hit them during the live show, depending on the element of surprise plus superior firepower to get Bia and me into the bucket and away before most of Fat Fat's soldiers knew what was happening.

227

The bucket was supposed to have been dropped ever so lightly on the roof. Instead, in the dark, Sombat had misjudged by twenty feet — after all, he hadn't worked in awhile and he was rusty. The rest was history.

Willie and Tommy had assembled something a bit smaller than the cast of *Ben Hur* in putting together this caper. I had to wonder: How did they propose to pay off this army with what Mu and I were giving them?

"We earn a little bonus," Willie tells me. "It so happens our people clean out the marks after they leave the casino. So we can forget about the extra expenses we charge you for otherwise. We take them out of our bonus instead. No problem."

Their expenses had been pretty heavy, though. Especially since they'd been forced to slap the master plan together so fast, what with me getting snatched and nobody hearing boo from me about where I'd gotten to. But most of the crew had earned their fees, or so I heard; though there was some question about whether others should even get paid.

"We should know better than to trust that old man to look after the fireworks," said Willie. "How does anybody sleep right through a rocket attack that way?"

"And to think Mu actually recommended him to drive the getaway car." Hip shook his head in amazement. "Cousin or not, the old dodger could hardly stand up, much less drive. And his car was in worse shape than he was. I believe that was the oldest Benz I've ever seen in Thailand."

"Wait a minute — was this car painted green, by any chance?" I asked, hardly believing it could be so. "With patches?"

"You got it," Hip told me. "So you've met the guy?"

You could say we'd met. This was the strangest thing. And here he was one of Mu's cousins as well. Of course I was beginning to wonder who wasn't, so maybe that part of it wasn't too surprising after all.

What an operation, though. There hadn't been a single casualty on our side, if you overlooked the geezer, who had gotten himself busted for unauthorized use of fireworks by the only cop in that part of the city who wasn't over watching the department store burn down.

One thing still bothered me: What made Fat Fat build that condominium right next to Luckyland that way? In most other respects he had struck me as being kind of obsessive about security.

"With the connections he had? Cops in his pocket and everything?" Hip was giving me the you-babe-in-the-woods look again. "Fat Fat never expected anybody to try busting him."

"That's why he had two walls and four front doors and crocodiles all around the joint, right?" I said, giving Hip my you-babe-in-the-woods look. "Get serious."

"Whoa. Come on, Jack. You've been in Thailand for awhile. That was mostly image. Self-presentation. You can't be somebody important if you don't have a mobile phone and a Benz and membership in a golf club; you can't be really important unless you've got bodyguards. And everybody's got dogs and walls. So if you want to be a *chao por*, a godfather like Fat Fat wanted to be, you're going to have even more walls; and it's always a good idea to have some lasers and video cameras because that's Hi-tech and Up-to-date. It also makes the cops look good if anything goes wrong and the public starts wondering why they are not closing down these dens of vice more often.

"Crocodiles, mind you, that was putting on airs. And the condominium itself — Fat Fat just wanted to have the biggest erection in the neighborhood. That's all. Lucky for us, nothing would have it but he also needed the biggest crane in the world on top of it. That was dead convenient.

"And if this security stuff had any real purpose beyond showing

229

everybody who was who and what was what, it was only to keep all the unhappy people in."

And Hip explained how he decided to come along on the raid. First, as he told me, he had felt somewhat responsible for the whole situation — on behalf of Izzy Scoop, that is. Besides that, he was a reporter. What the hell, anyway; he had attended parties in Vietnam that made this one seem tame enough, when everything was said and done.

"But you listen to me, Jack," he said. "Even though all this grief was meant for Izzy, it could have just as easily been meant for you. Come to that, it should've been meant for you, the way you carry on, a loose cannon in this Land of Smiles, here."

laying the ghosts to rest

Selections from Arno Petty's *Intelligencer and Weekly Gleaner*

UNIDENTIFIED FALLING OBJECTS. This past week a rogue construction crane dropped a 10-ton steel bucket through the roof of the headquarters of one of this country's most feared 'dark influences.' The operator subsequently fled the scene, which no doubt seemed a good idea at the time, given that the building belonged to none other than Mr Hung Fat, better known as 'Fat Fat,' though not to his face.

NOT-SO-LUCKYLAND. Those of you who have always worried about maybe slipping up and calling this notorious mangda Fat Fat to his face can now relax, however. He has suffered a massive loss of face, one occasioned by an 11mm slug, and he has no face to talk to anymore. While UFOs were ventilating one building, Bangkok's finest were tearing up the adjacent Luckyland Casino, in the course of which raid Fat Fat's luck ran out and he was shot while trying to escape custody. RIP, Fat Fat.

I DON'T KNOW WHY I look forward to the mail. Here's somebody trying to sell me a subscription to *Asian Business Investor*. I haven't got the capital to subscribe to the magazine, much less invest in a condo. And here's an investment plan. I get a pension, life insurance for myself and my loved ones, a burial plot, and a genuine leather carrying case for a portable computer complete with embossed gold monogram. That's great. I get the whole lot for one low monthly premium that happens to be more than my total income, these days. Oh, boy. And I couldn't afford the portable computer to put in my personalized carrying case, much less the mobile phone that would slide into the conveniently attached pocket they talk about here.

And there's a letter from my Dad. This is an occasion.

> Jack: I don't pretend to have ever understood you. Or
> your Mother, for that matter. You do what you think
> you have to. The Bears are doing terrible this season.
>
> Love, Dad.
>
> P.S.: What are you doing about a retirement plan?

Propriapist Publications have responded to my query about up-
ping my fees. They want to know if I can run the entire alphabet.
They are willing to double my take if I sign a contract with some
kind of penalty clause I don't understand. I'd better talk to Hip.

The *Bangkok Globe* is busting at the seams with news today. The
cops are taking credit both for the Luckyland raid and for Fat's
timely demise. It seems that one hero, a police captain, had directed
undercover operations from inside.

And you get the feeling, from reports, that everybody was quite
keen on seeing the end of Fat Fat's video library, many of the features stored there having been recorded through hidden cameras at
the Shaking Heaven. The police took all these interesting records
away, in any case, and the other powers-that-be must have been
quite grateful for this, because the newspapers are saying what a
surprise it was for the police department to get such a generous
slice of the budget for the coming year.

And we finally had the coup after all. Just a couple of days after
the raid. The only reason we knew about it was that the three ra-
dios going at once all had the same music on, even though they
were as usual tuned to three different stations. This same music,
moreover, was martial tunes of a kind designed to make right-
thinking citizens march about admiring their own country.

But none of this was half as exciting as revolutions in Burma or walkathons or even merely hanging around this apartment I live in on your average Sunday morning. Nobody buzzed us with helicopters, and the only difference to anybody's life I could make out was that the PA system at the army base down the road blared fusion jazz so relentlessly, meaning to keep the citizenry calm, that finally it was enough to make you edgy, especially if you hate fusion jazz, which I do.

Anyway, I am writing some stories about how nice and quiet and bloodless this unscheduled change of government has been, which is in no way considered first-class copy by editors, though one or two are buying it anyway. I am writing these stories, furthermore, on my computer, which some of Mu's cousins were kind enough to get out of hock with part of the take from the casino mob. Of course I still have the old Royal as well, which is useful when my computer is being used by Maem to conduct her classes in Lotus 1-2-3 and dBase. Which is most of the time, now that I think about it.

There is indeed money on all hands. Money to get my computer out of hock. Money to fix Bia's eyes, though it was Tommy offering to fund this operation, and this Mu did not consider appropriate. Finally it was agreed they would add the plastic surgeon's fees to the rest of the money we had to pay for Willie and Tommy's services.

Yeah. Pretty well everybody but me is rolling in dough, right at the moment. What it is, Willie and Tommy's friend Dit organized the phony police raid on the front gate of Luckyland, enlisting several of Mu's cousins and friends of cousins plus a couple of his own. They painted one of the Bug-I-Cide panel trucks over so it looked something like a paddy wagon. This had made it a dead cinch to divert some of the community pillars who were fleeing through the hole in the wall. Then, in the spirit of Robin Hood and his Merry Men, they drove these citizens away to a quiet area and appropriated all of their money, which, if they had been left to their own devices, they would have no doubt lost at gambling anyway.

Though Mu says her cousins couldn't have had any part in this. Sure, they might dress up like cops for an evening and carry on a bit, but rob a bunch of rich people? Not likely.

Bia seems none the worse for wear, on the whole. She has had her eyes opened in more ways than one, however, in the course of these events I have related. And if she doesn't start keeping a better distance from one Tommy Two-Toes, she's going to learn a lot more about life than any proper nineteen-year-old Thai girl would ever want to know.

Bia has new eyes, as I have said already. Not only that, she's gone and cut her bangs back enough that she might be mistaken for a genius. You could post bills on her forehead, if you wanted to. She still falls down the stairs a bit, but that's only habit, and she should gradually adapt to being able to see again. And I have to admit it, she does look pretty good with her new eyes, though she tends to keep them open too wide and she doesn't blink much; what's the point of having all these beautiful big eyes if people can't see them?

Another good thing: Bia has stopped wearing my shirts. The bad news is that the marker-pen girl has already turned a couple of them into patchwork skirts, which is worse. Mu says they were old ones anyway, but she'll see it doesn't happen again.

Two of the performers from Luckyland One are now living in our house, the ping-pong girl and the marker-pen lady. One of them is in Cousin Maem's computer class, and the other is proving a dab hand at creating stylish clothing out of odd bits of cloth. Mu has put her in charge of the sewing contingent for now.

Sombat may finally be on his way to Saudi Arabia. And his performance on the crane went a long way towards compensating for the fish box full of dead arowanas, in Mu's mind. But what I want to know, if he's such an artist with a construction crane, and seeing as how there are more cranes than stray dogs in the city these days, is why he has to wait till he gets to Saudi Arabia to get a job. But nobody listens to me on this matter. It probably has something to do with the Thai Way.

Esther and my mother haven't arrived yet.

My sense of impending doom, I find, has not let up to speak of, not even with Fat Fat and the coup both out of the way. This leads me to believe that coups or even the prospects of getting shot to death and worse were not the significant factors in this sense of unease I have been carrying around with me these past days. It makes you think.

And that is not all that is worrying me. Some people might call me a wimp, but I am a bit perturbed about having shot a man to death. Although even that doesn't seem to bother me as much as the total mayhem that Willie and Tommy and the rest of the wrecking crew managed to come up with in the space of just a few minutes, and the people that were killed without so much as a chance to explain themselves.

But not to worry, Hip tells me: "War is a time when laws are silent. That was Cicero's opinion, Jack; and Cicero was a person who knew a lot about life.

"Now, what we went through the other day was war. But war is war, and peace is peace; and now you got to settle down to doing something about the peace, my friend. What are you going to do about Mu?"

A few days ago Mu took me to the temple to put in the fix for bumping Fat Fat off. At first I said no; then I thought it over and I said okay. And maybe it did lay some ghosts to rest, after all, because I'm sleeping better these past couple of nights.

Still, I told her, ghosts were mainly malarkey. This got her steamed up, and when I said "Have you ever seen a ghost?" she answered "No, but my cousin in Lamphang did." And this is more or less what she related: One day her cousin, a rice farmer, opened his door to find a group of excited chickens standing there. This was not standard chicken behavior, so he chased them away; but they came back. This time the excited chickens ran into the kitchen and tried to hide under everything. He chased them away again but still they came back, so the cousin began to get the idea something was wrong. He finally went out into the farmyard, and what did her cousin see but the figure of an old man glowing with a funny light and hovering two meters off the ground.

"Yes?" I said. "Go on."

"What do you mean, 'go on'?" Mu looked at me as though I was thick. "That's it."

I thought about that for a minute, and then I started to laugh. I laughed and laughed, and after a while Mu ceased being pissed off and she started to laugh too, until neither one of knew what we were laughing about but it felt good anyway. So we made love. I didn't have any problems, and Mu didn't have any problems; and in fact I didn't remember it being this good since the time I fell down between the beds in Pattaya.

Mu saw I was feeling good, and she was feeling good, so she decided this was probably the best time to tell me that she was the one who hired the two men on the motorcycle — the ones who took some shots at me in the taxi.

"You remember?" she asked me, no doubt figuring it had long since slipped my mind.

"What?" I said. "*What?*"

"It was me, Jack. I hired those men. I'm sorry; I was only trying to protect you."

I had to jump out of bed and stride up and down the bedroom for awhile, trying not to fall over things in the process. No matter how good I had been feeling, this news came as something of a shock to me. I kept throwing looks at Mu, just to check that this was the same woman I had been living with all these past months. Then I stopped for a minute.

"Mu. Back then… You borrowed some money from me. Five thousand baht."

"I paid it back, Jack. And it was only for your own good. I told them not to hurt you, my darling. Just scare you a little bit."

After a while I left off saying "Jesus Christ!" and I stopped striding around the room. Mu managed to explain how that whole scheme was supposed to be something like an inoculation. If only she could throw a scare into me, show me what could happen if I didn't cool down some and start doing as the Romans did, then maybe she could save me from getting ventilated for real. Or so had gone her reasoning.

But now she was sorry, she told me. These bozos she had hired were cut-rate bozos and hadn't show a lot of finesse. As it turned out, you could say, there hadn't been a lot of difference between the inoculation and the real McCoy. Of course if only I'd lent her ten thousand baht, like she'd asked for in the first place, maybe she could have got somebody decent to do the job.

Still, she could see I might be taken aback at the news that my own girlfriend had hired some gunmen to take a few shots at me.

"But you wouldn't listen, Jack."

She offered to hire Willie and Tommy to rough up the gunmen she hired before, just to teach them a thing or two; but I declined with thanks. I said we could let bygones be bygones, and *mai pen rai*. Like, "never mind," and so on.

When I told her this, and I got to the part about mai pen rai, she looked at me fondly and kissed me. She said I was learning how to get along in this life, and she was proud of me.

"Jesus Christ!" I said once more. Just when I thought I was getting to know this lady, and now look.

Then she tapped her tooth a bit, and she started to wonder if maybe she shouldn't hire somebody to shoot Tommy, though, the way he had been hanging around telling Bia how good she looked. But Mu was kidding about getting Tommy shot, I think, and really she kind of liked him herself, I could see that.

Mu has bought me another amulet this one, I am told by those who know, so potent I couldn't do better with armor plating all around and a bunch of bodyguards on the side.

Not only that, it looks as though I'm signed up to do a *vipassana* meditative retreat. This is what is sometimes prescribed, in these parts, for jai rawn, for burning hot on the temperamental front. For ten days I'll get eleven scheduled hours of meditation every day, plus any more I want to do merely for fun. I won't be able to talk to anybody the whole time except the meditation masters, and even that is only if I have some technical problem, such as for example I come to know myself and I don't care for this jerk. Or maybe my knees lock and I can't get up out of the lotus position. That kind of thing.

Two vegetarian meals a day, God help me, and I'm pretty sure there'll be no beer, though I didn't ask. No smoking. No women. No thinking of women. You can't leave the joint till the end of the session, unless you want to quit altogether. You can't even make a phone-call. No smoking. And get this — you're not supposed to bring in any magical objects or books, no lucky rabbit's feet or anything like that. So no amulet.

So no problem, right? Wrong. If you had said a year ago I would feel nervous about leaving behind a little silver figure of a fat man with his hands over his eyes, I would have told you you were nuts. But there you go. I'm probably going native.

Mu believes I am, anyhow. And so does Hip, I think.

Hip has been telling me how this trip to the temple is both

going to help me give up smoking and learn all about the Thai Way besides. He has explained the idea of *khon suk*, and how traditionally Thai girls wouldn't marry a boy until he had been "ripened" through a term in the Buddhist monkhood.

But Mu has told me in her opinion I am already no longer entirely a *khon dip*, merely a callow dipstick. I have ripened, I guess, at least to the point she is willing to make an honest man of me. And maybe I'll let her at that.

I sense some funny changes in myself these days. For example I was downtown, walking through the heat and the exhaust fumes and the screaming din of motorcycles and tuk-tuks and tape vendors and Gods knows what all. I was strolling along, almost ambling, and I happened to look across at the new Universal Commercial Tower, one more modern temple to Mammon, already enormous and reportedly growing to ninety-one stories. The gigantic department store that is the base of this monument was already doing business, no matter there were still cranes all over the top of it adding more floors for later. Hanging on poles around the surrounding plaza were big red banners with dragons on them, lending a fine mythic quality to the scene. Suddenly I had to smile, a good smile. I saw the fun in it all. I *liked* it, and I found myself looking forward to the new surprises this city and this life in general were bound to come up with. I even looked forward to the day, any day now, when Bangkok achieved gridlock, and what fun it was going to be to see that. And the flood. Soon we were supposed to get the worst flood in the city's history.

For one thing alone, what good is it to be a journalist, or even only a reporter, if you're going to flee the scene just when things get interesting? After all, this is where the action is. And what's life without risk? Interesting times may be a curse for the average citizen, but they are a writer's bread and butter. Somebody's got to witness this stuff, to get it down for posterity and suchlike.

239

Maybe that's when I decided to ask Mu if she would marry me. Her and all her cousins and Bia and other ones I haven't even met yet, but whom I now look forward to meeting. What the hell. Marriage to Mu can't be any more dangerous than a lot of things. And there are bound to be some good stories in it.

*

This morning I have the strangest feeling, lying here in bed with Mu. She's still sleeping, not quite snoring, and the sun is sneaking in around the curtains and warming the skin on her tummy. She's also got one leg sticking out from under the sheets. Things are quiet, as quiet as they ever get, anyway. I feel a peace — a shagged-out, I-don't-give-a-damn, nobody-can-blame-me-if-I-never-move-again, downright luxurious lull in the course of events.

I know I've got a lot to do today, but I am content to lie here. Simply lying here seems enough in itself. All these other things I have to do will get taken care of when their time comes. Right now is my time. Mine and Mu's. She is asleep, but I can see from the way she is sleeping she is with me on this matter. I lie still so I don't wake her up; I want this moment to go on and on.

From outside in the street I get the sudden hysterical blat-blatting of a tuk-tuk decelerating from about three-quarters of the speed of sound for the turn into the soi. And it is as though something in me precipitates out. I feel a calm excitement that takes me back to when I was a kid, waking up to the sound of birds singing and to all the familiar voices of the neighborhood drifting in through my bedroom window. This was feeling purely good and at one with things, though with a hint of urgency, a sense I might miss something if I didn't get out and about without further delay.

The feeling this morning is even better. That tuk-tuk is immediate and real to me in a very personal way, and I suddenly see that I am equally part of the traffic, the kids in the street, the dogs, the rustle of the wind in the palms. And they are part of me. Like that.

It's not easy to explain. It's as though I have this comfortable certainty everything will still be there later. I can experience all these new things in their proper time, and meanwhile I can lie here cocooned in happy anticipation of simply being there — of being whoever and wherever, of a future that's going to be basically fine and exciting, give or take a bad time or two now and then.

I'm closer to understanding Mu than I've ever been, to understanding her as a woman and as a Thai. Or so I believe.

There's a clatter and a clumping from outside the bedroom that could be Bia falling down the stairs. "*Arai na?* What?" Granny is awake and demanding clarification, even though the rest of the household isn't up yet, and nobody is talking to her or to anybody else, so far. But Mu is waking, stirring and stretching. Her eyes open and she grins lazily at me.

From outside, I hear the tape vendor start up for the new day. Here it is some hour of the morning, so early I can't even look at the clock, and we are getting music. And the first selection of the day is Milli Vanilli.

Made in the USA
Las Vegas, NV
29 March 2023

69794604R10142